TIDEWATER
HIT

TIDEWATER HIT

M. Z. THWAITE

TIDEWATER HIT
Copyright © 2017 by M. Z. Thwaite

Publisher's Note

Published by Spartina Publishing
Beaufort, South Carolina.

Printed in the United States of America.

Cover and author photo by Steve Weeks.
Interior by Roseanna White Designs.

First Edition (Hardcover print)
ISBNs: 978-0-9991812-0-1 (Hardcover)
        978-0-9991812-1-8 (Paperback)
        978-0-9991812-2-5 (Digital)

To Steve, my love and the best playmate I have ever had.

Consequently, this Rule of Right and Wrong, or Law of Human Nature, or whatever you call it, must somehow or other be a real thing—a thing that is really there, not made up by ourselves.

— C. S. Lewis

ONE

August, 1986
Coast of Georgia
USA

Abbey Taylor Bunn glanced in the direction of the obnoxious voices. Too loud and querulous for this time of day. They sounded close but noises carried great distances over water so the fact that she heard them meant little. Fishing boats were always present on Georgia's tidewaters, mere background sound like ceiling fans on Southern porches, but the fact that she heard the voices at all over the rumble of their powerful outboard motor meant they were almost shouting.

Her rowing shell barely rippled the greenish-brown brackish water as she navigated the watery landscape between salt marsh and dark mud banks; that she sat backwards on a sliding seat a mere fact, not a complication. She saw where she had been, not where she was going. A tell-tale rolling wake from a motorboat would have tossed around her twenty-six-foot shell like a child's bathtub toy. She continued to row down the creek undisturbed, with an occasional glance over each shoulder so she could steer around obstacles like oyster rakes or sandbars.

The outboard must have been in the wide-open sound on the

1

far side of the marsh to her left. Fishermen more than likely, and from the sound of it there was an animated discussion going on. Cocking her head, she tried to listen. One person talked over the other or others; difficult to tell how many there were but they were definitely men.

She couldn't be bothered. It was too beautiful a morning not to enjoy her workout and to breathe in the rich fragrance of the familiar salt-laden air as she glided back to catch the water again with her oars. Gas fumes wafted across the grasses on a slight breeze. Her nose crimped. "You stink. Go away," she mumbled, as she tried to ignore the intruders.

As if her complaint had reached the men's ears and really ticked them off, whatever they had discussed before seemed to have developed into a full-blown disagreement. Her peace and quiet were shot, but there was only one way for her to get back to the cottage at Kings Bluff and that was to row. She stole a look at her watch and at the quickly decreasing edge of bank. Incoming tide would give her a little push back to the dock where she had started out at daybreak that morning.

The day was still young. Most folks were sleeping in because it was Saturday but that was usually a work day for her. Though she was on vacation, she had promised herself she'd make calls for an hour. Real estate had its drawbacks, but clients didn't need to know she was cooling her heels at her family's cottage five hours south of Atlanta and her office. All she had to do was stay in touch; let them know she hadn't forgotten about them, that they were important. At least she wouldn't have to make appointments to show houses for another week.

Annoyed at the yo-yos who had disturbed her peace, and tired, sweaty, and hungry to boot, she turned into the river at the end of the creek and headed for home. The outboard motor suddenly growled to a higher whine … *woooooo…* as though it was coming straight toward her; then *ahhhhhh*, like it was going away … but then *woooooo-ahhhhhh* again. *Is he circling?* Her stroke rate slowed as she listened. *Why would a fisherman pull tight circles like that?* It sounded like a boat coming back for a fallen skier, but no one in his right mind would ski out there where sharks bred like rabbits.

There was a yell and then disturbed-sounding voices. She squinted as though that might help her to see better but it didn't. Again, the boat circled. A yelp, a shout, something – and then a loud thunk.

"Damn." Her oars stopped mid-stroke. Tiny hairs crinkled all over her body and tickled her neck; her shoulders tightened in a protective hunch. Something or someone was either busted up or seriously injured.

TWO

August's rising sun quickly warmed any hint of morning's cool and bore down on Abbey as she listened over the sound of her own heavy breaths and imagined what could have just happened. Although the noise itself frightened her, the frantic voices or whatever was going on out there made her sit up taller and crane her neck to try to get a better look, but the marsh between her and them was too high. Her shell sat mere inches above the water. The boat sounded as though it was going away. No more loud voices, only the roaring of the departing motor. Maybe differences had been settled and the men were looking for a spot to drop anchor and fish. It was none of her business anyway.

Sweat dripped into her eyes and ran down the creases beside her nose. It was bloody hot. She swiped each sweaty cheek across a shoulder, then held both oar handles in one hand and grabbed her water bottle from in front of her feet and drank. She wished there was a scale back at the house, but this was a fish camp and hunting club and the only thing that got weighed was raw meat. Didn't matter. Today's heat would be worth several pounds in sweat. She could eat whatever she wanted.

She argued with herself. *Not my problem anyway. Gotta get back to make those calls.* Wheels whirred on metal tracks beneath her sliding seat and oarlocks clicked with the plop-whoosh of each stroke. Familiar sounds. Unlike what she'd just heard. *But anything they hit could have made that noise, a board, a log, a huge raft of marsh grass.* Just like a paved highway, the Intracoastal Waterway picked up an odd assortment of trash, even abandoned boats or dislodged dock parts. It was dangerous. *Fools probably weren't looking where they were going. But it wasn't a hard sound like a whack; it was more a soft, sickening thud like running over a dog.*

As it moved through the water, her port oar hit something causing the shell to tip momentarily. "Damn." She regained her balance and continued to row while she looked between the parallel puddles left by her oars. A white object bobbed in her wake, maybe a paper plate or a big blob of a jellyfish, which locals called a jelly ball. Curious, she stopped, then backed several strokes.

I'll be damned. With one hand on the oar handles, she reached in the water and plucked out a cotton baseball cap. It wasn't waterlogged. Its shape was perfect and it hadn't been discolored by days on end in salt water. A large P was embroidered on the front. It might have just been separated from its owner. She tucked it beside the water bottle. *Well, damn.* Without hesitation, she turned the shell around in the middle of the river.

"Hold on," she muttered. She had no idea what, if anything, she might find out in the sound. If it was debris, no big deal. If it was a person, she'd figure out what to do when she got there, when all she had at her disposal was a skinny woman powered boat built for one. While her brain figured and calculated, muscle memory took over and rowed.

All morning the water had been a rower's dream, flat and glassy. Luckily, conditions held. Blinding sun reflected and made seeing difficult even with sunglasses. She glanced over her shoulder to see if anything looked unusual ahead. Something dark stuck up in the water. It didn't roll or flip so it wasn't a dolphin, and crab pot buoys were usually white or light-colored so they could be spotted easily at a distance. She angled forty-five degrees, stopped, and spotted the object again. It wasn't swimming or moving. She had a feeling, and it wasn't a good one.

This new orientation allowed her to finally see the boat she had been listening to, and it seemed to be hightailing it away, not looking for a fishing spot. It was difficult to tell at this distance but it appeared that one dark-skinned person stood in the stern. If there were additional people seated or on the floor she couldn't tell, but there must be at least two on board, the one standing and a driver. If she could see them, they could see her, so she sat perfectly still. Rowing shells were almost impossible to spot unless they were moving and the sun caught the movement of the oars or their back-splash; if you didn't know the shell was there and you weren't looking for it, chances were you wouldn't see it.

It took a minute to locate the floating object again but it was being pushed with the tide as she was so it wasn't anchored in any way. There it was. Still afloat. It showed no movement on its own. Finally the other boat went around a protrusion of marsh and disappeared from view. *Allright.* She realigned her shell and went to see what the drifting thing was. The closer she got the more the black blob looked like a person.

Oh, shit. Not again. She rowed harder. *It looks human. Acts human. Hell, if being still is an action, of course. It is the act of doing nothing. Of floating. Damn Abbey. Shut-the-hell up.*

She made out eyes and a mouth. *It's a man. Lord help me.* At twenty-five feet long and ten inches wide at its broadest point, her single shell didn't have a whole lot of room for a rescue mission, but right now she was the only game in town so she pushed hard and closed the distance between them.

There was no obvious blood in the water but that didn't matter. Sharks and bloodhounds had superior noses. *Do something.* Glancing to her left and calculating the distance to land, she realized that somehow she needed to get him onto the bank of the nearby marsh island.

"Hey, mister." She slipped up beside him, but out of his reach in case he grabbed and put them both in the drink. He lay on his back with his hands roughly beside his head. Fat man's float, easy for those who carried a few extra pounds, difficult for skinny folks. He didn't move but he looked harmless, sort of the preppy type judging by his shorts and shirt. He'd lost his shoes somewhere along the way.

"Hey, mister," she said again, then held her breath as his eyes fluttered open.

"Hey," he said in a raspy whisper, turning his head toward her voice. "Where have you been?" His eyes closed again.

Where have I been? I was going to ask you the same thing. She maneuvered a rigger over his hips and started to talk as though somehow this would all make sense to him. "You look pretty strong so I'm going to tell you to do some things. We need to get you out of the water so listen to me, okay? I'm going to have to touch you in a second and I'm going to tell you how to help." *Okay, okay, okay. Be calm. Think this through.*

"I'm in this little boat here and I'm going to show you how to hold on to a rigger. Don't go wacky on me and grab my boat, okay?"

"Wacky. You're funny." His eyes didn't open this time.

"Yeah, I'm a real comedian." She grabbed the compact personal flotation device wedged below her shoes and beside her water bottle and her new hat. It was getting crowded down there. She'd never used the PFD but she'd promised her mother and Tom Clark, the man she'd been dating, that she would keep it with her when she rowed alone in the Intracoastal Waterway. Small concession to keep them happy but she wasn't fooling herself. It was a damn good idea.

"Here's what we're going to do. I have a brand-new never-been-used floating thing here." She held her oars with one hand, grabbed the PFD, and unbuckled the waistband for the first time ever. *This thing had better work.* "I'm going to strap this onto you and it'll help to hold you up. I know you're tired of having to stay afloat on your own. Good job, by the way."

She backed until she was even with his shoulders. Except for the occasional eye twitch and the chest moving up and down, he did a good job of looking dead. His half-buttoned shirt revealed a chest and abdomen with a strange resemblance to a raw London broil. One side of his face was deep red and swollen.

"Now remember, don't reach for my boat." *Hope whoever did this to this fellow doesn't come back to finish the job. Wouldn't he be surprised? Yeah. Like I'm a big threat.*

The man's eyes opened wide. "You here already? What's going on? Where did they go?"

"I wish I knew. Now listen. I am going to touch you. Please stay still. You're hurt and I want to help." If he heard her, he didn't acknowledge. His eyes were shut tight again.

She wedged both oar handles between her chest and her thighs and stretched toward him. If she let go of the oars, the shell would turtle like an airplane without a wing. "I'm going to put this thing around your arm." She maneuvered the PFD under his near arm and worked at the clasp one-handed. "That'll do." She tugged on the clasp's strap to tighten it.

"Now when I pull the tab, this thing will inflate and help to hold you up." *Until I decide our next move. How the hell am I going to get you to shore?* The marsh bank was only about fifty or so feet away. Maybe he could hold on. When she touched his palm, his fingers closed around hers like a baby, so that reflex was alive and well.

"Okay, good." She took his fingers and placed them on the rigger, then wrapped hers around his. "Here's what I want you to do. Hold on here just like you're doing and I'm going to…" Just then, the wind changed and she heard the loud drum-drum-drum of a diesel engine. The sharp tip of a boat's bow appeared over the marsh in the river she had just exited.

THREE

Rigged like a shrimp boat with long hanging nets, this new-comer churned along at a leisurely pace and didn't appear to be looking for anyone. Her befuddled new friend said, "What's that damn noise?"

"A working boat just came into the sound." Whose captain could have pitched your preppy ass overboard and run over you. But my money is on those fishermen who raced out of here.

"Who brought the beer?" Though the man's voice was a little shaky and uncertain, she thought she detected a touch of sarcasm.

"We'll have one back at the house after we get you taken care of." Humor him. Poor guy could use a beer after that lick. Being a sitting duck—which she might be, if the captain of that working boat possibly had anything to do with the injured man—was not high on her bucket list. "I sure hope you're a good guy," she said under her breath. "Hold on. We're moving toward land."

Rowing slowly toward the bank with her added weight and drag, Abbey watched the working boat slink into the sound like a lioness, its long, sloping hull now fully visible and moving straight ahead as though Abbey was of no concern. He's not coming after us. Memory ticked in. I know that boat. Her unusual hull and deck loaded with working gear made the boat stick out among the fishing boats tied up at Kings Bluff. Abbey's shoulders dropped from around her ears and she let out a breath she hadn't realized she was holding.

She stopped rowing and yelled, "Hey," then waved furiously with a free hand. "Hey, Sarge!" No way he'll be able to hear me.

She looked at the PFD on Preppy. Tom had insisted on attaching a bright yellow ear-piercing "raise the dead" whistle to it when he gave it to her. She unclipped the whistle and blew it for all she was worth. The captain leaned his head out of the wheelhouse on Abbey's side of his boat, so she blew until her cheeks hurt and waved like a Daytona 500 flag man. The captain looked up and his boat eased her way.

"Yes." Abbey yelled, "Sarge, help!"

Preppy's eyes blinked open. "You're loud. What's the problem?"

"I am loud. I have to be at the moment. Hang on there just like you're doing. Help is on the way and we're going to get you out of the water."

"Where am I?"

"You wouldn't believe it if I told you. We'll talk soon."

It seemed to take forever, but eventually the shrimp boat's wake rolled under Abbey's boat. The man moaned.

"Hold on, mister." Abbey touched the top of the man's fingers, which held the round rod of her rigger like bird claws on a telephone wire. "Help is on the way." How in the heck are we going to get him into that boat?

Sarge's engine down-shifted to neutral. "Whatch'all doin' out heah?"

Abbey pointed to the man. "He's hurt, Sarge. I think he was hit by a boat. We need to get him to land."

Ten minutes later, having rested her boat and oars on a flat stretch of sand, Abbey picked her barefoot way across broken oyster and clam shells on the bank. Amazing how quickly things could change. An hour ago, the morning had been about getting some exercise.

She jumped in and swam to Preppy. His eyes opened. "Who are you? What's going on?"

"Not much. You're a damn good floater is all I know." And you'd be a dead man if I'd headed home.

Sarge tossed a white life-saving ring tied to a rope, which she retrieved and pushed under Preppy's knees. Between the ring and the PFD, he was well supported. She hung onto the ring and treaded water while Sarge turned cranks and dials and swung a shrimp net her way. As the net lowered into the water two feet from her, she grabbed it and pulled it around Preppy as best she could. Thankfully he was out of it again and pliable as a sausage so she draped an arm across him, then gave Sarge a thumbs-up and they began to rise. The net gathered around them like a soggy skirt but it worked.

The man's eyes opened wide. "Whoa. Is this a hammock? I love hammocks."

"Yeah, me too."

As they were lowered to the deck, Abbey scrambled to her feet. "Bet that's a first, Sarge." She disengaged Preppy, then Sarge raised and repositioned the net and joined her. "I wondered how you were going to do that but this boat was made for it." Sarge nodded.

"You sure you want to try to get my boat? We need to get him to a doctor. I can row home later." Unless the tide comes up over that bank and takes my boat with it.

He looked toward her boat. "How long's that thing?"

"Almost thirty feet," Abbey said.

"What does she weigh?"

"Twenty-nine, thirty pounds, give or take."

"Yep," Sarge said. "Go get 'er. Take ten minutes."

Abbey dove off the shallow stern and swam back to the shell bank. Within minutes she was in her boat and back at the rear of the shrimp boat, where Sarge was busy with something.

"Can you get to this?" Sarge lowered a ladder, of sorts, over the back of his boat and hooked it over the gunwale.

"What is that thing?"

"Ladder." The "ladder" had massive U hooks that fit over the gunwale, wide steps, and a generous platform at the bottom that hung only inches from the water.

Abbey looked from the platform to Sarge. "Can you turn sideways and float with the current so I can get up to that platform and grab it, Sarge?"

"Yep."

Great. I'm aiming for a moving target. Piece of cake. She watched the shrimp boat get in position. "Okay. Here goes."

As good as his word, Sarge matched the current so Abbey rowed right up to the back of the boat and grabbed the ladder with her left hand. She pushed up and swung her buttocks to the platform as if it were a low-profile dock, and with her legs holding her shell close, she unfastened her oars and handed them one at a time to Sarge. Then she stood and picked up her shell, held it to her hip with one hand and used the other hand to hold on as she sidestepped up the short ladder. Sarge met her at the top and helped her bring the shell on board and secure it. Once again, the long, low open deck of Sarge's boat allowed it to be used for something for which it had never been designed.

"Did we just do that, Sarge?" He nodded and walked away. She let out a big breath, then wrung water from the tail of her tank top. Sarge appeared with a folded stack of colorful towels, handed her one off the top, then motioned toward the man with the remaining stack.

"Softer'n the deck," Sarge said.

Preppy was out cold. She gently placed two towels beneath his head. The warm sun would dry him in no time. She studied him. His lips were parted and he breathed deeply, occasionally blowing up his cheeks and emitting a phhhhhhh snore. His fingers were balled into soft fists on top of his belly. She straightened them gently and noticed a roughness, perhaps calluses, on the underneath side of his long, tapered fingers. His nails were short-clipped without a speck of dirt or oil under them, not those of a fisherman or someone who fooled around with boat motors. A tan ran from the bottom of his shorts to his feet, much like hers, so he obviously spent time outside.

Water dripped from small clumps of hair around her face and she wished she had a visor to keep it out of her eyes. She wondered if the hat she'd found belonged to this fellow. Lucky. If the tide had been going out instead of in, both the hat and the man would be well on their way to Florida. She stood back to see if there was anything else she could do for him.

Preppy's eyes opened. "Are we there yet?"

"Not yet. You just rest."

She called to Sarge, who was fooling with his shrimp net. "Got any ice or water on board?"

"In there." Sarge motioned toward a covered hatch at the stern. Abbey nodded and went to the cooler, where she scooped ice into the towel she had used and grabbed a gallon jug of water. There was a sleeve of Solo cups beside the cooler so she filled one.

"Look yonder," Sarge called back to her. Abbey walked over and followed his gaze.

"What is it?"

"Beer can. Musta been whoever hit this feller 'cuz most folks around here is better 'bout takin' care of the 'viromet." Sarge waddled back to the steering wheel.

Icy water from the towel dripped onto her foot. Abbey went to Preppy and knelt beside him. After helping him drink, she unbuttoned the one remaining button on his shirt and put the ice pack on the large, purple bruise on his chest. It looked like it would ooze like a ripe peach if she pressed it with her fingertip. His shirt was nice, not a fisherman's shirt but a fastidious dresser's shirt, similar to the one from Brooks Brothers she had given to Tom for Christmas. The man was in decent shape, not cut like a gym rat but fit enough and looking like he enjoyed the beer he had mentioned several times. Dark hair. No tattoos, wedding band, or shoes. Kinda cute. Clean cut anyway.

"Where to?" Sarge called.

Abbey joined him up front. She had spoken to him before but they had never had a real conversation. Sarge was known as a man of few words, and she had noticed that he cupped his hand over his ear when spoken to at Kings Bluff, so she stood as close to him as she could without getting in his way.

"He was hit pretty hard, Sarge. We're about midway between Brunswick and Jacksonville but I know Jacksonville Medical has a trauma unit." Tom Clark in a hospital bed, with his shoulder bandaged and tubes running from him to beeping machines, flashed through her mind. He was why she knew about the unit. She took a deep breath. "I know they're good with trauma. No telling what kind of injuries this guy has. Jacksonville's our best bet."

"I'll contact DNR," Sarge said.

Abbey thought for several seconds. "We're closer to Kings Bluff than Jekyll, St. Marys, or Fernandina."

"DNR'll meet us there. They'll call everybody else," Sarge said.

Diesel noise drowned out the squawking gulls who followed the boat in anticipation of handouts. She looked back at the man passed out in the sun. What kind of people would run over a person and leave him to die in the river? The world was full of sorry people, it seemed. It remained to be seen whether this fellow was a bad guy or just an unlucky one.

She turned back to Sarge. "What's the story with that ladder?"

"Sometimes I need to get down to one of my crab traps if it's tangled up or somethin'. I gotta git real close to the water."

"Worked for me. You pull many crab traps?" She had followed gallon milk jugs tied to crab traps all morning.

"A few. Crab man's got 'em too." Sarge aimed his lips toward the water on the right side of the boat and let go a stream of brown. "I do mostly swimpin."

"Unh-hunh." Abbey watched the juicy blob of spit airstream until it landed with a splat on the deck inches from the man. Now she understood what Sarge had been doing right before he turned his boat her way. He hadn't heard her whistling and yelling—he'd seen her when he turned to spit. "Were you headed out to shrimp this morning?"

"Yep. Heard sumpin' wuddin' right." He pointed a thumb at the man on his deck, then tuned his VHF radio to channel 16.

"DNR, right?"

"Yep."

"You know Jim Godwin who works for them?"

Sarge nodded, then tilted his head like she was pulling his leg. "You know Godwin?"

"Yes. He helped me with a little problem here last year."

"Drug deal?" Sarge said.

"Yes."

Sarge spat again, straight down into the river. Better aim this time. "I took time off from caretakin' at Kings Bluff last summer. Blood clots in ma laigs. Club put me back on after they's fixed." He handed Abbey a thermos. "Give him a drink. Caffeine. Might do him some good."

Abbey walked back to check on their passenger. She knelt beside the man, raised his head slightly and dripped coffee between his lips. They moved.

"Ummm," he groaned.

"I'll give you as much as you want." She dripped until her arm grew tired and his lips closed.

She stood and walked to the stern as they passed the dock at Taylor's Point, a place full of memories, of childhood fishing outings and so much more. Her mother was always after her to write. This adventure could be a chapter in her first novel. Maybe it was time to start. She didn't want to die without realizing her childhood dream to be a writer. There was the money aspect. How would she support herself? If you wanted to do anything badly enough you could. It was worth thinking about. Her head was full of things to think about, the insistent Mr. Thomas Clark being one of the main ones. He wouldn't believe today's adventure.

When she went back to the wheel, Sarge was talking. He handed her the phone. Jim Godwin said he would make the necessary calls and would meet them within the hour at the dock in front of her mother's cottage at Kings Bluff.

Abbey looked around the boat as they made their way down the river. "Sarge, I have never seen a boat like this. What is it?

"Deadrise workboat. Use 'em up in Virginia."

She wondered if she had heard him right. "Did you say deadrise?"

"Yep. See that sharp bow? Foller that to the stern. It flattens out into that wide V. If'n you was to look at her from the side, you'd see a gradule slope on up to the bow. Reckon that's why they call it a deadrise 'cause it don't get up to that bow point in no hurry. That's a deadrise angle, gradual like. Makes a good stable workin' boat. That's why I can haul shrimps, crab traps, and fish offen her."

Abbey moved to the side of the boat. "Don't forget rescue people, carry rowing shells…" Sarge nodded and kept on driving while Abbey watched white egrets feed along the marshy mud bank of the meandering river.

FOUR

As they rounded the bend, the first of several Kings Bluff docks came into view. A young father gathered a cast net into one hand, while he talked to the small boy at his side, then he tossed the net. Clad in shorts and a striped t-shirt, the boy hopped up and down and pointed excitedly at the deadrise slipping up the river toward him. The man looked up, nodded at Abbey, and emptied his catch onto the dock. Abbey remembered her father teaching her and her brothers how to throw the cast net. The focus was always on the river and what it was doing, what was its tide stage and what it might provide for dinner that night. Abbey smiled and waved and the little boy waved timidly, then stuck his thumb into his mouth and watched them move on.

They continued up-river slowly so as not to wake boats tied up at docks along the bluff. Word traveled fast. People watched from shore. Emergency vehicle lights flashed on the bank up ahead.

"It looks like they're waiting for us, Sarge."

They pulled up to a dock midway down the bluff, the one in front of Abbey's mother's cottage. Several men moved boats to make room for Sarge and another man waved him into the vacated spot. Sarge acknowledged with a wave, then nudged into the space.

"There's Godwin," Abbey said. She tossed a bow line to Jim Godwin of the DNR while Sarge dropped a rope to a man at the stern.

"Holy smoke, Jim. Is the National Guard on its way too?"

Jim pulled Sarge's boat up close to the floating dock and secured it to a metal cleat.

"Nah. Just the usual. EMTs and sheriff's office, since it was a hit-and-run. Sheriff will want to talk to you, of course. What kind of trouble have you gotten into this time?"

"I swear I didn't go looking, Jim. It finds me down here."

Two young men in identical emergency garb carried a stretcher down the narrow ramp, then hopped on board. Abbey introduced herself and Sarge and explained what she knew about the boating accident, which wasn't much.

"I iced his chest and gave him water and a little coffee." The two men went to work so she backed away and stood nearby. Maybe she'd learn something.

Sarge busied himself putting things back in place, his movements slow and as deliberate as a three-hundred-pound tin-man outfitted in baggy, faded britches and a parachute of a shirt. An unlikely savior. Sarge's white rubber boots squeaked on the wet wood deck as he stacked buckets, wound ropes, and secured the ring float in a storage box. From the looks of it, this was the first time in a good long while that his boat had received such painstaking attention. He worked a chaw in the back of his left cheek like an oversized chipmunk with a wad of acorns. If he hadn't shown up, that fellow could be dead by now. Sarge glanced at her. When their eyes met, he looked away and went back to coiling his ropes.

A young policeman appeared on the dock. Square-jawed and muscular, he stood straight as a hickory stick and looked to be all business. Serious. She watched the way he attacked his gum and decided if he went after her like that she had better organize her thoughts. Clutching a clipboard in one hand, he jammed his other fist on his hipbone and lit into Sarge, not her.

"That boat yours?" The cop shot the question up at Sarge just as the shrimper dropped a bumper over the side of his boat to keep her from rubbing against the dock.

"Yessir." Sarge stopped what he was doing, wiped his chin, then stuffed his hands into his deep pockets like a disobedient child and continued to work his chaw.

The cop stopped chomping on his gum and shook his head. "You put in the call to DNR?"

Sarge nodded.

"DNR called the sheriff's department," the cop said. His jaw muscles were back at it, his arms were crossed over his chest, and his thigh and butt muscles squirmed under his tight-fitting britches like snakes in a barrel.

Abbey glanced at Godwin, who walked along the dock until he was beside the cop.

"Like I said when I called it in, this was a hit-and-run," Godwin said.

Abbey detested the cop's bully attitude. His voice matched his black-mirrored don't-let-them-see-my-eyes sunglasses and I'm-tough-as-shit separated foot stance. Whereas she knew Jim to be a nice man, she wasn't getting a whole lot of warm and fuzzy from the cop.

"What happened here, big guy?" The cop looked in the direction of the techs, but who could tell what he was looking at from behind the shades. "You didn't see him swimming or what?"

A brown stream of saliva slipped over Sarge's lip, which he swiped with the back of a hand, which he then dragged across the seat of his pants.

Abbey walked to the edge of the boat and looked down on the cop. "I don't know where you're from but you don't swim in the sound voluntarily. Sharks do though. Plenty of sharks out there. DNR knows what happened. Talk to Godwin."

The cop lifted the brim of his hat, then resettled it on his head.

"This man," she touched Sarge's shoulder briefly and studied the cop's clipboard, "had nothing to do with the hit-and-run, Sheriff Jerkoff."

The cop stopped chewing and followed Abbey's eyes to the clipboard, on the back of which his last name was printed in bold black letters.

"Name's Terkoff," he said through gritted teeth, which immediately restarted the vicious mandibular assault on his gum. His stance widened and his hips thrust forward.

Oh, please. Is this intimidation? Abbey dismissed him with "Whatever," and started toward the EMTs.

"Yeah, well, hold on, lady. If you know so much, what the hell happened here, ah, Ms...."

Abbey stopped and turned back. "Bunn," she said. "Abbey Taylor Bunn, as in hamburger but with two n's. I was rowing this morning and found a man doing the backstroke in the shark tank." She cut her eyes to Sarge. His bottom lip quivered and his shoulders moved, then he looked at his boots. A chuckle maybe? She gave Terkoff the Cliff Notes version of what had happened early that morning.

Godwin said, "That fellow is damn lucky, Terkoff. If they hadn't come along when they did, we wouldn't be standing here having this conversation and that fellow would probably be a legless torso bobbing toward the Atlantic or on the bottom of the sound by now. You wouldn't have a crime to investigate now, would you?"

"Exactly," Abbey mumbled as she stepped to the dock.

Two additional EMTs received the stretcher as it was passed down from the deadrise. Terkoff looked at the injured man as he passed by. Abbey, Godwin and Terkoff walked off the dock together. In a somewhat chastened voice, Terkoff said, "Ms. Bunn, you mind walking with me to my car so I can get your contact information? This is a hit-and-run now, but..."

"But what?" Abbey said.

"Brain injury. There's always a chance he won't make it."

FIVE

When all the excitement died down, Sarge helped Abbey take her boat and oars to the cottage, where she hosed off the salt water and secured everything. Her stomach rumbled. No wonder. One cup of hot tea at dawn. Lunch time.

Watch Dog wagged and danced at the back door when she opened it. "I know, I know. I have to go too."

Moments later she re-emerged in dry shorts and a t-shirt and grabbed a peach and a dog biscuit on her way through the kitchen. "Come on, fella'. Let's take a long walk." She scratched his ears. "You're such a good boy."

The yellow lab darted through the opened door and bee-lined to the hickory tree by the porch, then he tore off across the dirt road to the river bank. With his nose to the ground, he vacuumed scents from tree to dirt to bush. Abbey went left on the road and whistled and soon heard the galloping thump of feet on hard-packed dirt. Watch Dog forged ahead down the sandy road adding his prints to those of raccoons, deer and humans, and the squiggly track of a snake.

When they returned from their walk, Abbey took a tomato-and-Vidalia-onion sandwich to the screened porch. It was the first time she had sat down for more than a moment since she got out of her shell that morning and she was whipped. On the first ring of the phone, she jumped up and flipped the remainder of her sandwich to Watch Dog. Tom, an attorney, was in Philadelphia for a trial. He was good about calling, being a man who was genuinely interested in how she spent her days. She hit the high spots of her morning, adding details she knew the attorney in him would want to know.

"Good grief, Abbey. Was he cut to hell and back?"

"No, prop didn't get him. I don't know how, but it looked to me like he took the brunt of it on his head and chest. He's a little wacky, talking nonsense, but I guess I would be too if I'd had a head-on with a boat. I can't believe they left him out there."

"No, that's some kind of evil person. But he'll be out of it for a while. That's pretty typical for a head injury. Football players get their marbles rattled all the time. Have you been to see him?"

"No. I just ate and I'm pretty tired. I'll call the hospital first to make sure it's okay to visit him, then I'll go. It'll be interesting to see if he even recognizes me."

"Good idea." A moment passed. "What is it with you and these river rescues?"

"You've got me. Amazing, isn't it?"

"It is, and I agree with what you said earlier. I bet that hat is his. It fits the scenario too perfectly not to be. I think you have fallen into your calling here on God's green earth. Some people look their entire lives and never find theirs, and these things just fall into your lap, or boat, or something."

She chuckled. "I guess. It would make an interesting line on my business card, wouldn't it? Real Estate and River Rescue. Sounds awkward, but I have seen agents who put every continuing education designation they have ever gotten on theirs. Mine might give me an interesting edge and it would certainly open up conversation."

"It would sure do that," Tom said.

"So, are you about to wrap things up in Philadelphia?"

"We're getting close and it's a good thing."

"Why is that?"

"I'm almost out of boxer shorts."

"You are so lame. Ever hear of a laundromat? I'm sure they have them in Philly. They usually take quarters. You can do your underwear while you read the Inquirer."

"Nah. There's a service here at the hotel. They do my shirts and shorts every day."

"You spoiled brat. Why don't you come down here for a few days once you're free there?"

"How long are you staying? I'm playing golf with clients this coming Friday in Atlanta but I have some time coming to me if you plan to stay for a while longer."

"I have the house for two weeks and I arrived yesterday. That was Friday, right?"

"Yep. Believe so."

"Right, so I'll be here a while. See what you can do. I can pick you up at the Jacksonville airport unless you need your car, in which case you can drive down. Your choice. Anyway, this hit-and-run guy might need a good lawyer."

"Hit-and-runs aren't really my thing, but I could use a break. We're working straight through this weekend and I hope to get away from here Wednesday or Thursday. Once I get to Atlanta, I'll see if they can spare me for a few days. I need that porch. And a cold beer. And a mess of crabs."

"Is that all?"

"No, my dear, that's only the half of it."

"Okay. That's better. I'll try to stay busy until you manage to get down here."

"Busy has never been a problem for you, Abbey."

"Oh la-di-da."

"Don't give me that bored stuff. You never have time to get bored. I bet you're glad you had that PFD with you. Is it back in your boat where it belongs?"

"Yes. Definitely. You never know who I might need to rescue next."

"Very funny, but try to be careful. You have no idea what this fellow is involved in. I know you're going to do what you want when you want because you have a mind of your own, but please don't do anything outrageous—or dangerous."

"Is that an order?"

"Yes."

She scratched between Watch Dog's shoulder blades. "There's a blonde-haired fellow licking my leg."

"What? Who—"

"Ha-ha-ha," Abbey said. "Gotcha."

"Oh," Tom said. "Damn. Watch Dog. Give him a scratch for me."

Abbey smiled. "I can't throw that bloody baton thing very far out in the river. He misses his buddy with the good arm."

"Yeah, well, his buddy misses the leg his pal is slurping. You two behave."

"I miss you, Tom."

"Yeah, miss you too."

Abbey hung up the phone. Tom was an unusual man. He had figured out early on that she didn't like to be told what to do so he didn't, most of the time. He offered suggestions and didn't get all preachy to try to make his points. They pretty much stayed out of each other's way.

She grabbed a glass of water and a legal pad and headed back to the porch. Outside was always better than in. Lumpy with layers of gray paint, the old wooden rocker emitted slow, low moans like a well-oiled saddle. Soothing and peaceful. She stared at the river. What a day. Before her impressions from the morning became all foggy and started to change shape, she wanted to write them down. Watch Dog scrambled to his feet by her chair. A rumble vibrated deep in his throat.

"Sit, boy. Stay." She patted the dog's head and looked around to see what disturbed him. The rumble stayed just below a growl.

SIX

U "Uh ... Ms. Bunn," a male voice said from the far side of the porch.

Watch Dog's toenails clawed for traction on the uneven wooden floor. Abbey stood and turned just in time to hear the collision of battering ram head and screen and to see the furry yellow rump pass through the frame of the destroyed screened door. "Whoa, boy. Whoa."

Watch Dog put on the brakes one foot from an open-mouthed Terkoff, whose hand froze on its way to his weapon.

"Damn," Terkoff said without looking away from the dog.

"Dead," Abbey said from the porch.

"What?" Terkoff hazarded a quick glance at her but then his eye went back to the dog. "Who, me?"

"No, the screened door." When she opened the mutilated door, the rusty spring screeched. "Once, I saw the little round bum of one of my nephews crawl through a hole in this screen made by another dog. It made a cute picture."

Terkoff took his eyes off of the dog and looked her way, his mirrored glasses reflecting blue sky peeking through pine boughs.

"Oh, sorry, Terkoff. Won't you come in?"

"Is he okay?" Terkoff dipped a shoulder toward Watch Dog. His hand hovered over his pistol. "Sorry about the door. I'll have it fixed."

"Screen's probably thirty years old. I'll tack this one down one more time. No big deal. It needs to be replaced anyway." She looked at Terkoff. "Are you coming in or are you going to stand out there in the yard and feed the sand gnats?"

He looked at the dog, who hadn't budged.

"Oh. Watch, it's okay, boy. Come."

Watch Dog inched up until his great wet nose tickled Terkoff's gun hand.

Terkoff stiffened. "What's he doing?"

"Saying hello."

Watch Dog's pink tongue slapped at the sheriff's hand. Terkoff's mouth opened and emitted a little squeak.

"He likes you. Relax." She waved him up. "Join me. Care for a glass of iced tea?"

Terkoff followed Watch Dog to the porch, his eyes not leaving the animal's head until the dog resumed his supine position beside Abbey's chair. Only then did the sheriff look up and allow his eyes to travel over the enormous expanse of marsh across the river. "I didn't even know this place was down here until today."

"Good. That's the way we like to keep it."

He nodded. "I had a long talk with Godwin. He told me about the drug bust near here last year."

"Okay. Now you know how we met. Busting scumbags, and here we go again. Another opportunity to bust scumbags, if we can figure out who they are, right?"

"Yeah, right." Terkoff looked up and down the road. "I didn't get a chance to look around here much this morning. What is this place?"

"It's a private hunting and fishing club. Members only. There are about forty cottages along this bluff. Folks come to fish, crab, hunt, or just get away. Have a seat. Be my guest."

He looked at her. "Yanking my chain again?"

Abbey moved the legal pad from her chair and sat. "No, just trying to make you feel comfortable. The membership and this cottage belong to my mother. Her father was one of the founders and her mother gave her membership and the cottage to Momma so her Atlanta grandchildren and her daughter would come visit now and then. Momma grew up in Wayside, Georgia, about an hour from here near the Okefenokee Swamp."

"Nice. What a great spot." Terkoff chose a rocker. "You hunt?"

"No, but I shoot."

"Shotgun?"

"Pistol. There's a range on the back of the property."

"That's good. You practice there?"

"On occasion."

He removed his sunglasses. "I like the way this place looks. It's so damn quiet."

"Thanks. I like it. I forgot about our tea. Sound good to you?"

"Sounds great. I'm dry as a bone."

Abbey returned with two tall glasses of tannin-colored tea and a plate of sandwiches cut in half. "I skipped breakfast so I had a tomato sandwich just before you got here, but I'm still hungry. Rowing and rescuing people are tough work." She put the plate and glasses on a small table between them. "All I have is jalapeno pimento. I'll warn you, it has a little kick."

Terkoff grabbed one. "I'm starved." He took a bite. "Wow. You aren't kidding it kicks. Excellent." He polished off one and took another.

"So, what brings you calling? I guess you're the new sheriff in town because Godwin and I dealt with an older fellow last year during that drug bust."

"He retired when I came on, moved to the mountains. I was able to get our John Doe checked in at the hospital okay. You wouldn't believe the nonsense that guy was spouting. None of it made any sense. I called the hospital just before I headed over here, and he's in and out of it, sleeping mostly. They're keeping a close watch on him. He'll have one hell of a headache when he comes around, if he comes around."

"He's going to come around, Terkoff."

"Yeah. Sure. It's obvious they intended to kill that poor sucker. Probably figured they had." He looked her in the eyes. "When he's better, I hope he'll be able to fill us in on who did this to him."

"He's smart." Abbey scratched Watch Dog's head. He panted and kept cutting his eyes from her to Terkoff. "Somehow he avoided a direct blow. You get hit by a boat, you're going to end up dead— usually—or at least chewed up by the prop. He stayed clear of those blades."

"True. Thank goodness we're not dealing with usually here." Terkoff sipped his tea. "Unfortunately, you're the only one with any knowledge of what happened."

"Yes, well, John Doe and the people in the motorboat and I have differing amounts of knowledge about what happened. We talked a little when I first got to him."

"Did he say anything that made sense?"

"No, not really. I mean, he acted like it was no big deal that I just happened by right after he was run over by a boat. He wasn't making any sense at all. Amazing how a brain can block something like that."

"We probably can't count on anything he says right now. I've seen this before. He's disoriented. I just hope it comes back to him pretty soon so we can go after the driver."

"He did say to me, 'Where did they go,' but he could have been talking about anybody any time. I think it just popped into his head."

"So, that's all?"

"Pretty much. I kept talking so he wouldn't be frightened and every now and then he would say something, but it didn't fit the situation. He wanted a beer. That was kind of funny. He never seemed frightened when I was with him."

Terkoff's lips pressed together in a straight line. "Can you think of anything else, anything at all? You never know what might be useful."

She sipped her tea and stood. "I left that dock early today." She pointed to the dock in front of the cottage.

Terkoff stood and his eyes followed her finger. "That's where I met you with our John Doe this morning, right?"

"Correct. I rowed around that big marsh out there and then cut to the left. You can't see it from here." They both sat back down. "I rowed from that river into a creek. I heard men talking over the sound of their motor." She thought for several seconds. "Actually, they were yelling."

"You didn't see the boat." The sheriff rocked tentatively.

"Not at first, not until I rowed around a bit of marsh and got out into the bigger water." Abbey's forehead wrinkled. "The boat circled." She drew an air circle with her finger. "You know how the sound goes away from you, then comes back toward you? Doppler effect, I think they call it. I could tell by the sound that it circled."

"Huh. Doppler's a ten-dollar high school science word, Ms. Bunn."

"Yeah, right. Anyway, I think it circled. Then I heard this loud noise like a thunk. Imagine if you dropped a pillowcase full of sheets from a balcony onto a wooden floor. That sound but much, much louder." She thought for several seconds. "Someone yelled or yelped or something. I don't know. I was too far away."

Terkoff scribbled notes on his pad, then looked up at Abbey. "Was the circling before or after the loud noise?"

She closed her eyes, then squeezed them tighter. "I think before." Her eyes opened. "By the time I got to him, the motorboat was pretty far away. I could be wrong, but I think there were at least two people in the motorboat. I saw one standing in the stern; then of course there was the driver. They headed south, I think." Terkoff wrote furiously.

"I had a feeling there was something going on." She remembered the hat and glanced at the sheriff jotting notes as fast as she talked. "I found a hat in the water before I found him."

He looked up. "What do you mean? What kind of hat?"

"When I was rowing. I found a hat. When I got to him, our guy didn't have on shoes or a hat or sunglasses or anything like that."

"If he had on any of that stuff, it was probably long gone by the time you got to him what with the current and all. Probably sunk dead away or was carried out on the tide."

"The tide was coming in, Terkoff."

"Oh, yeah. I remember now. Maybe I ought to take the hat." He turned pinkish, then looked down and vigorously erased something he had written.

"Yeah. Maybe you should. You might find one of his hairs on it or something." She waited a minute. "You ever run over anything in your car, Terkoff?"

"Dog once."

"Yeah, me too. Remember how it sounded?"

He nodded. "Made me sick."

"You never forget it. That's what that thunk sounded like, a soft hit, not hard like a board or another boat. It sounded like it hurt."

"All of this stuff is important. Hell, everything's always important. There was a robbery on Sea Island last night in one of those big houses on the beach. Made a pretty good haul from the looks of it, all the wife's jewelry."

"When did you learn this?"

"This morning on my way over here."

"No way these could be connected, is there?"

"Who knows? Maybe they were splitting up the goods and the two you saw got rid of John Doe so they'd have more for themselves. We can't rule anything out. You never know what people's motives are."

"I hear you."

Terkoff said, "At least our John Doe's accident wasn't fatal. It could have ended up differently."

Abbey looked at him hard. "I wouldn't call this an accident. Incident maybe, but that was no accident."

He gave her a quick look, erased a word and wrote something else. "Right. Better description. You an English major or something?"

"Matter of fact, yes."

"Are you a college professor?" Terkoff studied Abbey's worn shorts and flip-flops.

"No. I'm an Atlanta real estate agent on vacation."

"Huh. You always spend your vacations rescuing people?"

"You'd be surprised."

"Oh, yeah, the drug bust last year—which reminds me." He gathered his things. "We need to keep a lid on this until we can check some things out, see if the robbery connects. I'll be in touch, but if you hear anything give me a call." He handed her his card.

The cottage sat on a corner. Its front faced the river and its right side faced the road into the club; across that road were the low red-brick clubhouse and the old tabby pool. Abbey and Watch Dog walked Terkoff around the side of the house just as a car pulled up with a family going for a swim. The dad who had thrown the cast net on the dock that morning stepped from the driver's side of the car and watched Abbey and Terkoff walk toward the patrol car. Mom exited the passenger's side. The little boy in her arms pointed at the patrol car and Mom looked Abbey's way. The dad flipped up both palms at waist level and mouthed "you okay?" at Abbey. She waved to him, then held up a circled thumb and middle finger and mouthed "I'm fine" back to him.

"I'll talk to them when you leave," she said to Terkoff. "The man and the boy saw us coming in this morning."

Terkoff scratched his chin. "I guess that's all I need for now. You have my card."

Abbey held up her hand to show him the palmed card.

"By the way. Godwin gave me his account of the drug arrest last year but I'd like to hear yours."

"Terkoff, I have a feeling we will have plenty of time to talk about that one once we get this one sorted out. Later, okay?"

"You got it. Adios."

Terkoff's tires whirred when they left dirt and hit asphalt. Abbey walked over to the pool and briefly explained to the couple what had happened that morning.

At the cottage, she refilled her glass of tea and headed back to the porch. Real estate had taught her the value of writing down dates, times, names, and who said what to whom. The habit had come in handy on more than one occasion. She wrote for a minute or two, then put down her pen. "He forgot the hat."

Late that afternoon, the crimson epaulets of red-winged blackbirds shone brilliantly in the setting sun as they flitted from one slender stalk of spartina grass to the next and sang oh-ka-lee, oh-ka-lee, oh-ka-lee, to a final sharp trill. Abbey stood on the bank and watched the fickle disquietude of their hopping from one stalk to the next, doing what God created them to do, singing and using their miraculous engineering.

Everyone has had a flying dream, maybe because of our fascination with how birds get around. Abbey's was a recurring one when she was a child. She would get a running start in her back yard, her little legs pumping harder and harder, then a Peter Paul Mounds candy bar would swoop down beside her and she'd jump on as it lifted her from the grass. Wind whipped through her hair; the dizzying height made her gasp. She flew and sailed on invisible currents, the sensation light and free. It was wonderful. Standing on the bank, she raised her arms to the breeze, and felt it move around her outstretched limbs.

A truck passed on the road behind her and a voice called out, "Pretty, isn't it?"

Abbey half-turned and waved, then watched the setting sun. The coppery pink glow deepened by the second to a rich raspberry-orange. Day is done, gone the sun, from the lakes, from the hills, from the skies… all is well, safely rest, God is nigh. Those days at summer camp were carefree and simple, but even with all of this day's goings-on, all was well. Trusting her instincts was something she had worked hard on since her divorce the previous year. Another relationship so soon after disentangling herself from that abusive one was the farthest thing from her mind but it had happened, and under the oddest of circumstances. At first, trusting Tom Clark had been difficult, but it was his screwed-up marriage that brought them together in the first place. He had been hurt too. Since then they'd had their ups and downs and managed to talk through things. Tom was a good man. No, he was an exceptional man.

That morning, instinct had led to another rescue. The man was in good hands now and would hopefully recover sufficiently enough to tell Terkoff what happened to him.

"Ouch!" She swatted her leg and brought back a bloodied hand. Mosquitos loved sunset too. Reluctantly, she walked back to the porch and watched the last bit of light hiss into the horizon.

SEVEN

As she dried her shell Sunday morning with an old towel, Abbey grinned at the thought of the children several doors down who had accosted her when she and Watch Dog walked past their house a few hours earlier. They had a proposition. Before school started in the fall, they wanted their parents to give them a dog, and to prove they were up to the responsibility of caring for a pet, they figured if they proved they could take care of someone else's dog, their parents might give in.

Abbey had agreed, but under the condition that she treated this like a job. If she used their services, she would pay them. If she wanted to do something with Watch herself, there was to be no discussion. That way, they would help her and she would help them by starting a "dog kitty" for food and toys and dog stuff. They'd shaken on it and the children had come over to the cottage for a half-hour for a dog tutorial and then headed out with their new charge.

The message light was blinking when she went inside. There was one from her mother "just checking in," and one from her office at Dorsey Alston Realtors in Atlanta which she hadn't picked up the day before. The receptionist's message recited a list of clients who had returned calls Abbey had made to them, but there was one from a potential new client who asked that Abbey call her as soon as possible. The woman's phone number was in the same area code as the cottage at Kings Bluff. Excellent. *Maybe she has a million-dollar cottage on Sea Island she wants me to list.*

Boonks, the affectionate nickname Abbey's grandfather had given to his only daughter, was shocked when Abbey recounted details of the rescue and only stopped with her worried-mother comments when Abbey changed the subject and suggested she come to Kings Bluff for a few days while Abbey was there. When Boonks found out Tom was due down soon, she said she wouldn't dare interrupt their time together but she might drive down after Tom left. Abbey said she'd stay an extra day or two if her mother could come.

She then dialed the number her receptionist had left. Vickie Croek's Virginia Tidewater accent sounded like warmed molasses. Abbey hung on every word and mouthed several delicious ones silently. Only a Southerner could make poetry out of vowels. After they exchanged the usual pleasantries, Vickie offered that she owned two homes, one in a new development in St. Marys and another in Orlando, Florida—a home she described as "substantial" and situated in one of those "McDonald's" kind of subdivisions. Abbey assumed she meant McMansion, a snarky term agents used to describe gaudy, overly embellished new construction built by people with new money, as opposed to the elegant old grandes dames in cities like Atlanta.

As Abbey listened, she formed an opinion about her potential new client. Vickie loved adjectives and details and there was probably a great deal of hand-waving and gesturing going on. Several times Abbey tried to steer the conversation back to real estate. It was clear Vickie wanted to gab.

Abbey glanced at the wall clock. After the long day yesterday, she planned to put out the crab trap, go for a swim, and sit by the pool with a book. It was Sunday, after all, and a snooze in a deck chair would be welcome. Vickie jabbered on and on.

"So, Vickie," she said when Vickie drew a breath, "my office said you specifically wanted to talk to me. I'm flattered but curious. I assume you need help with real estate." She stretched the phone cord to the refrigerator and took out the remains of a chunk of New York sharp cheddar and put it on the counter to get to room temperature.

"Why, yes, Abbey, of course." The rise in Vickie's voice on course indicated she was surprised Abbey might think otherwise.

Abbey pulled up a nearby chair and sat. "You know, Vickie, I basically work metro Atlanta. I'm happy to talk to you but I'm wondering just what—"

"Oh, honey, I know. Please let me explain. I know I tend to go on and on, or so my husband tells me." Abbey pulled the phone's curly cord to its full extension, then let go and watched it corkscrew to a white wad of plastic spaghetti.

"I read about you in the paper."

Abbey jumped to her feet. Watch Dog rose and poked her thigh with his cold nose. "Oh. You did? When? Which paper?" Terkoff and Godwin had both sworn no details would be released to the newspaper until they had a grip on what had gone down. Of course, Kings Bluff was twelve miles from civilization and she hadn't turned on the television since she'd gotten here two days ago. News of the rescue could be plastered all over the newspapers and the TV, and she wouldn't know a word of it.

Vickie "ummmmed" into the phone. "It was after you helped with that drug bust last year. I don't remember the paper. Probably the local one in Brunswick. I happened to be on St. Simons with an acquaintance, a real estate agent actually."

Abbey took a deep breath and dropped back into the chair. Watch licked her toes, then flattened his soft warm body onto her feet.

"We stopped for lunch and it was on the television. I hate it when restaurants have TVs on, but I was mesmerized. It was terribly exciting. I mean, you were actually there when the plane dropped the marijuana and then you helped capture those druggies and then that fire afterwards. My word. I couldn't believe it, and you being a real estate agent and all."

As Vickie babbled on, Abbey stood again and let out held breath. She walked the length of the curly cord and back, picked up a pencil, and added a note—saw drug bust newspaper article—below Vickie's name and number.

"And I was so impressed I could have just split a seam. The fact that you were right there on that bust, well, I ditched that little meapy agent I was with right then and there. Thanked her and told her goodbye and that I no longer needed her services. After all, my husband and I already had a place to stay, well, sort of. It was a dump on this little creek, but at least it was a roof over our heads. Anyway, the only reason I was with that agent in the first place was we chatted in line at the grocery store and she just sort of latched on. You know how they do."

No, don't believe I have ever snagged anyone in the grocery store line, but I know an ambulance chaser or two.

"Of course, I had told her about my house in Orlando so I think she thought she'd found Mrs. Got-rocks and she could sell me something huge and get a big fat commission." Vickie took a breath. "After all that drug bust stuff on television, I decided right then and there you were the woman for me if I ever decided to buy in Georgia."

"I see." Although the celebrity felt good, Abbey waited. Vickie rarely paused for long.

"Listen, you don't know me from Adam's house cat, but let me fill you in a little bit. Bart, that's my husband,"—Abbey mouthed the way Vickie said Baht and couldn't help but smile—"well, Bart has dabbled in real estate over the years." Vickie paused again as if to choose appropriate words. "I feel stupid asking him business questions. Now I know that's silly because you'd think I could ask my husband anything. Right?"

No stupid questions, blah, blah, blah. She'd hated to ask her ex questions for the same reason. "Don't worry, Vickie. Ask away."

"Okay. Abbey, I don't think I can do this over the phone. It feels, I don't know, it feels sneaky or something, like I'm talking about Bart behind his back."

You haven't said anything about him except he dabbles in real estate. Abbey tapped her eraser on the pad.

"I know I'm beating around the bush, but I need some real estate advice and I feel like you can give me what I need. I want you to know that I will buy something from you. I won't waste your time. I have friends at home who are in the business and they tell me they spend half their lives showing people around and then they go buy a for-sale-by-owner or something. That's just not right."

"Good, Vickie, I'm glad you feel that way. I look forward to talking more about what you might want. What works for you?"

"Could we maybe meet today for a late lunch? I have an appointment in a minute that'll take about an hour so could we say one-ish? My treat."

She thought for several seconds about the swim and snooze she'd looked forward to but eventually gave in as she usually did. Another closing down the road wouldn't hurt. If she got cleaned up, she could even drop by the hospital before or after. "Sure. Sounds good. Where shall we meet?"

"There's a great little place over here if that's not too far for you. It's right across from the marina, where there's always plenty of action. We can sit inside, of course, but there's a nice deck so we can look at the water. I love to look at the water. Does that work for you?"

Abbey waited for several seconds but Vickie was finished. "And where is here, St. Marys?"

"Oh, silly me. Didn't I say?"

"You said you have a house in St. Marys and your number has a local Georgia area code, but I just wanted to make sure."

"Oh, you're good with the details, Abbey, but I already know that about you. What other real estate agent could help split up a drug ring, for crying out loud?" Abbey rolled her eyes.

"If you're not familiar with this area, St. Marys is just north of Fernandina. It's an adorable little village in Georgia, not Florida, and there's a little curvy creek which runs through the marsh there." Vickie giggled. "That's why my development is called Crooked Creek."

"I'm familiar with St. Marys." Abbey stared at the cheese. Her stomach rumbled.

"Oh, okay, great. The lunch menu is good there and I insist on paying. No arguments. What do you say?"

"Sounds good. I know where it is. See you one... ish." *Bet she's late.*

"Perfect," Vickie said. "And, Abbey, just so you know, I am serious. I will buy something from you."

That was all Abbey needed to hear.

EIGHT

Vickie Croek had arranged a private tennis lesson for that morning. Her instructor had helped her work on her serve and her stroke. Funny, she had never thought about addressing the ball, whatever that meant. She thought you just whacked the thing when it got close to you, so he assured her that wasn't true at all and showed her by wrapping his arms around her and placing his hands on hers. His arms were tan and ripped and his veins poked out like those of a racehorse after a trip around the track. When they moved through an entire swing, their bodies melted together as though they were dancing. Aftershave was the other thing. His was divinely sexy, manly with a hint of spice, and just enough so as not to drown out his own personal scent.

Private lessons with her instructor didn't involve as much running around as her group lessons did, so she wasn't that sweaty and it was a good thing. She was a little short on time before her lunch meeting with Abbey. Good impressions were important but she didn't have time for a shower. A shirt change would do. In front of her house she parked and sniffed her pits just to make sure. Stinky was never an option. Her deodorant was working just fine and, she reminded herself that too much water on the skin dried it out.

She hopped out of the car, all the while justifying the way she looked in her tennis outfit. The darn thing had cost her a fortune and she saw women all the time at the grocery store in riding boots,

41

tennis outfits, and golf skirts, so why should she be any different? Abbey didn't sound like the type who would care anyway.

Over coffee that morning Bart had told her he had somewhere to go; he always had somewhere to go so she hadn't paid much attention to the where or the why. It had been ages since she'd had a Sunday to herself and she planned to enjoy it.

Dashing up the stairs, she dropped her purse on the bed and ran to the bathroom. Above the flush, she heard tires crunch oyster shells in the driveway and then a knock at the front door. It wasn't lawn service day and the cleaning lady had come yesterday. She peeked out the bathroom window but the roof overhang hid the visitor's vehicle from view.

"Hold on. I'm coming." Her rubber soles tapped hardwood risers on the curved stairs. Breathing heavily, she opened the massive front door without looking through the peephole.

"Oh. Gosh. Hey," she crooned in two syllables as her body slid from curious greeting to left-hand-on-hip sultry slouch in a matter of seconds. "Bart isn't here, Cutty." *Thank God I put on the full face this morning.* "He went someplace for supplies, Jacksonville, I think. He might be gone all day long."

"Uh, yeah. I just met a friend for a long run and thought I'd stop by on my way home." Bart's partner raked fingers through his damp hair. His body glistened with perspiration and his tank top and nylon running shorts clung to his skin. "Bart said I could borrow his extra set of golf clubs."

Vickie's lips pushed into a pout. "Oh, shoot. And I thought you came to see me."

"Well, sure. I mean, it's always good to see you, Ms. Vickie. I just thought as long as I was out I'd go on and get those clubs if it's not too much trouble and—"

"Do say. Sweetie, please just call me Vickie. Ms. Vicki was one of Tiny Tim's wives. Remember him? He played a ukulele and sang 'Tiptoe Through the Tulips' in this strange little falsetto voice. Probably not. You're too young to remember that, I imagine, but goodness then, let's not stand here and beg for heat stroke. It's hotter than the hinges of hell out there and we don't want to melt. Not out here on the porch anyway. I'll fix iced tea or whatever you want. It's a little early for a drink and I have a lunch date, but I'm not in that big a hurry. Come on in and let's find those clubs for you." Vickie pushed the door wide open and retreated into the foyer.

NINE

Abbey had decided there was time to get to Jacksonville and back before meeting Vickie. As she drove into the hospital's parking lot, Abbey saw a dog asleep under a mature crepe myrtle tree at the corner of the building. Poor guy. Her last image of Watch Dog had been him chasing a ball in the children's yard next door.

Inside, Abbey was directed to the Intensive Care floor, where she found a nurse flipping through paperwork at the nurse's station. "Hi. My name is Abbey Bunn. The nice lady at Information said I should check here before I visit a patient." The nurse looked up and her eyes probed as though looking for the right vein to poke.

"Yeah, she has a habit of doing that, gets paid for being nice and giving people directions. I might try that line of work in my next life." She grinned. "Hi, Abbey, Maurine Travis. And who is it you want to see?"

"The man in the boating hit-and-run. He was brought in yesterday." Abbey assumed there was only one person who met that description.

"Ah. Our John Doe." The tall, dark-haired nurse came around the desk. "I need to prepare you a little. He was moved from ER to a semi-private room today. Don't be surprised if he doesn't recognize you at first. Head injuries are like that." They walked.

44

"I don't expect him to recognize me, because he doesn't know me. He was sort of out of it when I pulled him out of the river."

"Oh. So you're the one. I thought maybe you were the little woman who waited patiently at home and wondered why her hubby didn't come home last night."

I guess it helps to have a sense of humor if you work in this place. "No, sorry. I never saw him before yesterday. I heard the boat hit something and went to see what it was and found him."

"Okay then, I get it. You're kind of doing your follow-up good Samaritan thingie."

"You need to meet my mother. She thinks I'm nuts to check up on strangers but, yes, I guess I'm doing my good Samaritan thingie." Abbey chuckled and Maurine gave her a lop-sided grin. They were on the same page.

Outside a door they stopped and Maurine said, "He's very confused. THI does that sometimes. They don't recognize people they're close to and it's upsetting for the other person. Of course, he doesn't get it at all because he doesn't realize he's not making sense. When and if you visit, just be aware that he might get agitated, he'll more than likely repeat himself, and he almost certainly won't remember what you just talked about only moments earlier. He was checked for a brain bleed and there's not one, and x-rays were done. Nothing's broken. Of course, we will continue to monitor him."

"What's a THI?"

"Sorry. Traumatic head injury."

"Guess that makes sense when a boat whacks you in the head."

"Yeah." Maurine's lip dipped to the right. "It must have been a glancing blow or he would have been knocked out. Then he would have drowned. No way would you have found him then. What exactly happened?"

"I don't know. I was rowing on a nearby creek and heard an awful noise but I didn't see anything. I went over to check it out and found him floating on his back in the sound."

"Good thing he has some meat on his bones or he'd be a goner. Skinny ones sink like a bag of stones. In the sound, eh. He's lucky he's not in the belly of a shark."

"Don't I know it."

Maurine pushed the door open. "I call him J.D."

"I guess it will have to do for now. May I talk to him?"

"Sure. He needs to sort things out so he needs to hear conversation, which is about the only therapy he can handle at the moment."

J.D.'s eyes traveled toward the door, then his head followed in a slow four-frame stop-action sequence. "Whoa. What happened?" His eyes looked from Maurine to Abbey, then back to Abbey and stayed there. "I'm thirsty as all get out. You're late."

Abbey looked at Maurine. "When we were going for help he kept saying he wanted a beer. I told him I'd get him one as soon as I could."

Maurine shrugged. "Maybe he's making a connection. Talk to him."

J.D. grimaced as his hand went to his head. "You're late. You're always late."

Abbey walked closer to the bed. "You look like you made somebody mad. What happened to you?"

"Whoa. Do you know me? What happened to you? Do you know me?"

Abbey glanced at Maurine, then said, "It looks like you hit your head."

"Damn, it hurts. I got kicked in the head, you know. What happened? Horse or something?"

Abbey looked at Maurine, who mouthed "tell him."

"I think you were hit by a boat yesterday."

"I was? Why?"

"That's what I'd like to know. Why were you out there?"

"Where?

"In the river. I found you in the river."

"Why?"

"I think you were out in the river with some other men and you ended up in the water. Do you remember what happened?"

His eyes slowly moved from her to the television set. "Game's on in a minute." His eyes closed, and in seconds his chest moved up and his cheeks ballooned in a soft snore.

Maurine dipped her head toward the door and they left the room. "See what I mean?" They walked toward the elevator.

"Holy smoke. That was like Abbott and Costello's 'Who's on First' routine."

"Like I said. It can be frustrating."

"What are the chances he'll get better?"

"Time will tell. What he needs now is nourishment, hydration, and sleep. His body is trying to make repairs."

"When he said I was late, do you think he connected to our conversation during the rescue or do you think he was just talking?"

"It's hard to tell. When you get a blow like that, your brain gets scrambled. You started to tell him about the accident and he looked at the television and talked about some game. He's having difficulty keeping track of the conversation, of what others are saying. He'll talk about one thing for a little while, then he'll skip to something totally unrelated. It's very typical."

"And like you said, he repeats things."

"Over and over and over. Head injuries are traumatic for the injured but they're very difficult for the caregivers, who sometimes have to throw reason out the window. There's a major disconnect and you can't just fix it. It's frustrating for everyone."

The elevator door whooshed open. Abbey handed the nurse her business card with the cottage number on it and stepped onto the elevator. "Thanks, Maurine. I'll be back. Let me know if anything changes."

Abbey turned in her visitor badge and walked from the chilly refrigerated air into Jacksonville's sauna. The dull breeze felt like a hair dryer on low blow. Often she found it helped to compartmentalize, to separate work from personal and tackle them one at a time. J.D. was in the personal box and Vickie Croek was in the work box. Maurine said time would tell. Work was a good distraction and she was eager to talk to Vickie about what she wanted. Atlanta had condos and townhouses galore. The trick was to match Vickie's wants with just the right spot, and Abbey the matchmaker was pretty good at ferreting out what turned people on.

Moments later, she turned her Jeep's radio to a local news station and hoped the man she had just visited was not the major story of the day.

TEN

I-95 was a short hop from the hospital in Jacksonville to St. Marys, but Abbey remembered the pre-super-highway route on US 17, a simple two-lane road with the raked yards of Negroes' simple frame homes and the occasional two-pump gas station. It had been years since she had been to the small riverside village and then only to hop on the ferry to Cumberland Island.

Her parents had taken her and her two brothers there once. The trip out to the island in the ferry boat had been a big hit, but Cumberland's other big tourist draw, the wild horses, not so much. Kings Bluff was a hunting preserve where feral horses and cows grazed on marsh flats and had the run of the woods; where armadillos dug potholes and dogs chased wild pigs under cottages elevated on brick piers. Eagles peered from the tops of the tallest trees in search of rattlesnakes and other prey, and alligators sunned on mud banks alongside the brackish waterways. It was truly wild and you didn't have to take a ferry to get there. All you had to do was drive around Kings Bluff day or night and open your eyes to see all the wild game you ever wanted to see.

Like toadstools after rain, grocery stores and fast-food chains had sprung up all along the ribbon of asphalt from the interstate over to St. Marys. Amazing what happened when you stayed away from a place for a while. Once past strip stores baking on asphalt parking lots, there were live oaks and palm trees crowded around

49

old wooden homes that had been turned into hair and nail salons and veterinary offices. The look was run-down old Florida, an image developers seemed hell-bent to erase but which was one of the state's main attractions. It took forever to get from the highway to the river, but there things hadn't changed much at all. She parked in the shade of a gargantuan live oak a short walk from the café where she would have lunch.

Vickie had mentioned the deck so Abbey went upstairs and scoped out a table with an operable umbrella in case the shade of the trees didn't do the trick. She ordered an iced tea and told the waitress she was waiting for someone and they would have lunch.

People were interesting to watch, and she had a prime spot to do so totally undetected. St. Marys was not as large or as crowded as nearby Fernandina, but since St. Marys was the gateway to Cumberland Island there was always activity. Locals were easy to pick out. Males dressed casually, usually in some kind of fishing shirt and shorts; they looked at the ground while they walked and seemed intent on getting somewhere. They were on missions. Women had easy no-fuss hairdos, wore shorts or sundresses and sandals, smiled at everyone they passed on the sidewalk and often walked alongside a friend and stopped to point to things of interest like shops or restaurants or historic buildings.

You could pick out the tourists, whose heads swiveled like they had to take it all in and had limited time to do so. Dolphins cruising down the river always brought open-mouthed gapes and smiles. Who didn't love Flipper? Adults sometimes looked serious or confused, walking with their mouths open as though they were overwhelmed by the charming simplicity of it all or wondering why they hadn't learned about this place sooner. Of course, none realized they provided entertainment and a much-needed distraction for the lone woman on the deck above the street.

Her mind wandered. Actions told truths about people. She had only seen one person in that fishing boat, but obviously someone was driving it. Stern Man had been looking her way, she could tell that much by the way he stood. Was he looking for the man they had just hit or was he just gazing back at the beautiful water? Not likely. He was either looking for the helpless man or he was watching her. Whether he could see her was the question. She shook her head. All she knew was that there was a disoriented man in the hospital and there was no guarantee he would ever get his marbles queued up again. And she had a hat that might or might not be his. If the boat had been closer, she could have seen more—then they might have come after her. She took a deep breath and hoped she had stopped rowing soon enough so they couldn't have detected the motion of her oars. They had no way of knowing who she was, she hoped. *Damn.*

Down the street, boats were lined up on trailers in neat rows as if someone had followed a pattern on some graph or grid. A small red tractor exited a shed, its towheaded driver head-flipping bangs from his forehead as he went back and forth, back and forth, and moved boats around, zoom-zoom-zoom like a child riding his friction toy. Blonde hair flew from his eyes as constant as a facial twitch. *Get a haircut, Beach Boy. It's even driving me crazy.* She glanced at her watch, then pulled a paperback book from the open-top canvas LL Bean bag at her feet. Vickie was late.

Two pages later, she looked up. A gold Cadillac crawled down the street, its driver's head moved from side to side as she hunted for a parking space though there were plenty available. She had mentioned she drove a Cadillac but had left out the gold part. Brake lights tapped and the car bobbed like a baby buggy. Abbey put her book face-down on the table and sipped her tea. It was entertaining to watch people attempt to park parallel. The Caddy inched toward a vacant spot between two trucks.

Abbey sat up. "Oh, boy." An index finger pressed her lip. "No, no, no… straighten up, straighten up."

An elderly man several tables over said, "Pardon?"

"No, sorry." She gave a dismissive wave, then pointed to the street. "Parallel parker."

"Oh, yes. I see what you mean. Oh, well. That's what insurance is for." He smiled and opened his mouth wide for another bite of sandwich.

Brake lights tapped once, again, and a third time as the Caddy lurched to a stop, then slowly pulled forward to start over. Two more tries before the driver pulled out and headed down the street.

"Huh." Abbey glanced at her watch again and motioned to the waitress for a refill. "I think the person I'm meeting will be here in a minute. She's trying to find a parking space."

"Gold Cadillac?"

Abbey nodded. "Afraid so, at least I think. We've never met." She clenched her jaw. Sometimes not being judgmental took more effort than she could muster. How could any driver over sixteen not figure out how to parallel park?

The waitress looked down the street toward the retreating gold car. "Too bad this is Sunday. Looks like you could use a glass of wine if she's anything like her driving."

Abbey laughed and checked her watch. Vickie was twenty minutes late already but it was a beautiful day and she was on vacation, or was supposed to be. Crows squawked, palm fronds flapped gently in the breeze, and she might get a new client. Life was good and she had nothing else to do but enjoy sitting in the sun. Picking up her book, she pushed errant wisps of sun-bleached hair behind her ears. The Cadillac floated back into view from the direction in which it had disappeared moments earlier. *Atlas Shrugged* lowered to her lap again. Two angled spaces were available at the marina. The Caddy aimed at one, turned in too sharp, then bounced up and over the curb and forward. Its right front tire rested on the sidewalk. It could have been worse.

First meetings were important so Abbey was all eyes and ears. Already she knew Vickie was a lousy driver. Abbey watched the woman scrunch her curls with her fingers and then with a look into the rear view mirror, Vickie applied something to her lips, then looked again before she opened the door. One chalk-white tennis shoe and a shapely Coppertone-bronzed leg emerged. Baubles glittered on the briefcase-sized silver purse that appeared next, hanging on a slim tanned wrist.

Abbey settled her elbows on the table, resting her cheek on her fist. It had to be Vickie. There were no other Cadillacs on the street and this person with her tan, her enormous silver purse, and her large black Jackie-O sunglasses looked like the kind of woman who owned two McMansions. Abbey cleaned her shades with her napkin and watched Vickie prance across the street. A truck loaded with bushel baskets and crab traps rattled to an abrupt stop at the crosswalk. The driver finger-played ten note riffs in rapid succession on his steering wheel. Vickie waved and mouthed "thank you," then disappeared below the deck of the café.

"Oh, boy." Abbey took a deep breath and sipped her tea. So this was Vickie Croek. She dropped the paperback into her bag and pulled out a legal pad and pen. Several minutes later, Vickie and her girlish giggle emerged through the restaurant door.

"Is this your friend?" The waitress, eyebrows raised, glanced from her to Abbey.

"Gosh, I don't know." With both hands, Vickie clasped the straps of her handbag, or satchel, or whatever the thing was, in front of her waist; her ankle bones touched primly. By contrast, the copper-red glow of her chemically treated hair was anything but Little Miss Sunbeam.

ELEVEN

"Hi, Vickie." Abbey gestured hello with one raised palm. Vickie smiled thankfully at the waitress, then walked over and grabbed Abbey's extended hand. Vickie's felt like it belonged to a parakeet so Abbey eased up on her grip though Vickie's was amazingly firm for such a small hand.

The waitress clumped over in sensible black lace-up rubber-soled shoes, took the pencil from behind her ear and removed a pad from her pocket, looking from one to the other expecting an order. When neither spoke, she sighed, cocked her hip and waited, the only thing missing from her 1950s era look was her smacking a stick of Juicy Fruit gum.

"I am so pleased to make your acquaintance, Abbey." Vickie dropped her purse into a chair and what sounded like BBs in a jar rattled inside. Abbey's eyes darted to the handbag as a chill tickled her neck. *Tic Tacs.* Her ex had always carried the breath candies in a pocket of his pants so she hated that sound. He was always rattling. She shook off the unpleasant memory. The waitress finally gave up and went to another table of customers.

Vickie pulled a lace handkerchief from her purse and dabbed at her forehead.

"We can go inside if you'd rather." Abbey grabbed the handles of her bag.

"No, it's like a meat locker in there. I got all goose-pimply just

54

walking through downstairs. I don't know why they have to do that. Grocery stores are worse." Vickie wiggled in her chair, then settled.

"Would you like something to drink?" The waitress had returned and stood there scrutinizing her two customers as if trying to understand what had brought this unlikely duo together. Again her eyes met Abbey's and said silently, *She's a trip, isn't she?*

Vickie pressed a lacquered red fingernail to her parted lips and squeezed her eyes shut. Seconds ticked by. Abbey shrugged to the waitress and sipped her tea.

"Was that pink lemonade I saw inside?" Vickie looked hopeful.

"Yes. Our bartender experiments, and next week his concoction has vodka and pink lemonade and probably several other alcohol ingredients. He's rather fond of coconut rum, so I'd bet on that being in there. You'll have to come back to try one."

"Oh, goodie." Vickie patted her hands together. "May I please have lemonade?" She giggled. "Lemonade reminds me of summer days, and pink is so festive." She looked from Abbey to the waitress and studied their expressions. "He can do one today without the alcohol, right?"

Abbey and the waitress shared a smile and said, "Virgin," at the same time.

Vickie again looked at each of them. "Oh. Does that mean plain? Without alcohol?" Her brow wrinkled. She looked confused.

"Yes," the waitress said and cut her eyes at Abbey.

"Yes, then I'll have a virgin lemonade today, please, and I'll come back for one of his specials next week. Virgin lemonade sounds kind of kinky or something, doesn't it?" She tucked in a section of the hem of her polo shirt and pulled at her short white skirt. She and Abbey both ordered salads.

"So," Abbey said, "you must have played tennis this morning after we talked."

"Now how did you know that?" Vickie's glossed smile revealed perfect white shoepeg-corn-sized teeth.

Abbey stared at her for several seconds. "Well, I just assumed. The shoes, tennis whites…"

"Oh, of course," Vickie said. "I forgot. I did have a lesson this morning. But you know what? I think I would wear this even if I hadn't played. It's very warm here, isn't it? You'd think after living in Florida I would be used to the heat, wouldn't you? I heard white is the coolest color and in this heat you need all the help you can get, right?" As she gestured with raised palms, the perfect orbs of her breasts rose to the occasion. "I usually have coffee with the girls after tennis. We go to this adorable little coffee shop here in town, but I had a private lesson today and then of course I had this important lunch date with you. I hope you don't mind that I came straight here."

People-watching took on a whole new dimension now that Vickie had arrived and allowed Abbey a close-up look at one of the watched. *Come on. Could anyone be this much of a ditz? Be nice, act interested, try to learn something about her.* "Certainly I don't mind. You look great. What kind of mileage do you get in your Caddy?"

"That big old thing? Terrible." Vickie flicked manicured nails toward the car, looked around, then leaned in and whispered. "I'm not very fond of it." She glanced around again. "It's my husband's idea, but between you and me, it looks like a rich old lady and I'm not rich." She unfolded her napkin and dropped it into her lap.

"And I'm certainly not that old." She smoothed out the wrinkles in the cloth, then looked up at Abbey. "You're tall, aren't you? I wish I wasn't such a pipsqueak."

"If you don't like the Cadillac, why drive it?"

Vickie looked toward the door, then studied the empty seats around them and whispered, "Bart insists." She thought for several seconds. "But he's funny. He prides himself on negotiating the rock-bottom price. He beats the salesperson up over the phone beforehand, then tells him his secretary will be down with the money and to have the car clean and ready to drive off the lot. He puts the money in my account and then he tells me where to go, which car to buy, and how much to pay for it. I really think he likes the game, and if I know Bart, he also likes to picture me walking in, writing the check, and telling the salesman I came for my new car, when he was expecting the big tough negotiator he'd talked to on the phone. Silly, isn't it."

Abbey thought she detected an eye-roll but maybe not. Bart didn't want the purchase of his expensive cars to run through his account, so he made Vickie run it through hers so she looked like the buyer. What was he hiding?

One pink lemonade arrived. "We buy new, what I call drive-around cars, every two years, black for him, gold for me." Vickie's voice returned to normal. "Once he bought me a silver one. Better, I guess, but really..." She sipped. "I mean, with all the makes and models and colors out there, and he insists on Cadillacs. Now he has others, collectible play cars according to him, but I don't know. Silly hobby if you ask me. And expensive. But he wants to see me driving that gold thing. Oh, well, it's a free ride, so what the heck?" Vickie giggled, then looked down at her chest.

"He insisted on these too." She cupped her hands beneath her breasts and bounced them up and down like water balloons. Her cheeks reddened. "I hate them. When I was a nice firm little A cup I could wear anything. They didn't flop, they didn't sag. They were cute and perky like creamy little pink peaches and now I look like a cow." Her smile disappeared. "He doesn't give a flip that I have no sensation in them. Oh, well. He loves them so I guess if they keep him happy that's what counts." Her eyes creased and her plastered-on smile looked sad.

That's sick. "That's not anything I have to worry about," Abbey said as she pointed to her God-given chest. Vickie's laugh was throaty, big and sexy for such a little thing. *Interesting.* Abbey stared for several seconds as she tried to match that laugh with the woman sitting across from her, but she caught herself.

"You're lucky. Yours fit your body," Vickie said. "I can't wear anything cute and chic anymore, but Bart's a boob guy, loves décolletage. Maybe he should get a pair to see what it's like to lug them around." This time her eye-roll was obvious. "What Bartsie wants, Bartsie gets." Her giggle was less than convincing this time.

Bartsie sounds like an A-number-one-jerk, Abbey thought.

They talked about local goings-on between bites. Vickie giggled at everything. When the dishes were cleared, Abbey decided she'd had enough getting-to-know-you-time, and the giggles drove her to distraction. She had important things to do at the cottage like mow the grass, cut back encroaching prickly vines, and vacuum. What fun, but Tom was coming soon and she wanted things shipshape. "So you wanted to see me about…" She let her prompt hang as she stirred her tea with a straw.

Vickie looked toward the water. "I bet you don't let anyone tell you what to do."

The suggestion poked a raw spot in Abbey's heart. "No, but I used to." She waited a beat. Vickie looked at her. "I married a control freak too, Vickie. It didn't take me long to figure out I didn't like being told what to do all the time." Now Abbey looked at the water and to Vickie's credit, she didn't interrupt and Abbey's flush of hurt and anger subsided.

"It felt like control, but he also had a way to make me feel like I owed him something. He was very good at using guilt to manipulate me. He really knew how to punch my buttons." Her eyes met Vickie's. "I don't like to be used and I don't like users."

Vickie chewed her lip and gave the slightest nod. "That's what it is, isn't it?" She tapped the nails of her left hand on the table; the serious cluster of diamonds on her finger sparked fire in the sunlight.

"Maybe I knew what he was doing, Abbey, but didn't want to admit it. I remember thinking that if I really loved him I should do things to please him. Sounds harmless, right?"

"Depends." Abbey's engagement ring was now two diamond

stud earrings. She wore them on rare occasions and had considered trading them for a really nice watch. All she had was a sports watch, which didn't do when she dressed up. The two women studied each other. Abbey wanted to crawl inside Vickie's head. "The day I divorced my ex was one of the happiest of my life."

Vickie's mouth opened partially, then closed. She nodded almost imperceptibly as one does when talking to a good friend to acknowledge that she understands what the other has been through. "Bart lives large. I knew I was spoiled, being an only child and all, but he's worse. More is always better in his book. You should see our house in Orlando. It's in this gated community and a pro golfer lives next door. Tacky, right? Oh, my gosh. You wouldn't believe it." She drummed her nails on the table. "It's… um, it's on the market." She looked at Abbey. "But who needs two big houses? I guess the one we built here in St. Marys is modest by comparison and it's, I don't know, it's different." Vickie shook her head.

Abbey tried to think between the lines. "What?"

"I'm sorry. I'm babbling like you're a shrink or something."

That was nothing new. Clients often spilled their guts in the confines of her car while they looked at houses, often sharing more of their personal lives than she ever wanted to know. "No, but I am wondering why you need me if you have two houses already."

"Two Bart houses. That's the problem."

Vickie looked uncomfortable so Abbey glanced at her watch. She'd had about enough anyway. "Well, I need to get going. Maybe we can get together again soon to discuss some options for you in Atlanta."

"I'd like that. I'll call you when I have my calendar in front of me and we can set something up," Vickie said.

After Vickie settled the bill, Abbey watched her bump off of the sidewalk and roar away. Straining to see over the steering wheel, she looked like a Barbie doll driving a giant toy Big Wheel, and from the sound of the engine, her short little leg must have been

59

stretched to its limit so the toe of her tennis shoe could push the pedal. Abbey shook her head. Was Vickie sizing her up as an agent or what? She already had two houses—two Bart houses, that is. Now she wanted one that was like her. *I get that.*

~

Late that afternoon after a refreshing swim, Abbey took her book and a glass of wine to the screened front porch and grabbed a rocking chair. Soft light lingered in the hushed sounds of dusk until engine noise whined across the marsh, probably a fisherman who had gone out earlier and now wandered back for dinner. Maybe he'd claim the two scrawny, bare-chested, barefoot little boys on the dock who took turns pulling up small square metal crab traps. Great entertainment for a child on a hot summer afternoon. She'd used the same kind as a child but also remembered tying a cord around a chicken neck and scooping up her catch with a long-handled net. That was fun. People these days were into quantity as quickly as possible. They weren't interested in taking the time to do it the old way. She'd spent hours with her mother and grandmother in that most rewarding pursuit, doing their share to put dinner on the table while the men were out fishing.

Childhood memories from the Fifties down here were rich and happy, Ozzie-and-Harriet days that seemed sweeter and kinder than today's world, days she sometimes longed for. She missed Tom, missed their long talks and his companionship. He had a business dinner tonight, so she knew she wouldn't hear from him until tomorrow. She wanted to pick his brain about John Doe—but where to start. There was a hat and an unconscious man who would hopefully wake up soon and tell her and Terkoff what happened. Then there was her potential new client. Tom would get a kick out of Vickie but would warn Abbey to keep it all business and not to try to make friends. She was eager to see why Vickie specifically wanted to work with her. She had a feeling the reason involved more than just real estate.

A boat with long, low lines rounded the bend in the river. Abbey's knees creaked when she stood. Watch Dog's tail thumped against the plank floor. "It's Sarge." She put down her pad. *Thump thump.* "Let's go help him tie up."

TWELVE

In the hazy light of dawn, the wind chime on the porch played soft harmonic notes while in the marsh a clapper rail he-he-he'd like a hyena. Long dangling clumps of Spanish moss waved like tattered gray flags from live oak, hickory, and sweet gum trees while slender fronds of palmetto palms clapped politely. Whitecaps raced up the river. Snug and happy inside, Abbey stirred Tupelo honey into tea, steamy hot and dark. So much for a row.

"Okay, Watch. Too windy to be out there. Want to go?" *Thump thump thump.* She patted the dog's big yellow block of a head.

Daylight inched across the variegated greens of the marsh. While she pulled on socks and running shoes, Watch Dog waited patiently, whacking her rocking chair with his tail, until a green lizard scooted across the screen and he jumped up and woofed. The lizard bailed and landed on the branch of a convenient azalea bush.

"Okay. Hold on a minute." Tom ought to be calling. The two of them loved to jog down here on the soft sand roads. As she double-knotted her shoes, the phone rang. *Ta da...* She ran to the kitchen and picked up.

"How's the weather," Tom said.

"Good morning to you too. It's beautiful here but a bit windy. We were just heading out for a jog."

"We?"

"My loyal canine companion and I. He does a good imitation

of you, tail wagging and tongue hanging out all the time. It's cute, exuberance over the little things."

Tom chuckled. She loved to hear him laugh. "Of course. We're a lot alike. Listen, I hope to finish up and get out of here tomorrow night. I'll be sucking down recycled airport air and drinking burned day-old coffee. Then I'll get to breathe reconstituted airplane crap while you two fill your lungs with unadulterated Kings Bluff salty sulfurous oxygen. I can hardly wait."

"Poor baby."

"Hey, eat your heart out. Yesterday, I went for a jog on Kelly Drive along Boathouse Row. It's amazing. Those boathouses were built in the late 1800s. We don't have anything comes close to that in Atlanta."

"Thank you, Sherman. You're killing me, though. What a fabulous city. Did you see the boathouses at night all lit up?"

"Incredible. Right out of Hansel and Gretel. But seriously, in the daytime there were boats everywhere. I couldn't believe it. I might consider taking up rowing after seeing that."

"You're on. I know someone who might be patient enough to teach you, or at least give you a pointer or two."

"Yeah, I bet. I don't think that coach is in my budget."

"She might cut you a deal. So what are your thoughts about getting down here?"

"Once I get to Atlanta I should be able to wrap things up fairly quickly. There's a golf tournament Friday I'm supposed to play in, so I'm thinking I'll leave early Saturday morning to head your way. I put in for some time off before I left for Philadelphia, so if all goes well, and barring any major catastrophes, I should be able to get away most of next week. I hope I'll be there by dinner time Saturday and…"

Dinner time. For the past several days, dinners had consisted of shrimp and crab right out of the river. Extravagant was shrimp salad or crab cakes or the occasional avocado on a salad. When at

Kings Bluff, grocery store visits were made only when necessary to replace milk or salad stuff, and the only other Jeep travel was to go to Taylor's Point to go fishing. No traffic to avoid or frantic pace, and no real work except for an occasional phone check-in at the office.

Alone wasn't half-bad at a place like this. There was always plenty to do, and she was only halfway through her book. Maybe when she got back to Atlanta she'd start writing, join a writing group, go to a writer's conference and try something new. A challenge. Change was good. Tom wanted to fast-forward their relationship. She got that. Men, for all their bravado, liked to be taken care of and often remarried after a divorce or losing a wife like Tom had. He deserved a good partner after what he'd been through, but talk about a challenge…

"Umm, Abbey… are you still there?"

Abbey shook her head. *Oops.* "Oh… yeah, yes, I'm here, Tom. Sorry. When do you think you might be able to get here?"

"Did you hear anything I just said?"

"I'm sorry. I'm really distracted. I'll be glad when you get here so we can have a normal evening together and talk face to face. Do you understand phone sex? I don't get it."

"Whoa. Are you okay? You didn't get hit on the head or anything during that rescue, did you?"

"No, I'm fine. There has just been a lot going on. And I miss you. I was teasing about the telephone sex. I just wanted to hear you laugh."

"You're sure you're okay."

"Yes. I'm fine. I think I have a new client. We had lunch yesterday, but mostly she talked about her husband and we never got around to talking real estate so we're meeting again. I don't want to waste your dime talking about all of that, so I'll tell you about her when you get here. I'm looking forward to that dinner you mentioned and a nice glass of wine."

"Okay, now you sound like Abbey, but telephone sex? I'll bring lots of wine."

"Red and white, please."

"Sure. And listen, I'd rather you focus on this new prospect than the fellow you rescued. Let the cops handle him, okay?"

"Okay, Tom."

"That's my girl. Several of my buddies will be down on St. Simons for a golf week. Would you mind if I got with them a time or two?"

"Mind? Absolutely not! I'd be delighted. I have plenty to keep me busy here, so you set up some games. That sounds like fun, and the weather is supposed to be perfect. No rain in the forecast." *And I won't feel guilty if I have to spend some time with Vickie.*

She hung up with Tom and called the hospital. There had been no change. She called Terkoff to see if he knew anything, but he wasn't in yet. The wind had picked up considerably so she went out to her Jeep and got tie-down straps and plastic tent stakes from an old camp duffle bag that she kept in the rear. She turned her boat right side up and saw the cap wedged beneath her shoes. She hadn't even noticed it in the half-light the morning before.

Pulling it out, she flipped it over in her hands. *DOC* was written in permanent marker inside the back rim beside a label from the Mad Hatter in Philadelphia, Pennsylvania. How odd. Tom could check this place out but he was probably too busy and she didn't want to interfere with his work. She secured her boat with the straps and tent stakes and put the hat on the screened porch. She could sure use it on a day like today but she didn't dare. It might contain some evidence and Terkoff would kill her if she screwed it up. Heck, it could even belong to one of the men in that fishing boat. Wouldn't that be ducky?

With Watch happily leading the way, she jogged down the bluff that separated the row of cottages from the river. A woman pulled weeds in her flower garden and waved. Toward the end of the houses, a fellow called from his screened porch, "Do one for me!" She waved. Her eyes were trained on the road, where roots and oyster shells were sure to catch a toe and send her sprawling if she wasn't careful. She had done three- and four-point landings more times then she cared to remember.

At Taylor's Point, she walked out on the dock and watched the turbulent water and the blowing grasses. She sat on a bench and thought about the letters DOC and the Philadelphia label in the hat. What would a guy from Philadelphia be doing down here in that sound? *Fishing, and I'm calling him Doc. Forget this John Doe business.* She had found him not far from this dock, and the drug bust in 1985 had happened right here as well, where there was virtually no outside traffic.

White froth rolled on top of waves. The more she thought about it, the more she believed that the man she found had lost his hat. If he was Doc, there was a good chance he had bought the hat in Philadelphia because that's where he lived. People in that city were active. There were rivers and parks, and everyone rowed, walked, roller-bladed, bicycled or jogged every day and at all hours. Doc looked in decent shape. If her assumptions were correct, he probably flew to Jacksonville, rented a car, and drove to St. Marys. The boat she had seen was a fishing boat and it had headed south. There were a lot of charters out of St. Marys. What else would he have been doing on that boat except going for a ride or fishing? *Something to think about. Hat and rental cars.*

THIRTEEN

For Abbey, Crooked Creek's proximity to Kings Bluff made it worth checking out. Any development along the US 17 corridor from Darien, Georgia, to Amelia Island, Florida, interested her. Developers responded to demand. When an area got hot, subdivisions popped up like mushrooms on manure, and Abbey's goal was to keep land-seeking developers and nosy purchasers with loads of cash as far from Kings Bluff's near-virgin acres as possible.

She loaded Watch in the Jeep and they headed south. You could take an agent away from her home turf, but you couldn't take habits out of the agent. Now that she had met Vickie, she wanted to see how and where she lived. As she drove she thought about her conversation with Tom. He wanted her to focus on her new client but what harm could it do to stop by to check on Doc after she finished seeing where Vickie lived as long as she was down here? She thought for about two seconds. *None.*

She found a parking spot right on the water in St. Marys and leashed Watch Dog. He pulled her to an overstuffed trash can where someone's discarded lunch leftovers of fried shrimp and French fries spilled out onto the sidewalk and emitted a noticeable stench as they warmed in the sun. "No, Watch." She pulled him away. "No, boy. Let's walk."

Maybe to assuage the guilt she knew she would feel when she ignored Tom's suggestion to leave Doc alone, she stopped at the quaint book store she had noticed on Sunday and bought him a copy of *To Kill a Mockingbird.* One night when they were talking about their favorite books that had been made into movies, he admitted he'd seen the movie but never read the book.

The night before, she had remembered that her mother used to visit an Atlanta friend who had a home on a river in St. Marys. She spotted a pay phone outside a weather-worn building. Real estate had taught her it was always good to know where pay phones were located when you were out showing houses. Store owners frowned upon you using theirs unless you bought something, plus it was a pain in the neck to have to explain the urgency of your call. There was a lot of talk about companies developing phones you could use in your car, and she hoped the buzz was true; not being particularly techie, she would be the last to know. It sure would make selling real estate a whole lot easier if all she had to do was dial from her car when she saw a for sale sign in front of a house she wanted to see inside.

St. Marys Marina was painted on a sign over the door of the old building. It looked interesting, like an old hardware store, and worth a look around inside sometime. The beauty of a small town.

Quarters plunked into the phone one by one. She dialed her mother's number. "Hi, Momma. Guess where I am?"

"Well, I thought you were at Kings Bluff."

"Not at the moment. Watch Dog and I are in St. Marys. I have been talking to a lady down here who wants me to show her some condos in Atlanta. She lives in a new development here called Crooked Creek, and that sort of rang a bell. Don't you have some friends who have a place down here?"

"Well, yes, but I'm afraid it's *had*. They are both gone now. I heard their children sold their place. Oh, goodness, Abbey, it was beautiful, thousands of acres, and it was on Crooked Creek so I bet this new development is their property. They had a lovely cottage there on the creek. It's probably still nice unless the new people tore it down."

"I'll go check it out and let you know."

"Sweetie, how is that fellow you rescued?"

"Still kind of out of it. I went by to see him yesterday. Seems he has amnesia or something. He doesn't remember anything about the accident."

"Now be careful, Abbey. Don't go getting all involved with him like you did with that German fellow last year. Prisoner of war, my word. Whoever heard of such a thing?"

"Momma, he turned out to be a pretty nice man and you know it. And what was I supposed to do this time, let this man drown or get eaten by a shark? Not likely."

"I know. You did the right thing, but let the police handle it from here on out. He's not your responsibility." Boonks hesitated. "What does Tom think about all of this?"

Of course I don't have the sense God gave a goat. "It sounds like you've been talking to him. He's trying to get down here and I'm sure I'll have plenty of time to find out what he thinks when he gets here. And speaking of getting down here, I know you're busy, Momma, but we would love for you to join us if you can break away from that bridge table for a while. See what you can do." She scratched Watch's head. "I'll let you know what I find at this new development. I'm going to go check it out, and I'll let you know about your friends' house. See what you can do about getting down here."

"Okay, sweetie. I love you."

"Love you too." Abbey's mother thought real estate was dangerous enough without Abbey's peculiar penchant for saving people who found themselves in dangerous situations. When she hung up, change rattled into the slot at the bottom of the phone.

She dialed Terkoff's number. His partner picked up and he

seemed to know who Abbey was. She wondered if Terkoff had shared her "Jerkoff" jab with his partner.

"Too bad he's not in. I was wondering if there was any new information on the boating hit-and-run."

"Can't do much with a vic who can't talk," the policeman said. He coughed, cleared his throat and snorted. Abbey grimaced. "Interesting you happened to be so close to this guy but you couldn't tell Terkoff anything about the boat that supposedly hit him. How come?"

It wasn't worth trying to explain anything to this dolt. "I heard it, that's all." *Jackass.* "I didn't see anything. When will Terkoff be back?"

"Later, I guess. I'm not his old lady so he doesn't run his whereabouts by me, you know. All I know is he ain't here."

"Ain't isn't a word. Please tell Sheriff Terkoff that Abbey Bunn called and would like to talk to him." She slammed down the receiver before he could respond and thrummed her fingers on the rectangular phone box in front of her. Phone numbers, names, and *Mary is a slut* were etched into the black-painted metal.

"Let's go see where Vickie lives," she said to Watch Dog. That suited him just fine. They hopped into the Jeep and headed out. She had seen a turn-in sign to the development when she drove into town, and when she approached it, the Crooked Creek sign indicated the development was a half-mile away. There was no guard at the entry gate. She followed the rutted dirt road and soon came to a trailer with a Sales & Information sign out front. She parked and went in and, not wanting to use her real name, she borrowed that of the author of the book she was reading, signed in as Ayn Rand and made up an Atlanta address on Peachtree Street. Atlanta had a million Peachtree addresses so she was safe there. A woman in a short, tight skirt teetered up on six-inch stilettos. *Wow. I hope you never have to go anywhere in a hurry.*

"Hi. I'm Ashley," the woman said in a raspy nicotine-tinted voice.

Jungle Gardenia, a fragrance Abbey hadn't smelled since high school, wafted over in a choking cloud. It was clearly one of Ashley's favorites.

Chestnut hair coiled around the woman's shoulders. Abbey guessed she was in her late thirties, but without her perfectly applied Neiman Marcus makeup she might have pushed forty-five. For a split second, Abbey imagined being a subdivision agent in Atlanta. She looked around the trailer. Nah. Being in a place like this all day would drive her crazy. Too claustrophobic.

"Pleased to meet you, Ashley." *Too bad her lift didn't include her hands. She's forty-five if she's a day.* "Pretty name, Ashley. Mine's Ayn." Not even a blink. Her alias was safe. Ashley wouldn't know she had been duped until her follow-up note to "Ayn Rand" was returned address unknown. Ashley wore a considerable diamond on her left hand, every bit as showy as Vickie's.

"I'm staying on St. Simons this week, Ashley, and thought I'd come by to pick up a brochure and have a look around. How do you like sitting on the development?"

"It's great. A friend suggested I take this job and I love it. I get bored sometimes, but I meet the most interesting people and if no one is here, I read my magazines. I always bring a stack."

What a thrilling way to spend a day. Not. To play the role of interested prospect, Abbey walked around a mock-up of the development in the center of the room and studied framed home renderings on the walls. She wondered if architects had been paid to draw up these designs or if these were available from Southern Living magazine. "So I see there are plans to put in a marina here. No golf course?"

"That's right. No golf course. We're a boating community. We have plans to build two marinas," Ashley said proudly. "But there are loads of golf courses near here if that's important to you."

"No, I like the idea of the marina, actually." Several minutes later Abbey headed toward the door. "I have your card, Ashley, so I'll give you a call when I get serious about buying." The lack of a guard at the entry gate and the fact that hers was the only name on the sign-in sheet spoke volumes. Still, she prodded. "Have you been busy?"

After a moment's hesitation and a concerted effort to smile, Ashley said, "Yes, of course." She did a little cough, which sounded as though something wet broke apart in her chest.

Yuck. "Good. I hope you do well here."

"Would you like for me to show you around the property? I have a golf cart out back all charged up and ready to go."

"No. Not today. Thanks for your help, Ashley. I really have to run. I have my dog in the car and I don't want him to overheat." Abbey spotted a list of approved lenders and architects on a table and picked one up.

"They have some great rates if you need to finance your purchase," Ashley said, her smile still plastered on her face.

Abbey continued walking and had her hand on the door when she turned and said, "Do you have a map of the development?"

Ashley's smile tightened. "We're all out. They were supposed to be delivered today, but the printer we use had a backlog of jobs. He promised he'd have them ready by this afternoon, so the agent who has the later shift is supposed to pick them up. I'm so sorry, but if you drop by after lunch they should be in the box on the front porch. If you come in, please tell her you already signed in with me, okay?"

She's dying to get back to those magazines. "No problem. I'll come back."

Ashley smiled. "Thanks, Ann. Don't forget to call me when you get serious about buying."

Abbey rolled down all the windows in the Jeep. Behind the trailer was a smaller lot where a brand-new two-door red Mercedes convertible was parked next to two golf carts with Crooked Creek logos on their sides. Abbey doubted she bought that car with her commissions from this place.

She wanted to see where Vickie lived, so rather than exit the property she turned left out of the lot. A distinct overgrown line ran from the trailer alongside the road. Dirt roads at Kings Bluff were better maintained than this one, which was nothing more than a path that had been beaten down by tires over the years. Not very impressive for a new development. Numerous offshoots split off into the woods but the most traveled tracks would surely take her to where people lived. Vickie did not strike her as the roughing-it type and there was no way that Cadillac had four-wheel drive.

At a V in the road she went with the more traveled of the two legs and came to a relatively new frame home on a beautiful marshy bluff. A gold Cadillac was parked out front. Large by any measure, the house dwarfed the lot and seemed to occupy every permissible square inch of dirt. An in-ground pool in the back yard twinkled between the wooden boards of a tall fence.

Driving on, she came to a large area marked off by stakes and orange plastic tape. The clubhouse, more than likely, but there were no structures, no materials lying about, no landscaping, and no equipment of any kind to indicate work was in progress. And there were certainly no tennis courts and no hole for a pool. She drove back by Vickie's house. The scarred line she had noticed at the sales trailer ran to Vickie's but not toward the clubhouse. *Where are the utilities? Strange.*

She drove back to the V where she had originally chosen to go right, and this time she went left. Below tall grass, her tires found well-worn vehicle tracks, which snaked through two-hundred-year-old live oaks. There were areas where pines and scrub oaks had been felled and piled. Watch Dog hung his head out the rear window and barked when an armadillo broke from a palmetto thicket and scurried deep into the brush. The creek glittered through gaps in the trees on the right.

"Watch, there's the house Momma was talking about." Watch answered with a short yip.

The house was a one-story wooden ranch with a silver-colored tin roof. It looked as though it had been charming until it fell into disrepair, probably after the Atlanta couple sold it to Crooked Creek's developer. Overgrown azaleas and camellias threatened to take over what had probably been gorgeous gardens on the edge of the creek but now were so out of control they blocked whatever view of the water the house once enjoyed. The grass hadn't been cut in weeks. Approaching the back right corner of the property, she noticed the tail end of a white Range Rover sticking out of the carport. She tapped her brakes.

"Okay, Watch, we're out of here." Her tone elicited a low rumble from Watch Dog.

It was easier to retrace her steps than to look for a place to turn around, so she backed all the way to the V and turned down the road she had followed from the sales trailer. From there she went off-roading on narrow tracks, probably those of the golf cart the agent used. She tried to imagine Ashley showing property that way but couldn't quite bring up the image. Areas which had been cleared of trees had small lot markers, many with stick-on Sold labels on them. But it was dead quiet and lacked the usual hammering and slapping of lumber one would expect in a new development. Everywhere she drove, things were at a standstill.

It struck her as odd that lot owners' names and the cities and states where they lived were not printed on the sold lots. Purchasers liked to see where other buyers were from, and the signs were good advertising for the developer to show how far and wide word had spread about his development. Perhaps the fellow who printed flyers and maps for the sales office also did the signs for the new property owners and he was swamped, as Ashley had said. But how likely was that? This was his business. She drove back by Vickie's house, where the grass and foundation plants looked like they had been in place for some time. Something was going on here and it looked all too familiar. Developers went belly-up in Atlanta all the time.

She made her way back to St. Marys, where she stopped at a real estate office and spoke to the duty agent, who introduced herself as Linda.

"If you drove around in there, you probably saw the cottage on the creek, which belonged to the original owners," Linda said. Abbey nodded. "The developer tied into gas and electric from that cottage, then put a septic field in another lot down the creek and built a model home. He had it open to agents while it was under construction and had a big open house one weekend with food, drinks, balloons, the works."

And Bart and Vickie bought the only house in the development? None of this makes any sense.

"His agent knew about as much about new construction as she did about flying a 747," Linda said.

"And would that knowledgeable agent be the divine Miss Ashley?"

"Oh, you have had the pleasure of meeting her," Linda said. "She's the developer's sister and word has it she's not sneaking by solely on real estate commissions. Anyway, next thing we knew, he moved into his show house."

"Wait a minute," Abbey said. "The developer lives in the new house with the pool?" *You've got to be kidding me.*

"Yep. He sure does. First thing he did was put a 'Private' sign out front so nobody would barge in on him, but by then word had gotten out and no one was showing out there anyway. He needn't have bothered with the sign or the big open house. Should have saved his money. It looks like he could use it."

"So, Bart Croek is the developer?" *Dabbles in real estate, Vickie? Really? Why lie to me about that?*

"You know him?"

"No. But I'm beginning to get the picture. I met his wife." She said no more. It would not come from her lips that Vickie wanted to look for a place in Atlanta.

The two traded real estate horror stories, and Abbey picked up a real estate magazine. "Are there any tennis courts around here?"

Linda dug through her files and pulled out the full-color flyer from Bart's one and only open house and handed it to Abbey. "Tennis courts? Gosh, not that I know of. The high school has a basketball court, but tennis? I sure haven't seen any, but that's not to say they're not there in the back of the school or something."

"Okay. Just wondering." She held up the flyer. "May I make a copy?"

"No, keep it. I don't think I'll be needing it. I was going to purge these files this afternoon anyway, so this will get me started."

"Okay, sure. Listen, thanks for your help."

Back in her car, Abbey tossed the real estate magazine onto the passenger seat and thought about Bart. *Some developer.* The Bart his wife had described sounded like the typical control-freak male jerk. A beard-bristled face with a pig's snout and floppy little ears popped into her head. *He must be incredibly hot for Vickie to put up with him.*

She glanced at her watch. By the time she got back to the sales trailer, the bin was full of maps. As she grabbed a copy, she glanced through the window panes in the front door and saw the back of a man in a floral Hawaiian shirt. A white Panama hat was clasped in the hands of the woman whose arms were wrapped around the man's back. Those hands didn't belong to Ashley; the nails were painted light pink and the rings on the fingers were silver and turquoise, no diamonds. Abbey backed off on tiptoe, then drove away, not noticing the flowery shirt that appeared at the front door as she departed.

FOURTEEN

It was early still, so Abbey hot-footed it to Jacksonville. The medical center had her number but hadn't called her yet. She was not one to wait around. It couldn't hurt to drop by again to check on Doc. He might have improved since yesterday.

Once on the road, Abbey's thoughts turned to Vickie. Atlanta was full of possibilities for her. Virginia Highlands had interesting shops and eateries and was fun, but maybe a bit too young and quirky. No. Vickie seemed more the type for upscale shopping and restaurants, more the Buckhead type. A condo or townhouse on or near Peachtree Street might work. Vickie would probably think she had died and gone to heaven if she awakened every morning near Atlanta's most famous street.

Vickie came off as ditsy, but something in her eyes and occasionally the way she talked said that wasn't the whole story. Boobs and the car pleased Bart, but it seemed there was more behind all the surface stuff—like hurt or anger or loneliness. Maybe all three, but why hide the fact that Bart was a developer, not just a dabbler in real estate? There was a pretty big difference. "Whatever Bartsie wants Bartsie gets." How pathetic. He probably felt threatened by a woman with any brains so she played dumb to keep him on the hook.

To heck with him. Vickie needed to qualify for a loan or come up with the cash to buy. If she was involved financially in Crooked

Creek and the place went under, she'd be toast. At least she could sell her car and that damn diamond ring to get a down payment— but then what? How would she live?

The next exit said Jacksonville. *Doggone-it, I hate it when I don't remember the drive.* She tied Watch to the crepe myrtle tree in the mulch where she had seen a dog tied the day before. "I'll be right back, Watch. Don't bark at strangers and no digging." She handed him a chew bone. "Be a good boy." He dropped to his haunches and chewed.

When she walked into the hospital's main entrance, she saw a familiar stance in uniform outside the gift shop. Terkoff looked up when she approached and stopped talking mid-sentence. The nurse he'd been speaking to looked over as well. Abbey flicked a wave and continued toward the Information desk.

"Uh, Ms. Bunn?"

Abbey turned and found Terkoff standing behind her.

"You here to see our John Doe?" he said.

"Yes."

"I was just going up. Care if I join you?"

"Not at all." The nurse reappeared with two guest passes.

On the way up in the elevator, Abbey said, "I think he goes by Doc."

"Why?"

"Remember the hat I told you about?"

Terkoff looked at her, then stared at the floor indicator light. "Yes. The one you were supposed to give me."

Abbey shrugged. "Hat hasn't gone anywhere. You left without asking me for it."

"And of course you didn't bring it."

"I had no idea I'd see you today, Terkoff. I called your office earlier. You were out. Your partner is an ass."

Terkoff cracked a smile. "Hang on to the hat. I'll need to pick it up and see what we can get from it."

Abbey rolled her eyes.

"What?"

"I'm glad I didn't wear it when I jogged this morning."

Terkoff shook his head. "Just put it someplace safe. The lab is pretty good. If it belongs to our guy, they'll be able to pick up hair samples. Don't wear it, okay?"

Abbey nodded. "Just pulling your chain." He shook his head.

Maurine was at the nurse's station. "Oh. You're here again and you brought back-up this time."

"Yes. This is Sheriff Terkoff. He's the investigating officer."

"I see. I could use a walk. Follow me," Maurine said. "Any luck figuring out who he is?"

"No," Terkoff said. "Is that a problem? I mean, he can stay here until we figure things out, right?"

"For now he's okay. Adult Protective Services will probably get involved if it goes on too long. They'll check around to see if anyone matching his description has been reported missing or anything. Not to worry. Something is going to break, always does," Maurine said with a reassuring look at Abbey.

The door was ajar, so they pushed it open and walked in. He was still the room's only occupant. A monitor with a squiggly line running across it beeped. Abbey's lips pressed together. The right side of Doc's face and his chest were putrid shades of black and blue and purple. She pulled her arms together around her middle. "That really looks painful."

"They're keeping him sedated to give his body a chance to heal itself," Maurine said.

"Did he talk much today?" Abbey said.

"Now and then. About like you heard yesterday. He still sleeps a lot, which is good."

Abbey glanced at Terkoff.

"Mind if we sit with him?"

"It shouldn't hurt," Maurine said. She touched Doc on the shoulder while she checked tubes.

"He's lucky the prop didn't cut him in two," Terkoff said.

"That's for darn sure. He's sleeping soundly so you can stay for a minute or two. Might do him good to know someone cares. Just don't touch him or speak too loudly." Her shoes squeaked as she walked out and pulled the door shut behind her.

Abbey said, "He's pretty banged up. You know that's gotta hurt."

"Ehhhhhh…" Doc groaned and his eyes popped open.

Abbey stepped closer to the bed. "Hi, Doc. It's me, Abbey. Do you need anything?"

"Who are you? Do I know you?" he said as though they had been conversing for a while.

"Sort of, but the main thing is you're safe, Doc. You're in the hospital in Jacksonville. No one is going to hurt you here."

His eyelids fluttered. "So thirsty. Where's my beer?"

Abbey held a cup of water to his lips like she had seen Boonks do when one of her brothers was ill. He sipped. "There you go. Good. Just a little. You're okay now. You're in the hospital." Terkoff stood on the other side of the bed across from her now. "Do you remember me? I think maybe you recognize my voice. I talked to you the whole time I was getting you out of the river."

The index finger on the hand closest to Abbey moved up and down. Abbey looked at Terkoff, who mouthed, "Keep going."

"You are in the hospital in Jacksonville, Florida. This is the closest one to where I found you. We pulled you out of the river with a shrimp net."

Doc said, "Do I know you?"

She looked at Terkoff, who motioned to her to keep on talking. "Looks like you were hit by a boat, Doc. I believe you go by Doc, don't you?" No response. "Judging by where I found you, I bet you were out there fishing."

His forehead creased and his eyebrows bunched. "Yeaaaaaah,"

he said so forcefully that Abbey stepped back. One of the monitors beeped loudly and the door flew open.

"I'm sorry, but I think he has had enough," Maurine said. "He's agitated, which is good. Shows he's trying to work things out. What did you say to him anyway?"

"I mentioned I thought he had been fishing before I found him and he said 'yeah' loudly."

"I heard it all the way down at the nurse's station. Fishing, huh. Well, maybe he was. That ought to help you find the so-and-sos who did this to him. He needs to rest now so why don't you come back tomorrow? You might want to bring your crystal ball."

"Why is that?"

"To see who is missing him. Just kidding, but the hospital likes paying customers so they want to find out who he is as much as anybody."

"Right." It had never occurred to her that Doc couldn't stay in the hospital as long as he needed to, but of course the hospital wanted to get paid. "Okay. We'll get on it." Abbey and Terkoff stepped into the hallway.

"Interesting," Terkoff said.

"He wasn't agitated until I mentioned the fishing trip." They walked to the elevator. "He's coming around, Terkoff. He wants to talk and I bet he has a whole lot to say. You know he has relatives somewhere who are at their wits' end."

FIFTEEN

Then sun was going down by the time Abbey pulled up behind the cottage and let Watch out. He trotted to the nearest tree and took care of business. It had been a very long day. She filled ceramic doggie bowls with dry food and water, then poured a glass of wine from the half-full bottle on the counter. Hoping the fridge fairy had popped in and left a culinary surprise while she was out, she was disappointed to find nothing new, so she grabbed an avocado half and the container of shrimp salad she'd been working on. There would be plenty of time to cook after Tom arrived; tonight she'd make do. Dinner took all of ten minutes; then Watch walked her to each end of the bluff in front of the cottages before they settled in for the night.

Sofa cushions sprung from years of use let out a soft *pfft* when she sat, the solid maple frame still sturdy and solid after more than its share of abuse by rowdy rough-housing boys and girls. She picked up the real estate magazine she'd gotten earlier and flipped through pages of slick copy. These mags were all the same, thumbnail-sized pictures of houses and smiling studio shots of agents. Bart wasn't even advertising his lots. Granted advertising was expensive, but nothing showed trouble faster than no building activity, landscaping gone to hell, and no advertising budget. He didn't even keep the place mowed.

Hopefully Bart had put up the cash for the development and the house. Vickie was too new an acquaintance to ask too much about her husband, but there were already plenty of X's in his undesirable column. She made a mental note to call one of the mortgage brokers on the list she'd picked up at the sales office. Lenders were cautious people. If the deal stank, they wouldn't touch it. Tom might caution her and tell her to keep her nose out of Bart's business, but it wasn't Bart she was worried about. Vickie had asked for help, though she hadn't been specific.

She tossed the magazine aside and picked up the file the St. Marys agent had handed her along with the Crooked Creek open house flyer that she'd planned to scrap. One newspaper clipping was dated December 1984. Bart Croek beamed at the top of the page with a hard hat pressed to his chest and a shovel in his other hand. The caption read, "Developer breaks ground in St. Marys."

She propped her feet up on a worn footstool and read. Bart grew up in Orlando. He moved back home and became a banker there after graduating from the University of Florida in Gainesville in 1961. While visiting with college buddies one weekend, he met "a lovely girl from Virginia" and was smitten. "She had a date with an old friend of mine but I knew the moment we met that I didn't want her to get away." *I bet he didn't.* They married six months later. He stayed in banking a total of four years but he had bigger plans for him and his new bride. He changed hats and used the knowledge he'd gained in banking to become a partner in a real estate development outside of the city. Bart said his first ten to fifteen years in the development business were a great training ground. He was having fun and things were booming, but it couldn't last. He wanted out of Florida so he started to look around for other opportunities and he found one, a beautiful tract of land in Georgia on a coastal river. *So if Bart found it, maybe he did put up all the money for the land.*

In another article, she found the names of two real estate agents who had put lots under contract in Crooked Creek early on. The agent who was quoted gushed about the property. The story included their office's phone number. *Free advertising.* She called the number and was able to get contact information for one of the agents from the answering service but had no success with the agent who had been quoted. Abbey called the first agent, Joy Smith, and introduced herself. She apologized for calling at night and told her she had found her name in a rather old newspaper article that mentioned her office. When Abbey said she had a client in Atlanta who asked her to check out Crooked Creek in St. Marys, the agent unloaded.

"I have no idea what's going on with that property, but the developer has major issues. He put the moves on me, scared me to death. I told my broker. He suggested I take another agent with me the next time I showed out there." Abbey let her talk. "He said he'd say something to Bart but who knows if he ever did. Typical good-old-boy deal. I suppose my broker didn't want to get involved. I'd have broken Bart's neck if he ever tried it again. You notice I wasn't quoted in that article. It was all the other agent."

"I noticed that," Abbey said. "What did you think about the development?"

"I'll tell you one thing, if done right, that place could be fabulous," Joy said. "The marina will be a huge selling point with all the boaters down here. There are plenty of golf courses already, and who wants to pay for them? I didn't want to give up on the lots so the next time I had a client who wanted to build, I took Samantha, the agent who was quoted, with me.

"By then, Bart insisted on being present for all showings. Maybe he thought he could sell better than all the agents around here, but I suspect it was because he wanted to put a little pressure on the buyers. He could be fairly aggressive. At any rate, I was very stand-offish with Bart and it was obvious he took a shine to Samantha. At first she thought he was cute; it gave me the creeps the way they looked at each other. It was too bad because I liked her a lot. I quit showing out there. There's plenty more around here without having to put up with that nonsense."

"There were no maps the first time I went out there and it's all overgrown. I don't know how he expects to sell anything," Abbey said. "Did your friend know Bart was married?"

"I don't know. I never saw him wear a wedding band, but I guess I found out somehow he had a wife. But after a while Samantha quit. I never really talked to her about any of this."

"Quit selling real estate?" Abbey said.

"Yeah. I mean, who knows. She just quit coming to the office, let her license lapse and everything. I don't know what happened to her."

"That's odd. Surely someone checked on her." Abbey remembered the agent in Atlanta who showed a vacant home to a new client and was later found dead in the basement. She'd been raped and strangled.

"Well, sure, I mean, I called the number my office had for her and no one answered. My broker got worried so he checked around and found the guy who owned the little house she rented. The lease was month to month and it was paid up, but she had vacated. We figured she had gone to California or something. Samantha was always talking about California, but I think she was from Alabama."

Abbey thanked her and hung up the phone. Something wasn't right. Where was Tom when she needed him?

When the phone rang she jumped. "Hey, it's me. I just wanted to say goodnight."

Abbey leaned against the kitchen counter and let out a deep breath. "Hi. I'm glad you called."

"You sound out of breath. Is anything wrong?"

"No, not at all. I just got off the phone with an agent. Part of the unfolding saga I'll tell you about when you get here. It's funny, though. After I hung up with her I was thinking about you, wishing you were here to talk to."

"Good thoughts, I hope."

"That goes without saying, knucklehead."

"Is that a term of endearment? Your idea of phone sex?"

"I don't do phone sex, as if you didn't know. But seriously, I just found out something that has me a little worried." She gave him the background on Vickie and the development and two-timing Bart and what she had just learned about the agent who up and quit. "I don't know. I don't trust Bart as far as I can throw him."

"I'll get one of the interns to check out this Bart fellow when I get home, which might be as early as tomorrow. I'll give you a shout when I get back. Go on and give me what you have on this guy." She gave him all she knew, and when she was finished he said, "Just for the record, I'm ready to see you."

"Me too." Abbey smiled when she hung up the phone. *I wonder what happened to that agent.* She took her wine and her book to the screened porch and turned off her brain.

SIXTEEN

With her eyes glued to the paperback in her hand, Vickie sipped her wine, then placed the glass on a small tile coaster on the end table. Snuggling deeper into the sofa's soft cushion, she exhaled a contented sigh. The swarthy swashbuckler had finally grabbed the red-headed wench by the waist and pulled her to a back-bending, hair-thrown-back embrace as promised on the book's cover. Vickie twirled a red curl of her own and turned the page. Her breaths quickened. Over the years, she had eschewed murder mysteries and thrillers for romance novels, which she didn't dare read when Bart was home. He thought they were trash, but she loved to get lost in their titillating promises of passion and sex.

This was the second night in a row she had been able to sip her wine and read in peace because Bart's daily cocktail hour had extended well into the evening. Accustomed to her husband's tightly wound nature, she had learned to cut him some slack, but she hoped this new twist of staying out drinking was just a passing phase and would not become habit. Surely this was a business dinner he'd forgotten to tell her about. Since they'd moved into this house, Bart seemed to have lost interest in her physically. Maybe it was his age. She hoped not, but more than that, she hoped it wasn't something or someone else. The bluster of the old rooster in the hen-house strut he'd had when they met was back, but he certainly wasn't chasing her around the bedpost. Tonight she had a sure-fire plan. What man could resist the feel of satin and the allure of delicate lace?

Shells crunched in the driveway. The electric garage door whined before bumping to a stop. She marked her spot with a paper marker from the bookstore, downed her last sip of wine, and deposited her glass in the kitchen sink before scurrying up the back stairs adjacent to the kitchen door. A nightlight in the master bathroom illuminated the super-sized mirror over the double vanity. Vickie's long hair hung loose and sexy. She ran a hand over her bare arms and legs and breathed in the light floral scent of the bath oil she had soaked in earlier that evening. The sheer black teddy she had purchased months ago looked even better filled out with her rounded curves. It just might do the trick. She gargled and swished mouthwash, then tiptoed to the far side of the king-sized bed, her side. Bart got up often during the night and liked to be close to the bathroom.

The alarm on the kitchen door beeped. Heavy-footed Bart could never sneak in. He always kicked off his shoes at the back door then clunk-clunk-clunked around the kitchen in his sock feet. A loud fart followed by a grateful groan traveled up the back stairwell. Bottles on the refrigerator door clanked. The silverware drawer bumped open, utensils rattled, the drawer bumped closed. Vickie had left dinner on the stove covered with aluminum foil in case he was hungry. It was right by the refrigerator so he couldn't miss it. Several minutes later, the television in the family room came to life with a burst of cheers.

She lay in bed and listened. Downstairs noise had two stairwells up which to travel, and insulation in the floors was minimal at best. Announcer Skip Caray might as well be in the next room instead of in California with the Atlanta Braves. West Coast games meant it would be a late night. Eventually, her eyes became heavy and closed.

Sometime later, the phone rang once. Vickie awakened and slipped her hand where Bart should have been. The sheets were cool and undisturbed. Caray's unmistakable play calls were sharp and excited. The game must be near the end, but Bart wasn't grunting his usual staccato game script. His voice was more a low growl, quiet, sexy, and anything but business or baseball. She glanced at the clock. It was past midnight.

She slipped from bed, used the bathroom, and looked in the mirror as she rinsed her hands. A tear sparkled on her cheek in the dim glow of the night light. Grabbing a tissue, she touched it to her eyes and almost collided with Bart as he stumbled to the toilet.

Vickie stepped back, balled her fists and said, "I'm sick and tired of this. Don't you think it's a little late to be talking to your girlfriend on the phone, Bart?"

SEVENTEEN

From the comfort of her bed the next morning, Abbey listened to cicadas and tried to picture how they made their shrill sound by vibrating a membrane on the underside of their abdomens—when all she had ever found of one was a crunchy, empty shell clinging to the bark of a tree. If it hadn't been explained to her by her father, she'd have never guessed. He had also explained how crickets rubbed their forewings together to make their chirps, but that was easy to imagine if you grew up with Walt Disney and Jiminy Cricket.

A seed-laden pine cone thumped to the earth. A mourning dove cooed. Her brothers could name most birds by their calls and certainly on sight, as well as identify them by their eggs. As young boys they had collected eggs, no more than one per nest. The oldest brother was the stump up which the younger one would climb until he could stand on his brother's shoulders and shinny up the tree the rest of the way. Whether their interest was just boyhood curiosity or something inspired by Scouts she didn't know, but she wished she had their knowledge. Darkness turned to gray dawn. Enough lying in bed thinking. There was much to do.

Abbey put the teakettle on the stove to boil, then filled Watch's bowls. She had puzzled over Vickie all night. She could have just come out and said Bart was the developer, but she didn't—so there must have been a reason. Maybe she didn't think it was important, but how could it not be important to a real estate agent? Obviously, Vickie only shared what she wanted you to know. That presented a problem unless you knew that about her and took everything she said with a grain of salt, or you pushed.

Vickie had to be deaf, dumb and blind not to see what was and what was not going on at Crooked Creek, so Abbey had to assume she knew at least some of it. Maybe she was embarrassed that things had stopped moving ahead, or maybe she thought it looked like any other development in the early stages. But Bartsie probably kept lots of secrets, business and monkey. No, she wasn't that dense. If a subdivision looked like a flop, it usually was, until someone came along and either invested a lot of money to get it out of its quagmire or took it over. *Damn. Does Vickie really want to use me because of that bust she read about or does she have something else in mind?*

The kettle whistle interrupted her thoughts. She dropped a tea bag into her Abbey mug and went to the porch to continue parsing her thoughts. Watch Dog circled and plopped down by her rocker. Abbey sipped her tea and scratched Watch's head. Being a developer was a far cry from dabbling in real estate and Vickie knew it, so why stretch the truth? There was only one way to find out. Vickie had mentioned a coffee shop in St. Marys where she and her tennis cronies went after their lesson. "Come on, Watch. We'll jog later." *I gotta see a lady about a lie.*

~

Watch hung his head out of the Jeep's rear window and didn't miss a moving thing alongside the road. There was no telling where the coffee shop was, but St. Marys wasn't very big and chances were it was near the water, where all the action was. When she stopped, Watch poked his head between the front seats and offered the leash in his mouth. "Good boy. Let's go."

A pelican atop a piling caught Watch's eye. He woofed. The odd fellow looked statuesque until it gazed around to see what all the racket was about and exposed its telltale beak. Watch dropped to his haunches and stared back, his mouth open, pink tongue panting, ears and eyes alert and fixed.

"Tom would love this little town, wouldn't he?" Watch glanced at her, yawned wide and *arfed,* then refocused on the pelican. *I'll bring him here one day for lunch.*

Tom's unhappy marriage had been brought to an abrupt and unexpected end a year ago when his wife was killed in a suspicious one-car accident just north of Jacksonville. Abbey had helped him discover the truth of Lucinda's death, and over time, he had come to grips with her lies and cheating, and maybe when he finally realized what she really was, it was easier for him to get on with his life. At any rate, he was ready for an honest relationship and a committed marriage, one that included Abbey, and he wanted it now.

She, on the other hand, had jammed on her emergency brake and said not so fast. Since she had divorced her controlling and abusive alcoholic husband, her life had gotten back on track. She was crazy about Tom, that wasn't the problem. It was the whole marriage thing, the forever-and-ever-amen part. It sounded so permanent, and she kind of liked the way things were. Of course, if her mother had anything to say about it, Abbey would march down the aisle before the end of the year. Tom was smart, fun, attractive and gainfully employed. He was a catch and he'd be a great mate and a terrific father. He made no bones about the fact that he wanted kids and, at thirty-seven, she knew time was not on her side. If she wanted children with Tom, that had to be at the top of her priorities. It deserved some serious thought.

"There she is," Abbey said softly.

Vickie drove down the street slowly, headed away from town. Abbey and Watch hopped back into the Jeep and followed her to a stand-up sandwich board with a steaming mug of coffee painted on it. She parked. Vickie slid out of her car like a twenty-year-old alley cat. The perky tennis-player-wanna-be from yesterday must have stayed home today.

"Come on, Watch. Let's see what's up." Outside the coffee shop, he plunked down in the shade of a huge azalea bush and dropped his head for a snooze. "Stay, boy. I'm in there." He did not acknowledge.

Vickie fluffed her hair and turned around when Abbey tapped her on the shoulder at the counter. "Good morning, Vickie."

"Oh, hi." Vickie's face went slack at first, then her eyes opened wide in recognition and she forced a half-hearted smile.

Abbey glanced around the shop, which was empty except for an elderly couple. "Are your friends joining you?"

"Oh, umm, they couldn't make it today." Vickie's eyebrows creased. "Busy girls."

Lame excuse. They ordered coffee and scones and took them to a table. Vickie's eyes darted around the room as though she expected to find someone there she recognized.

The pancake makeup was new, or was it? If it had been there Sunday it hadn't been quite so noticeable, but then, the parking exhibition had been so extraordinary who would have noticed foundation makeup? However, this was a thick smear. No, this was new—as was the bluish tint on Vickie's left cheek. Okay, so something was going on here. "Did you bump your cheek?"

Vickie's hand flew to her face and she winced. The corners of her mouth dropped. "No, I'm clumsy. I tripped. Last night I, um, I stepped out of the tub and slipped on the tile. Dumb me. I forgot to put out the bath mat."

I bet Bart's right-handed. "Ouch. Ice it. That'll keep the swelling down."

Vickie gave a weak smile. "Thanks. I'll try that."

She looked like a bird ready to take flight should a cat jump onto the table. Something was going on with her, personal stuff. If she wasn't honest about Bart's involvement with Crooked Creek, she sure wouldn't 'fess up to his abuse. "When we had lunch the other day, you said you wanted to know what I really thought about Crooked Creek," Abbey said, "so I picked up a map from the sales office and drove around out there."

She leaned in closer and rested her elbow on the table to support her chin. This close, it was obvious that the cheek was swollen and bruised. If Vickie had hit the tile she would have split the soft tissue wide open, not just bruised it. "Funniest thing happened, Vickie. I stopped at a real estate office in St. Marys and talked to an agent who told me Bart is the developer at Crooked Creek." Abbey put on a big meet-the-boyfriend's-old-girlfriend smile and watched Vickie react.

"Oh." Vickie sat back in her chair and looked as if she had just swallowed an unripe persimmon. "Didn't I mention that?"

"No, you didn't. You can imagine how surprised I was. Actually, I felt rather stupid because I had just told this woman that I was going to work with you in Atlanta." Abbey sipped her coffee. Vickie's mouth hung open and she looked as though she expected Abbey to wallop her. "Your home is lovely, by the way."

Vickie's mouth snapped shut and she adjusted in her chair to a more upright posture. "Thank you. It's nice enough." She looked down at the table while the red receded from her face. "That's awful for me to say. No, really, it is lovely. It's just not me. We did it all for Bart and he adores that house."

"I wondered about something. For the life of me, I can't find tennis courts anywhere, and I have looked all over St. Marys. Where do you play?"

Vickie turned red. "The high school. Nothing fancy."

"And you get a pro to go over there to give lessons to you and your friends."

Vickie's thumb and index finger swiped down the corners of her mouth as if removing milk from the creases. "Not exactly a pro. PE teacher at the high school. He played all through high school and college so he's pretty good. Most of all, we get along, my friends and I. They're local girls and they knew him growing up, so we have a good time."

"Oh. That's nice." *That explains that. How about the development?* "Crooked Creek looks a little sleepy for you, Vickie. There doesn't seem to be much going on out there."

"Well, it has slowed down some lately—we sold a lot of lots when we first opened though." Vickie's attempt at sincerity sounded forced.

If she had money in this deal, she was probably scared to death she was going to lose it all. Abbey remembered her earlier thoughts about it going in the tank. Vickie's voluptuous chest heaved as she ran a hand through her hair. *She's nervous as hell.* "You said 'when we first opened.' Are you involved in Crooked Creek monetarily?"

"Well, no, of course not." Vickie shook her head. "Heavens, no. I know nothing about building houses. Bart wants to take care of all of that. I only work in the office part-time, the administrative office, Bart calls it." Vickie sighed. "Some administration. I guess my official title," she did air quotes, "is 'Girl Friday.'" Her mouth twisted as though the title tasted foul.

Vickie was too well-spoken to be stupid, but for some reason she seemed to like to play the role. "And your function is…"

"I pay bills, make coffee, answer the phone, that sort of thing. Bart's out a lot so I take messages for him, things like that." She frowned.

"All of that is important, Vickie. Trust me. To make sales you need names and phone numbers. Without them, you're dead in the water. With them, you can build a database." Vickie bit her lip. "What's wrong?" *Abbey the psychologist.*

"Oh, nothing. It sounds silly. Answering the phone isn't exactly demanding, but some days I hate it. People can be so unbelievably pushy."

Emotions worked with Vickie's delicate features so Abbey

lobbed an easy one. If she was a Girl Friday, she probably read the mail so she had to know what was going on. "Do you get mail delivery out there or do you have to come in to St. Marys?"

"We have a post office box in town. Bart has the key so he picks it up every day." Vickie glanced around as if divulging top-secret information. She spoke softly. "I thought it was an expense we didn't need, but he insisted. Checks were supposed to come rolling in, Abbey. Buyers were going to be knocking our doors down to buy property." *Ah, a glimpse of the real Vickie Croek. She's pissed.*

Vickie shook her head. "Fat chance, though. Nobody's knocking. Nobody stops in. How can we sell anything if nobody even comes to look?"

"Tough job keeping up with all the invoices what with contractors and all. You said you pay the bills."

"Well, yes, of course."

"Wow. I was an English major, didn't give a flip about numbers. I guess if you write the checks you keep a handle on finances for the development and all of that. I wouldn't touch that one with a ten-foot pole."

Vickie tapped a nail on the table and licked her lips. Her eyebrows pinched together. "Come to think of it, I haven't written a check on the business account for a while." She sighed. "Things have been a little tense lately, and Bart has kind of been off his feed, if you know what I mean."

And it looks like he has taken to roughing up his wife. Bet there's another woman. "Slip him a little horny goat weed in his morning orange juice."

Vickie's mouth dropped open. "That sounds interesting. Does it do what it sounds like it does?"

Abbey nodded. "Supposed to."

"Now how do you know about that?"

"I read Cosmopolitan once when I was stuck at the hospital for a while, and there was an article about it."

"Do you think it works?"

"You never know 'til you try." *So that's definitely part of the problem and the other is money.* "We were talking a minute ago about the messages you take, and you said 'they' are so pushy. Who's pushy? Buyers? Real estate agents? Don't let them boss you around, Vickie. Push back. It's okay."

Vickie glanced up at the ceiling for several seconds, then she looked directly at Abbey and crossed her arms on the table. "Um, no, not them."

Abbey didn't rush her. Vickie was procrastinating, maybe putting two and two together. Judging by her facial expressions, she was concerned.

"There's one banker who—I swear—calls about every other day. He's a real pest. Probably wants us to get a credit card or something. Then there's this lawyer." Her tone bordered on huffy. "Well, there was this one lawyer who always used to leave messages for Bart. But yesterday one called and he actually wanted to set up a time to talk to me. I can't imagine why."

Abbey had been with Tom long enough to know that lawyers didn't just call people out of the blue. And she had been a real estate agent long enough to know that when developers got into financial trouble, anyone and everyone who had anything to do with the developer could be deposed. *Oh, damn. Bart's in over his head so that's why she brought up all of that business about the drug bust and the newspaper articles. He's in trouble and she knows it and she's scared to death and she thinks I can help her somehow. Okay. I get it now.*

She waited. Vickie acted like the bankers and lawyers were annoying telemarketers, but that could all be part of her act.

"Oh, well, they're all jerks if you ask me." Vickie looked around conspiratorially. "The one who calls Bart all the time is an A-number-one-ass, if you want my opinion."

Your opinions are always interesting. Abbey took several minutes to consider which way to steer the conversation. She planned to call a mortgage broker on the list she had picked up at the sales trailer, but she'd see what she could get from the horse's mouth.

"Paying the bills is a huge responsibility, Vickie. I guess that means you pay the taxes and insurance and balance the bank statements and all of that, right?" She smiled and leaned in closer like she was talking to the chairman of the board of the bank. Vickie stopped chewing, laid down her fork and sucked in a deep breath. "Vickie, are you okay?" *Money talk always upsets her but she's giving today.*

Vickie nodded.

"When I was here yesterday, I spoke with an agent in town who doesn't show property at Crooked Creek anymore," Abbey said.

Vickie's eyes opened wide. "Why not?"

Hunh. That was a voice I haven't heard yet. The real Vickie? "Because she heard there are problems. And I was out there. No dirt's being moved. No infrastructure is going in. There's one road going into the development and it's not even paved. Utilities go to the sales trailer, the office, and your house and that's it."

"Bart said they were behind but..." Vickie stared off for several seconds. "He said it had something to do with the city. I heard him talking about it but he didn't want to discuss it with me, said it was nothing. They were just a little behind schedule."

"Vickie, without roads you can't get plumbing and electricity, and without utilities, you can't sell houses. If work was started and contractors weren't paid, there will be liens put on the property." She waited several seconds.

"Abbey, no one has set foot out there in weeks."

More like months, but there was that new voice again.

"I'm not stupid, Abbey. I know the development is in trouble. That's why I wanted to talk to you in the first place. I have to cover my... you know, I have to be able to live."

Now we're getting somewhere. "Yes. I know. And I'm sorry you have gotten into this mess."

"Oh, damn, Abbey." Vickie looked at her hands and slowly tore her napkin into strips. "I'm going to lose all of my money, aren't I?"

"I was afraid to ask. How much have you invested?"

"Everything, so far. My father bought the land, so I got it when my parents died. But Bart said I'd get everything back and more when the marina went in and houses went up on those lots we sold. People were supposed to be in their homes by now. Bart said it was a sound investment. He promised me, Abbey, damn him, he promised. It just hasn't happened yet." Her hopeful look faded and turned to doubt when her eyes met Abbey's.

Yes, you are probably going to lose all your money. "You brought up lawyers a minute ago. You should have one." Vickie winced as though she couldn't imagine why Abbey suggested such a thing.

"I have some things I need to go do, Abbey. You kind of took me by surprise when you showed up here." Vickie grabbed her purse. "Listen, I know it's a lot to ask, but could we get together for a long lunch? I really want to talk about possibilities in Atlanta."

"Sure. How about tomorrow?" As they walked out the door, something she had heard thousands of times in her business popped into her head: Buyer beware. An unsettling feeling came over her.

"Oh, Vickie," Abbey said as she turned and walked backward toward her waiting dog. "I told you I was an English major. What was yours?"

Looking over her shoulder Vickie said, "Psychology." As she walked to her car she said, "With a minor in drama."

Nice exit. Oh, boy. She's playing me for sure.

EIGHTEEN

Vickie floored it as she pulled away from the curb. Abbey watched, amused, a relief from the feeling moments before. Vickie knew exactly what she was doing, but she was still a lousy driver. She seemed worried or frightened, and rightly so. She could lose everything, but what about the folks who had already closed on lots? Where was their earnest money?

The agent in St. Marys had raised a question about Ashley and implied that maybe she was getting family benefits. If Bart was slipping money to her from funds that should be in a trust account, he was in big trouble. The Real Estate Commission would be all over him. Then there was the lawyer who wanted to talk to Vickie.

She rubbed her throbbing forehead. *What did I do to deserve this?* "Come on, Watch." He had been perfectly content with his nap, but she needed to walk. Scones were not on her normal diet, and the one she had just consumed felt like a ball of yeasty sourdough batter on the rise.

It was warming up. Near-perfect weather had held for her entire vacation and she hoped it would continue for Tom, but wet weather was forecast. Rainy days were good; one held a special place in her memory, the one soon after she and Tom met. They were caught in a downpour on the dock at Taylor's Point and had driven back to the cottage sodden and chattering with cold. She'd never forget that shower together, not in a million years. She smiled. Good memory, one of those she called up often in thunderstorms.

The waterfront was active for a Tuesday morning. Self-describing acronyms spoke volumes about drivers in the concise space of their license plates. WLDMN. *How charming.* GODWGS. *Woof-woof.* PRTY WMN *How original. Party or pretty?* Tags identified many states, mostly Georgia or Florida. On the sidewalks you could pick the Yanks out of the crowd. Men with lily-white legs and dark socks and sandals and women with the skin tones of Martha White flour or frog's bellies had to be New Yorkers or north Jersey folks.

She switched gears. "Let's walk." Doc was on her mind, and he didn't give her a headache like her new client did. She was sure the hat belonged to him, and Tom the inquisitor agreed. It was no coincidence that the hat and the man were in the river at the same time and so close to one another. A year ago when she met Tom, she discovered she liked to investigate and she liked to help good people solve their problems. Doc had the hands of a doctor. The golden eagle was a Philadelphia Eagles emblem, verified by the Philadelphia hatter's label in the cap. Having little else, she decided to go with it.

Boats were lined up for gas at the St. Marys marina. She'd come over with her brothers years ago to fill up their boat. St. Marys wasn't that far from Kings Bluff, which meant it was relatively close to the accident by water. So was Jekyll Island, but she would have seen the boat had it headed north. Fernandina in Florida maybe, but that was pretty far away. A group of seagulls laughed overhead. *Okay, you figure it out.* Watch was interested in the seagulls, so they followed them while she thought.

The squat building she had noticed earlier had Marina in black block letters over the front door and a red neon Open sign in the front window. She had tried to recreate the boat she had seen driving away from the accident in her head, but maybe it would come back to her if she looked at several. A white-chinned golden retriever's head protruded from the doorway. He snored and twitched, chasing rabbits in his dreams. Abbey picked her way across his outstretched legs and Watch followed, giving him a sniff-down as he crossed the old boy's legs.

A small handwritten scrap of paper thumbtacked to the door said "Dog biscuits at counter." The sleeping dog raised his head and touched noses with Watch Dog, then resumed his chin-on-paws nap. Nail salon fumes competed with *eau de gasoline* and motor oil. Abbey's nose twitched and she sneezed; then Watch Dog sneezed. "Excuse us," Abbey said.

A gasp came from behind the counter. "Oh, shit." A young girl jumped up, reached below the counter and did something frantically with her hands. Abbey walked over. A puddle of orange pooled around the base of the cash register beside an uncapped bottle of nail polish. Fearful eyes begged Abbey for help. "He's going to kill me."

"Yep." Abbey nodded. "Is the, umm, is the manager in?"

"Unfortunately." With glistening marmalade-colored fingernails splayed in drying mode, the heels of the girl's hands pushed downward on cutoff jeans that threatened to split her in two. "He's in there." The girl cocked her head toward the back of the marina.

"What?" said a voice on the other side of a partially closed door. A young man with long beach-boy blonde hair and eyes the color of Caribbean seas exited a small room with cluttered shelves. Beach Boy wore cut-off jeans too. The dress code here was relaxed. A huge blue swordfish leaped from frothy water on the front of his t-shirt. His flip-flops had blown out last season, if not before.

"Go outside to do that, Sis, after you clean that stuff up. Good Lord, it smells like a French whore—" He stopped when he saw Abbey at the counter. "Sorry. I didn't know anyone was out here except her." He frowned at the mess of wet orange paper towels in the trash can. "Find something to cut that shit with. You've got to get it off the counter, okay? I can't have receipts and stuff sticking to that…

that… whatever that is. Clean it up and get some air freshener from the cabinet under the sink in the head."

Beach Boy flipped hair from his eyes as he rounded the end of the counter and looked at Abbey dead-on. His frown reversed into a broad smile, which Abbey matched. He was the fellow who had been moving boats around with the little tractor the other day.

"Hi." He smelled like a rum-and-coconut cocktail. All he needed was a cherry stem sticking out of the corner of his mouth and a small turquoise paper umbrella behind his ear.

"Hi, yourself," Beach Boy said, as his eyes scanned her from stem to stern in one efficient glance. "Something I can do for you?" His rakish grin said he had more than a container of Coppertone or a pack of gum in mind.

She extended her hand. "My name is Abbey."

His tanned hand took hers. "Cliff." He flipped the grease-stained blue cloth in his left hand onto the counter without taking his eyes off Abbey's.

"My boyfriend and I are thinking about buying a boat." She might just as well have tossed a wet blanket over his head. No more flirty Cliff. Abbey paused to give him a chance to get his breathing under control. *Damn testosterone. Amazing stuff.* "We're looking in magazines but I'm really visual. I have to see it to get it."

Cliff crossed his arms and nodded. His "all business" frown wasn't nearly as appealing as his flirty smile, but still interesting in a young Robert Redford sort of way. "I need to see what folks are going out in down here. My brothers had a little jon boat growing up, but that's about all I'm familiar with."

"Those are fun boats. Every kid ought to have one. You going to be around for a while?"

"Unfortunately, no. I drove down from a little north of here and met a friend for coffee. I have to get back, but I thought as long as I was here I would look around and get some ideas. I don't want to waste your time or anything."

Beach Boy took a deep breath and seemed to grow an inch. "I'm happy to help you. That's what I'm here for." He stuffed his hands into his back pockets, or what was left of them, and said, "Let's look around the yard. This is for fishing, right?"

"Yes. We want something we can use in the creeks, but we also want to be able to go to Cumberland, Fernandina, offshore maybe. Definitely bigger than a jon boat." She smiled. He grinned. Friends again.

Twenty minutes and a boatyard of possibilities later, Abbey said, "Okay, thanks again for your help, Cliff. I really appreciate your time."

"Sure. Looking's free." Blonde bangs flipped back from of his face as he gave her the sexy, bad-boy grin again. "Later, Abbey. Come back if you have any more questions about boats. I'm here dawn to dusk most days."

"Yeah, okay. Thanks for showing me around." *No memory sparks, but it was worth a try.*

"Hey Abbey," he said as he walked back inside. "Nice dog."

NINETEEN

Abbey and Watch walked back to the waterfront. Beach Boy was doing a good business at the pump today. Funny job, that. She wondered if he had gone to college and gotten a degree and, if he had, what his parents thought about his current managerial position.

The breeze had picked up. Hair blew into her face; she wished she had a hat to hold down flying strays. She usually kept one in her car in Atlanta for that very purpose when she rowed. She needed to get Doc's hat to Terkoff. Doc's hands were sort of rough and he was tan and fairly fit. If he rowed in Philadelphia he was accustomed to being close to the action so he was probably staying close to the water, not near the airport. If he flew to Jacksonville, chances were he rented a car at the airport.

She turned her back to the water and looked down the street she had driven in on. There had been a charming, pink, two-story Victorian. Had to be an inn or a bed-and-breakfast. "Let's go exploring, big boy."

The temperature had climbed into the high eighties, but there was a sea breeze. Cars drove slowly as drivers looked for the parking place closest to their destination. Funny how most Americans did everything in their power to avoid walking a few extra steps. Her stomach gurgled. She had already blown her budget with yesterday's lunch and this morning's coffee with Vickie, so she ducked into a sandwich shop and bought an iced tea with a lot of ice. Watch Dog snatched cubes she tossed as they walked. Three blocks later, they arrived at the Osprey Inn Bed and Breakfast. She walked around the parking lot and though there was no car with a Philadelphia tag, there were several rentals.

She tied Watch to the banister on the front porch and went inside. Windows dripped with moisture in the near-Arctic temperature. Amazing that in summer when it's supposed to be hot, some chose to refrigerate inside air to wintertime outdoor temps. Red rose wallpaper, worn oriental rugs, and the aroma of just-baked cookies warmed the foyer and invited Abbey to step back in time. A glass cake plate heaped with chocolate chip cookies sat on the check-in desk in the front parlor. The round-faced, white-haired woman who greeted Abbey was identified as the clerk, by the gold badge on the shoulder of her pink cotton twin set, and the baker, by her ample posterior.

"Good afternoon. I am looking for a friend from Philadelphia who said he would be at a beautiful B&B in St. Marys, but I can't remember the name. This is the prettiest one I have seen, so I thought I would start here. Would you mind checking your register to see if you have a guest from Philadelphia?" *Don't ask me his name.*

The middle-aged clerk's smile looked like a little red rosebud. She clasped her hands as she spoke. "I'm so sorry, dear, but I can't give out that kind of information. Perhaps you could come back later and talk to the manager though. He's very accommodating. He's such a nice man."

"I understand, but I live some distance from here. If I leave my name and number, would you mind asking him to phone me?"

"Not at all. I will give him your information the minute he arrives."

Abbey wrote her cottage's phone number on back of her business card along with a note that asked the manager to please give her a call as soon as possible. *Please let me be right.*

TWENTY

Vickie took her time at her favorite nursery on her way back to work after lunch and found several things she'd come back for on her way home later. In the gravel lot behind the temporary trailer that served as her office, she parked to leave spaces available in front for agents and buyers, though neither had shown up in ages. "Administrative Office, my patootie," she muttered as she passed the two-by-three-foot glossy white sign with a large arrow pointing to the front door.

A white Range Rover occupied the space closest to the door. Though not personalized with a sign or marked with white paint, Bart considered this his space and had made it known to her and to Cutty Faulkner, his partner. This transgression could start World War III. She fluffed her hair, threw back her shoulders, and gave her chest a quick appraisal. *If you got 'em, smoke 'em.* She licked her lips and smiled as she paraded in the front door and was met by an empty reception area. Her smile faded, her shoulders relaxed. "Oh, well," she sighed.

Cramming her silver bag into a large, empty file drawer, she moved the white plastic Receptionist plaque to the most visible space at the front right corner of her desk. She plucked a shriveled red carnation from a skinny glass vase and dropped the spent bloom into the trash can. With a quick look around the room, she

107

eyed the file cabinet by the front window as though it was a homeless person who had sneaked in during the night for shelter.

Last week, Bart had asked her to make up a list of the names, phone numbers and addresses of persons who had either visited or requested information about the property and the dates on which they had called, visited, or been contacted. She'd assumed her next task would be to make follow-up calls to everyone on the list she put together. When she had told him that was her intention, Bart told her that was a dumb idea. She wasn't qualified to give out any information because she wasn't a licensed agent. Then she had offered to go to real estate school and to take the exam so she could get her license, but Bart told her that was an even dumber idea and that she would never pass the licensing exam.

As much as the insult angered her, she had let it go. When Bart asked her father for her hand in marriage, he had said no wife of his would have to bring home the bacon. Why not let him play the proud Southern man who wanted his wife to raise the children and take care of the home? There were two sides to every coin. For a split second she wondered how Abbey would have responded to Bart's slight. She let that one go too.

Vickie brushed her hands together several times as if she was tackling an ominous project before she opened the top drawer of the file cabinet and stared at the loosely packed row of hanging folders. The first one seemed like a good place to start. January was printed on its tab and inside was a stack of papers in her handwriting. "Oh, yeah," she muttered as she flipped through the sheets. *Easy peasy.* It all came back to her. She had made a file for every month and an information sheet for each visitor or contact. Now all she needed was a little time to go through and make a master list of names and numbers. With the January folder in hand, she smiled and closed the drawer. Now she had purpose.

A cough startled her. A toilet flushed. She darted to her desk and whipped a tube of lipstick from her purse. He was here! With her eyes glued to the bathroom door, she applied color to her lips, then finger-fluffed her hair and sat down ram-rod straight, chest out, professional. She picked up the phone and scribbled nonsense on a notepad. Cutty walked out of the bathroom with his eyes still on the section of newspaper he held.

Vickie spoke into the receiver, "Yes, that's fine. I'll take care of it." She jotted down her maiden name and her own phone number, then hung up.

"Good afternoon, Cutty." She pushed her chair back. "I thought you were out on the property or something when you weren't in here. How about I make us a fresh pot of coffee?"

"Oh, hi." He stopped abruptly. "I didn't hear you come in. But that's okay. I'll finish off what's there."

"It looks like it's from this morning. I know I didn't make it. Why don't I start a fresh one for you?"

Cutty plopped on the sofa amidst scattered newspaper and continued to read.

Vickie walked over to open the blinds by the cabinet to let in natural light and noticed movement outside the office. Bart's black Cadillac pulled into the space beside the Range Rover. "Uh-oh, Bart's here, Cutty." She watched her husband get out of his car. "And he doesn't look too happy." Her face fell when Bart hocked a wad of phlegm into the bushes. *Gross.* She sent an apologetic look to Cutty, but his nose was still buried in the sports section.

The front door jerked open and banged against the wood veneer wall. "Bah-aht," Vickie said as though scolding a child who had been told not to do something a million times.

Cutty looked up. Smoke spiraled from his cigarette to the lamp on the table beside the sofa. Vickie shrugged an apology.

"Uh, sorry, Bart. I didn't think you'd be in this afternoon. I'll move my car."

"Where the hell did you think I'd be? We need to talk. In my office." Bart stomped off. The trailer's cheap floor bounced under his weight. Deep creases in his yellow oxford-cloth shirt suggested he had slept in it. Vickie frowned. His shirts had just come back from the cleaners, but this one didn't look nice at all. She tore off the page where she had jotted her number earlier and dropped it into the trash. Grabbing her pad and pen, she rounded the corner of her desk as Cutty stubbed out his cigarette and stood.

In a scornful tone Bart said, "Not you, him." He cut his head toward the sofa on his way to his office. Vickie stopped dead.

Cutty refolded the newspaper and dropped it on Vickie's desk. "I might take you up on that fresh pot of coffee now." He wasn't smiling.

Vickie nodded and squeaked, "Sure, Cutty. I'll get right on it."

Cutty tapped on Bart's door.

"Come in," Bart bellowed. Cutty pulled the door closed behind him.

After waiting several minutes, Vickie tiptoed across the room and brewed a fresh pot of coffee. She hated this cheap excuse for an office. Everything squeaked: floors, doors, drawers... but she had figured out where the supports were long ago, so she moved around with impunity. Bart's floor was the worst, so she crept to his door to listen. It sounded like a frog pond in there, but she knew where all the frogs lived. Her husband had a habit of walking in a circle when he was angry or thinking about something. Of late, he was angry a good deal of the time. At the moment, he circled the track he had worn in the beige-and-navy carpet she had personally chosen for his office.

"Why the hell did you park in my space, Cutty. It's not like there weren't others available."

"Sorry. I ran in to use the bathroom and just pulled in. I didn't expect you back so soon."

Squeak, squeak. "We need to make some damn money." Bart's voice was gruff and angry.

"You're right, Bart, we do. But it's only money, and I think we have bigger issues at the moment."

The phone rang. Vickie pulled off her sandals and picked her way over on tiptoe to answer. She dropped her shoes in her chair and took a message. The bank again and this time the manager didn't even try to make small talk. She stuffed the message in Bart's message slot and scurried back to her post and leaned in to try to pick up on their conversation.

"All the time asking me questions, driving me crazy. I'm tempted to tell her to go play tiddlywinks or bridge or whatever-the-hell women do."

Vickie's hand flew to her chest. Was Bart talking about her?

"Her new girlfriend keeps her out of my hair some, so that's a relief."

Vickie's lips straight-lined as she stood up. Her hands nested together and covered her mouth.

Cutty said, "Maybe we should hire a temp."

"Yeah, well, maybe. They cost a fortune though. We need to make some damn money is what we need to do. Project's at a stand-still. No offers, going on six months now."

"I'm sure it hasn't escaped your attention that we're behind on our construction loan and who knows what else," Cutty said.

There were more squeaks on the far side of Bart's office. Vickie knew them all. Someone was over near the table where she had placed knickknacks to make the space homier.

"Vickie is from Virginia, right?" Cutty said.

"Yeah. That's her on the horse. Son-of-a-bitch must have cost a fortune. Thank goodness she was on her daddy's dime back then. Talk about being born with a silver spoon in your mouth, shit, that's my little woman," Bart said sarcastically.

Vickie loved that photograph. She was sixteen, hadn't a care in the world, and her horse was her life. Cassius sailed over fences. He had been the best Christmas present her parents had ever given her. For a split second she remembered that girl, and how the most difficult part about going to college in Florida was leaving Cassius and Virginia's hunt country. And now this mess. Vickie swallowed hard, then waited for a kind word from Cutty. But no such thing ever came out of his mouth. Her eyes stung.

Abbey had been adamant about her need for a lawyer. Maybe she was right. It was time to take care of some things, so she grabbed her shoes and purse on her way out. Gravel shot out behind the large wheels of the gold Cadillac as it sped from the parking lot.

TWENTY-ONE

The list she'd picked up at the sales trailer on Monday was on her passenger seat, so Abbey went to the phone booth at the marina and called one of the mortgage brokers. Unfortunately, he no longer financed property at Crooked Creek, and she was determined to find out why.

"Listen, I sell real estate in Atlanta. I know nothing about what's going on in your market except what I see. I drove around Crooked Creek yesterday and there doesn't seem to be much happening. What's the deal? It's a beautiful piece of property on the water, and I would think this close to Jacksonville it would be going gangbusters."

"You got that right."

"Was there a problem out there?"

"I'd say there were and are several." He didn't elaborate but his voice intrigued her. Stiff, serious, and almost comical, it reminded her of Dudley Do-Right of the Mounties on the Rocky and Bullwinkle Show.

He's not going to give me anything. "Okay. I understand." *Toss him a cookie.* "Do you by chance know Vickie Croek?"

"Of course. She's the developer's wife." His tone lightened up.

"Yes, the developer's wife. Between you and me, Vickie asked me to show her some things in Atlanta." *Include him in the conspiracy and maybe he'll give something back.* "I need to know how

113

she stands financially. I'll have her prequalified by a mortgage broker I use in Atlanta, but after I drove through Crooked Creek I'm a little leery. I think she probably has family money, but I don't know how heavily involved she is out there in her husband's development." Phones rang in the background. As she waited she imagined wheels turning in his head.

"Are you in the area, Ms. Bunn?"

"Yes, actually. I had some other business here today."

"Why don't you stop by?"

He knows all about her finances. She's involved all right, and those fake boobs won't keep her afloat when she starts to sink. Damn. "Okay. I'm a little casual, but if you don't mind…"

"Everything is casual here. Come on by. You're an Atlanta girl so I'll even give you a cold Coca-Cola."

"Great. I have your address but I don't know my way around town that well." He gave her directions.

The only thing about the broker that even remotely resembled Dudley Do-Right was his wave of corn-colored blonde hair. After talking for well over an hour, she thanked him and hopped back into her Jeep. Watch poked his head between the front seats and plopped it onto her shoulder. She scratched the top of his head. "Oh, boy. She's in it big time."

She pulled the Crooked Creek map from the back of her legal pad and flattened it on her steering wheel. Watch stuck his head between the seats for a scratch. Softly she sang, "The bear went over the mountain, the bear went over the mountain, the bear went over the mountain to see what he could see." Watch slurped her ear and wagged his tail at the sound of her voice. "Let's go see what we can see."

She glanced at her map, then headed back to Crooked Creek thinking about the cottage on the creek once owned by the Atlanta couple. It had probably been fantastic once upon a time. She remembered the couple and their beautiful home in Atlanta. She wanted to see the cottage from the front. Locating the house on the map, she followed the main road onto the property until she spotted a dotted line that could designate the original drive up to the house, though it was not on the map's legend. Her tires found deep impressions under grass and weeds more than likely made by years and years of car or truck travel and too wide to be those of golf carts.

This felt right. Tall, skinny pines poked through voids left in the canopy of gigantic lumbering live oaks, through which the sun peeked and shot dappled light onto the layer of pine needles covering the road like a blanket and muffling the sound of her Jeep. Yep. The creek should be straight ahead. After several minutes, the road ended at the house, which from this angle appeared charming. The other road had come in to the back of the house at the carport, obviously just a convenience and not what the original owners ever intended for an entrance. The Range Rover was nowhere in sight this time so she drove past the house, turned around in the carport, and headed her car out the way she had just come in, should she need a speedy exit.

The house hadn't been maintained, but if the choice was hers, she'd have taken this river cottage over Vickie's boring box any day of the week—but that was her. Paint peeled from trim and windows were encrusted with spring's leftover pollen and crud from salt-laden air. Several shutters hung from stubborn screws and grass spiked through leaves in the front and side yards. On the front left of the house an overhead light was on. She left the engine running, opened her door and said, "Stay." Watch sat at attention and licked his chops. His eyes said he had her back.

Just as her foot hit the dirt, a car came through the woods from the other road, from the V. She jumped back into her car, put it in gear and headed out. In her rear view mirror, she watched a white car approach and turn into the carport. *Security,* in bold black letters, was on the side of the car. A uniformed man got out and watched her drive away. He looked down, maybe at her tire tracks, and then disappeared behind the bushes, a whole lot farther than she had made it.

Glancing into her rear view mirror every few minutes on the way into town, her heart still raced. How had Nancy Drew stood all of her narrow escapes? A cold beer or a glass of wine would be great when she got back to the cottage. She drove back to St. Marys and was in and out of the package store in five minutes. A white Range Rover squealed around the corner and gunned it, the same one she'd seen yesterday at the little house she had just left. *Interesting.* The driver lurched to a spot in front of her and Vickie's lunch spot, then took the stairs to the café's deck two at a time. Great muscular legs, tall frame, and dark skin and hair, a hunk by anyone's measure.

Clutching the brown paper sack full of libations to her chest, she started down the street. The new tall dark stranger's head poked up over the chair railing, and who should be sitting across from him but a man wearing a Hawaiian shirt and the same hat she had seen yesterday in the sales trailer. She stared at Hat Man's face and realized she'd seen a picture of him the night before in a newspaper article. *Holy shit. That's Bart.*

This was too much. She had to get closer to see if she could hear what they were saying. The waitress appeared, then left. The two men talked loud enough for her to hear them fairly clearly from the street. She was all ears.

"Dammit, Cutty, we don't know that," Bart said loudly, and just as she looked up he fist-pounded the table so hard the silverware rattled. "We don't know a damn thing."

The dark one's Range Rover was parked right in front of her and beside it was a black Cadillac whose tag was easy to remember. She got back in her Jeep and headed home. *"Dammit, Cutty, we don't know that… we don't know a damn thing." What was that all about?*

TWENTY-TWO

Tom worked out at his club in Atlanta early Wednesday morning before going to his office at Hollenbeck & Dunn to sort out messages and return phone calls. By the time he looked at his watch, it was mid-morning. Fast Eddy, the intern he mentored, usually went to lunch around one o'clock, so Tom buzzed him and gave him the information about Bart Croek that Abbey had given to him.

"See what you can dig up on this guy. I know this isn't much to go on, but a friend asked me to check him out."

"Would that friend be Abbey?"

Tom chuckled. "As a matter of fact, yes. How did you know?"

"Well, this guy is a developer and Abbey sells real estate, and his area code is coastal Georgia and Abbey kind of likes that area, so I figured..."

"Pretty obvious, eh, Watson?"

"Yes, sir, I guess so." Eddy smiled sheepishly.

"Is that a problem, Eddy?"

"Hell, no, sir. I like her a lot. Is she down there now or something?"

"Yes. Anything you come up with will help. What's today?" Tom looked at his desk calendar. "I flew in late last night so I'm a bit off. I'm here through the firm's golf outing on Friday then I'm heading south first thing Saturday morning. Until Friday, if I'm not here I'm at home and you have my number there. I'll give you where I can be reached after Saturday if you find anything worth reporting." He gave Eddy the number at the cottage.

"Remember, I've been on a case in Philadelphia since Monday a week ago and I'm going to spend some quiet time with a lady friend. I know you're busy, so don't kill yourself on this, but see what you can dig up."

Eddy cleared his throat. "Yes, sir. I get it. After this Friday, contact you only if I find out something I think you need to know."

"That's right."

"And, sir, you gave me a 912 area code for your contact number. Please tell Miss Abbey hello for me when you get down there."

"Right, Eddy. Will do." Tom continued to make phone calls.

Several hours later, there was a knock on the door. "Come in."

A tall, skinny red-headed young man with a crisp plaid bow tie entered and laid papers on Tom's desk.

Tom picked up the stack of double-spaced typewritten copy. "What's this, Eddy?"

"You asked me to check out Bart Croek. That's what I found."

Tom motioned to the chair by his desk. "Talk to me."

The intern sat up on the edge of his chair. "Croek is a developer from Orlando. Oddly enough, his development in Georgia is on Crooked Creek so that's what he calls the property. It's eight thousand marsh and waterfront acres in St. Marys, Georgia, just south of Abbey's place."

"Odd name, isn't it? Don't think I've ever run across a C-R-O-E-K before."

"It's Nordic, means crook," Eddy said.

"Ah. Well, let's hope not."

Eddy cleared his throat and crossed his arms. "I'm afraid the name might be appropriate. He's in arrears on his construction loan, and he has never managed to put in a paved road. That makes selling lots difficult. How does he expect prospects to get onto the property? At the beginning, enough lots made it to the closing table to get things started, but when things came to a screeching halt this guy Croek continued to live the good life. There's some question as to where the money put down on the lots has gone. It should be in a trust account, but I'll have to do some more digging to find out who banks this deal. So far the only thing that has been built on the development is the developer's own house."

"How about taxes?"

"Oddly enough, they're current."

"Did he finance the home?"

"Nope. His wife did, and her father paid cash for the dirt before Croek was even part of the family."

Tom shook his head and tapped the eraser of his pencil on the desk. "So is dear old Dad still involved?"

"Nope. He was a big-time lawyer in Virginia who speculated in land. He bought that piece in St. Marys outright and paid taxes on it for years. He was an investor so I imagine he thought that piece was better than money in the bank, only dear old Dad and Mom went on a golf weekend in Florida and met their maker in a friend's private plane. Poor man had one child, and Croek was married to her and all her assets."

"How much is she in for?"

"I couldn't nail that down in so short a time. I'll work on it if you want. Maybe just the house, but Dad had already bought the property outright and if he was savvy enough to set up some way to pay the taxes, which it appears he was, I bet there are deed restrictions or something which protect his daughter and the investment."

"Hold off for now. Abbey can chew on this for a while. I don't want to overstep my boundaries and do more than she wants me to do." He thumped the papers again with the pencil. "So this guy's an opportunist, lives high on the hog, and has managed to run his development into the ground. Is that it?"

"No, sir. That's only part."

"What, he has other developments so he's really strapped?"

"Well, yes. That too."

Tom rocked back in his chair and clasped his hands over his head. "Go on."

"The long and short of it is Bart likes the ladies. He must have had a dust-up with one of them because she took out a restraining order on him."

"Before or after he married the rich girl?"

"After. This woman was an agent who sold some of his lots when the development opened."

"So what's the story?"

"Crooked Creek was the hottest thing going because it was the only thing going in that area. St. Simons was on fire, but nothing had happened in Georgia south of there yet so when this new place with marsh and waterfront views hit the market in 1984, agents were all over it. Apparently an agent from St. Marys wrote several offers, and when she got them to closing, Croek gave her nice presents. She returned them all and told him she couldn't accept his gifts, but he didn't take the hint. He showed up at her house with flowers one night, and the next day she took out the restraining order.

"There must have been more to it than a bouquet of flowers, if you want my opinion. When dirt stopped moving, agents stopped showing. The restraining order agent announced at a sales meeting that it looked like Crooked Creek was in trouble."

"And how did you find out all of this so fast?"

"I date a real estate agent who lives on St Simons so she filled me in and gave me some names in St. Marys. I tracked down an agent who knew the one who took out the restraining order."

"Knew?"

"Yeah," Fast Eddy dropped his elbows to his thighs. One hand kneaded the fingers of the other hand then cracked several knuckles. "After that sales meeting when she told everybody about the development going down the tubes, she sort of disappeared."

"Disappeared. Did you check around?"

"I couldn't find her. The agent I talked to said her broker had tried but found nothing."

Tom clasped his hands in his lap and reared back in his chair. "Any arrests?"

"They brought Bart in for questioning, but he had an alibi. His wife vouched for him."

Tom didn't even bother to ask if Fast Eddy had checked out the alibi. It wasn't necessary. This guy never said anything he hadn't already confirmed.

"Thanks." Tom collected the papers on his desk and stapled them together. He looked at the young man. "On your way out, would you ask Benjamin to stop by my office? I saw him when I came in this morning."

Fast Eddy stood. "Sure." He headed to the door.

"Great job," Tom said.

"Thanks, Tom. Any time."

"You must have worked up an appetite doing all of this. Go eat." Eddy's lips hinted at a smile as he walked out of the office. Minutes later there was a tap on the door and a man strode in on legs the length of telephone poles.

"You're back. I thought you'd be booking it to the coast by now," Benjamin said.

"Saturday, as soon as I can get away. I have the golf outing Friday."

"Oh, right. Me too." Benjamin took the seat Fast Eddy had just vacated and Tom told him what he had just learned. The two covered for each other when one was out of town. Benjamin knew as much about Tom and Abbey as Tom did, almost. "Okay. If you need me to do some digging round on this, just say the word, and as far as next week, keep a close eye on that real estate sleuth of yours."

"You got it."

TWENTY-THREE

Vickie put the potential buyer list she had worked on all morning in her drawer and closed it. Bart had gone out, the phones were quiet, and she had just enough time to do a little shopping before she met Abbey for lunch.

Last night had been a sort of Mexican standoff in which she and Bart had barely spoken when he finally got home. That was fine by her. He'd gone straight to the family room and flipped on the television. She hated the room's heavy furniture and dark paneling. His Man Cave. Good for him. He could have it. She had retreated upstairs and watched an old Doris Day movie in the cozy fourth bedroom she called her Girl Cloud. Bart had fallen asleep on the sofa and she hadn't bothered to awaken him when she turned out the lights. This morning she'd run out the door for her tennis lesson and left him grumbling in the kitchen, all cranky and stiff and out of sorts.

Now she would spend her way out of the doldrums. It was another beautiful sunny day and Bart's glum attitude wasn't going to get her down. It had felt good to have a serious conversation with a woman yesterday. She hoped she hadn't said too much, but Abbey was a good listener and a sympathetic ear. Over the past two days she had done a lot of thinking and had decided Abbey was right about a lot of things. Bart was a manipulator and that's how he got what he wanted. He tried to control everything she did, and he was pretty good at it. That was about to change.

Then there was Cutty. He was a delicious thing to behold and an excellent buffer between her and Bart's nastiness. Besides, she hadn't had anyone to flirt with since she'd met Bart and flirtation was harmless, most of the time—nothing but innocent fun, and who knew what the future held? She liked to keep an open mind about that kind of thing. But Cutty sure hadn't jumped to her defense when Bart ragged on her. Nothing helped settle her down like spending money. Fernandina wasn't that far away and the shopping was excellent.

In front of her favorite casual clothing shop, she found a spot and parked, then looked in her wallet and pulled out Bart's American Express card. "Yes," she said with the vigor of a player who had just lobbed a winner. He would pay for his nasty little comments and his sour attitude—with his wallet.

Bright colors and cool light fabrics were spun around the shop in every available space. Blouses and dresses and skirts and pants she had selected awaited her in a dressing room. Parting stacks of neatly piled shorts and polo shirts, Vickie found her size and handed those to the sales girl to add to the others. It wasn't like she needed any of these things, because her closets bulged with beautiful clothes, but when she was out of sorts and got all riled up and knotty inside, like she often did these days, shopping took the edge off. Her selections would do for starters, but what she had in mind to do before she went to Atlanta to house hunt was a trip to Worth Avenue for haute couture.

The idea of a condo in Buckhead or a townhouse in Ansley Park started to sound better and better. An hour later, the dressing room was littered with clothes and hangers. Vickie picked through piles and grabbed a handful of items, leaving the rest for the staff to sort and put away. Handing the credit card and the pile of clothing to the saleswoman, she went to the sunglasses counter while her bill was rung up.

Moments later, a soft voice at her side said, "I'm sorry, Mrs. Croek, but this card was denied."

Vickie turned, wearing a pair of red sunglasses with faux diamonds encircling the lenses. After a moment, when what the other woman had said registered, her mouth dropped open. "There must be some mistake. Just run it again. It'll work, always does." She removed the glasses she had on and proceeded to make another selection.

"Sorry, ma'am, but I tried it twice already. I'd be happy to try a different card for you."

Vickie scowled. "Of course."

Taking the card from the woman, she looked at it as though she had never seen it before. "How silly of me. Did I give you the American Express? My husband canceled that one a month ago." She pulled another from her wallet. "His was stolen and I just forgot."

Vickie looked around to see who might have overheard her little white lie, but she was the only customer in the shop. She handed the second card to the clerk. "This is my old standby, had it since college. My husband probably has his new card at home and forgot to give me mine." The woman nodded, offered a tight smile and ran the other card. A good minute passed. Vickie's eyebrows arched as though she was getting ready to say something ugly, when the card finally went through. She exhaled. "That's more like it."

"Pardon?" the woman said as she passed over the slip for Vickie to sign.

"I just said I like it, all of it. The things I bought." The clerk pulled a plastic garment protector over the hangers and knotted it under the clothing.

"The sales items are final, Mrs. Croek," she said as she handed the bundle to Vickie.

Vickie's mouth dropped at the corners as though she had been slapped. "Of course they are." She hurried from the store, laid the clothes on the back seat of her car, and then sat there for several minutes before she started the engine. What an embarrassment. She took a deep breath. This wasn't what she needed on top of the humiliation of what she had overheard yesterday.

Fuming, she drove back to St. Marys for her lunch appointment. Just wait until she got this straightened out with Bart. Then she'd really shop, but not in this podunk little town. No, sir. It was Worth Avenue or nothing and that would require some planning. She'd see when Abbey wanted to take her to Atlanta to look around and would go to Palm Beach the week before.

TWENTY-FOUR

Vickie was already seated at a table on the deck when Abbey arrived and said, "You look nice," acknowledging Vickie's crisp cream-colored linen slacks and three-quarter-length-sleeve linen blouse.

"Thanks." Vickie didn't smile or return the compliment and didn't offer anything else, so Abbey took the hint and sat.

"So today we talk business, right?"

"You bet," Vickie said crisply.

Okay. So maybe the new voice is here to stay. They perused the menu and ordered.

"You know what I really want," Vickie said.

Abbey shrugged. "I've seen the outside of what you currently have, but apparently you don't like it, so no. Tell me."

Vickie stared out over the water. "I want something with my name on it."

Yep. She wants a safety net in case life with her idiot husband blows up.

"Call me crazy. Most women would kill to have what I have, but those two houses are not mine, really. They're stuffy and stiff and formal and look like Macy's showrooms. You know what I mean? They're not me."

"You and Eleanor Roosevelt," Abbey said.

Vickie looked puzzled.

"I read a book about the Roosevelts. Eleanor wanted her own place away from the Roosevelt mansion and her mother-in-law."

Vickie still looked puzzled.

Okay, so maybe she's into romance or cozy mysteries. That's okay. "So what are you thinking?" Abbey said. It was easier to change the subject than to explain.

Vickie tapped the table. "I'd like a townhouse in Atlanta, maybe in Ansley Park or Buckhead or somewhere close to Lenox Square. I love to shop, and I'd like to be able to walk to all of those lovely stores. Smart Atlanta stores are all over the magazines."

"Did you ever consider New York?" Abbey smiled when Vickie looked at her open-mouthed. "Just kidding. You're a Southern girl and Atlanta is growing. No need to go to New York since all the Yanks seem to be headed south anyway."

"Well, okay. I was worried there for a minute. Thank goodness I don't have to move to New York. I'd be terrified to go there all by myself. Wouldn't you?"

"No. I used to live in Chicago."

Vickie gasped. "It's full of gangsters, isn't it?"

"It has had its fair share. So go on. You were telling me what you want."

"Okay, so I'd paint it in soft, inviting colors and decorate exactly the way I want, none of that frou-frou stuff that looks like it was lifted straight out of a catalog. I'd have comfy club chairs and a sofa so big I could curl up on it with a good book." Her look was dreamy. "And I wouldn't be afraid to put my feet up on it. My dog could put his head in my lap and I'd scratch behind his ears."

"You have a dog?"

Vickie's dreamy expression melted. "Had." She reached into her bag and took out a bulging rectangular red billfold. She flipped through several plastic-coated photographs and slid one across to Abbey. "Bart thinks they *smell* bad. He made me give my Sophie away when we got married."

"King Charles spaniel, right?"

"Yes. She was adorable."

"I have a yellow lab downstairs in the shade. There is a gang of kids where I stay and most days I let him hang out with them, which he loves." Vickie gave no indication that she had heard or cared.

Abbey noticed the Vickie-look-alike photo on the facing page. "And who's the pretty girl?" When Vickie's expression went dark she bit back the you-could-be-sisters cliché that hung on the tip of her tongue.

"That's Bic, my daughter. I –or rather we– bought her a nice condo in Jacksonville." Vickie grabbed the wallet and dropped it into her purse.

"Do you and Bart have other children?"

"No, just Bic. I wanted to try for a little boy but Bart was satisfied with her. I love nasty little boys. I don't know, sometimes I think he didn't want the competition, but it doesn't matter. I'm too old for any of that now. I turned forty-five in June."

Damn. Don't start crying on me. "I understand. I don't have any children, but I love my nieces and nephews." She waited a beat. "Bic's an unusual name. Is it short for something?"

"Abigail. My mother's name. But when she was four, my precocious daughter stomped her foot and declared that Abigail was too hard. She insisted her real name was Bic. Bart fell head over heels for her the minute he laid eyes on her, apple of his eye and all of that, and this little show of attitude only cemented their relationship. At our house, she's the princess and I'm the—well, I guess I'm the pea—or the also-ran." She adjusted the collar of her perfectly laundered blouse.

"He spoiled her rotten from day one, and of course he paid for it by the time she was a teenager. No child needs a hot fancy new car in high school. It attracted the boys and the girlfriends and nothing but trouble, but he wouldn't listen to me. A horse would have served her better, kept her away from boys until she was older, given her something to do after school and weekends, and taught her some responsibility."

Change the subject. "So look, if you're serious, I'd be happy to help you find something in Atlanta." Again, Vickie acted as if she hadn't heard a thing Abbey said.

"I did all this stuff," Vickie fanned her hands down her chest, then gestured toward her car, "for him." She chewed her lip.

"Look, Vickie, what's done is done. You need to stand up for yourself, be a little more assertive, and tell him you are perfectly capable of making your own decisions. It's never too late. It won't hurt a bit. You'll feel great after you do it once or twice."

"I guess." Vickie's lips poked out thoughtfully. "I really do want something in Atlanta but I need you to help me sort out a few things, and it might take more than a lunch or two to get to it. I know you have other things to do than listen to me and my problems all day."

Okay, so now we're getting to the real reason she wants my help. Abbey waited.

"If I had a place in Atlanta, I could make some nice friends and you know, meet the girls for lunch. I could even go to the theater, couldn't I?"

"Sure."

"Maybe we could work out together." Vickie's eyes were glued to Abbey's sleeveless shirt. "My arms were nice and toned like yours when I rode horses all the time."

"I used to ride, but horses aren't in my budget anymore. Now I have a rowing shell; no feed bills, barn bills, or vet bills."

Vickie did the typical circular motion that most people did when Abbey mentioned what she did. "Like rowboats in little lakes and stuff?"

"No, like the long skinny ones you might have seen in the Olympics."

"Where the little guy yells at the big guys?"

Abbey laughed. "Yes, but mine is made for one person, so I don't have a little guy yelling at me."

"That's so cool." Vickie nodded and then fell silent. "Bart and I sort of had a falling out last night, and he wanted to know who I was meeting for lunch today. When I told him an acquaintance from Atlanta, he got all nosy and wanted to know how I knew someone from there. I told him you were a friend of a friend. He doesn't have to know everything I do."

Abbey liked to keep her private life private. She wished she hadn't said as much as she had.

"Where's your place? It must not be far from here," Vickie said.

"Not too far."

"Last year the newspaper article said you have a place at a hunting club or something, right?"

The waitress stopped and refilled their drinks. Abbey welcomed the interruption. That article had created an enormous trespass problem at Kings Bluff, nosy curiosity-seekers who ignored the Members Only sign and drove in wanting to see where the big drug bust had taken place, like there would have been a big sign to indicate exactly where it had happened.

"So, you want something just for you in Atlanta. Condo, townhouse, cozy cottage…"

Vickie pursed her lips, looking like a deflated balloon at the end of a party, but with one head-toss her expression changed to determined.

"You rescued someone, then you assisted in the arrest of those drug dealers," she said.

Damn, she's persistent. "Yes."

"I kept all the articles." Vickie studied her manicure. "You call yourself a real estate agent." She shook her head. "You're way too modest."

Vickie wasn't about to give up. "I didn't go looking for any of that. It happened, I was there." Suddenly, Abbey felt very tired and fought back a yawn. She'd been up at dawn.

Vickie stared at her. "God put you in that spot at that time, and you put two and two together and acted on it. That's how He operates, you know."

Yeah, I know. I get that. I'm Superwoman and being a real estate agent is my cover. Abbey smiled and let it go.

Vickie did a little head shake. "No, I'm serious. You are one fearless woman. I could never be as brave as you."

Why all the build-up? But she remembered the insecure quality she heard in Vickie's voice, from the time she'd been in an abusive relationship. She wanted to say "yes, you could," but instead said, "So let's figure out what you want in Atlanta."

Vickie slapped both palms on her thighs. Abbey jumped. "You mean you'll help me?"

Earth to Vickie. Does she listen or just talk? Abbey held up both hands. "Let me be clear, Vickie. You know the old adage, time is money. I can't afford to waste time. If you're serious about buying, I'd be happy to work with you, but it is work. I don't do tours around Atlanta unless I think there's something you absolutely must see that is near something I'm showing you."

Vickie clasped her hands under her chin for several seconds, then lowered them to her lap. Her mouth twisted and she licked her lips.

"If we're going to work together, I need to fill you in on a few things. You're smart, so you can come to your own conclusions." Vickie signaled the waitress and pointed at their drinks and empty plates.

"I had a life before Bart. My senior year at U of F—that's University of Florida—I married my high school sweetheart." Her lip trembled. "Billy was the love of my life. My parents adored him, and Daddy was going to give him a job the minute we graduated."

Vickie wiped a tear from her cheek. "We were in a terrible car accident. I walked away from it... but he didn't."

She avoided Abbey's eyes and stared at something distant in the water. "I was a wreck. Then Bart came along, right after the accident. The papers had been full of all the gory details and way too much info about me." She touched a finger to her lips. "People huddled and whispered, like I couldn't tell what they were talking about. It was awful, until Bart swept me up and took me away from it all.

"As I look back, I realize I should have gone home to Virginia or off by myself for a while. I was so hurt. There was a huge void in my life so I stupidly let Bart fill it. I should have waited, but," she flushed scarlet, "I was careless. I hadn't been able to get pregnant with my first husband."

Vickie wiped her eyes with her napkin, then pulled a pale blue monogrammed hanky from her purse and blew her nose. "Damn. Excuse me. I was lonely and devastated. I soaked up Bart's attention like a sponge. I guess it felt good to be taken care of again, but I sure as hell didn't need to go and get pregnant with someone I hardly knew."

Abbey moved her chair back from the table and stretched her legs out in the sun. This was the typical horror story laid on her and all her friends in high school, which was supposed to keep them from doing the dirty deed with boys; it had worked, for most. Abbey was thankful she'd been a prude and had spent her spare time at the barn and not in the back seat. She sensed there was more.

"Mom and Daddy were devastated on the one hand, but delighted on the other. They had lost the son-in-law they loved as much as I did, but they were getting a grandchild. They were so gracious about the baby, but they were hurting too." Vickie choked—or hiccupped. Abbey looked up. Tears pooled in Vickie's eyes.

"Are you okay?" She put her hand on Vickie's arm. *This woman needs a friend.*

Vickie shook her head. "There's more. My folks needed to get away from it all, so they flew to Florida for a golf weekend with another couple from home. They were on the friends' private plane, and on their way back home they ran into a horrible storm and the plane crashed." Her chin dropped to her chest. "Bart and I had only been married a short time and there was a baby on the way. I was a wreck."

The waitress walked by and looked at Abbey, who gave her raised eyebrows and said, "Would you mind bringing us some more napkins, please." *Wow. And she makes more over a picture of her dog than one of her daughter. Bart saw an opportunity and jumped on it and he's a cheat. Major manipulator.* "Remember yesterday I said you should have a lawyer. Have you thought about it?"

Vickie dabbed her eyes and blew her nose again. "I don't have any lawyer. There was the one in Virginia who settled my parents' wills and their estate, but why would I need a lawyer?"

"I bet Bart has one."

"Well, of course." Vickie waved the hand that grasped a sodden napkin. "But he needs one for business."

Abbey stared at her. "Lots of people have lawyers, Vickie, or know one they can call on anyway. I think you should have one just in case. You never know when you might need one."

Vickie licked her lips while she considered the idea. "Do you know any I could call?" She wrung her hands and looked around the deck, then said in a low voice, "It's probably nothing. I had a problem with a credit card this morning. Bart probably forgot to pay it or something. No big deal." Her lips trembled when she smiled. "If you think it's a good idea, maybe I should look into it. It just never occurred to me."

Abbey said, "I date a trial lawyer, but I have a lawyer friend in Atlanta who might be able to talk to you. If he can't help you, he'll know someone who can. And when you talk to one, get a will. Wills protect people." *And you need protecting.*

TWENTY-FIVE

By the time she got back to the cottage after lunch with Vickie, she needed a jog and fancied following that with a nice long swim, then a glass of wine while she watched the sun set. Watch Dog was cavorting with the children so the rest of the afternoon was hers. It was pleasant out, not too hot, and a brisk breeze kept the sand gnats at bay.

Moving at a comfortable pace Abbey spoke to walkers and enjoyed looking at the familiar cottages along the bluff and listening to the calls of the birds. Lawns were well-kept and flowerbeds were beautifully tended; some cottages were original, dating to the early 1900s when the club was first formed, and they had a charming look all their own. Newer ones were built to fit in with the setting, and all took advantage of the sweeping marshland view.

At the last cottage, she turned left and followed the sandy road through hovering live oaks and palmettos, which then gave way to straight rows of planted pines. As children, she and her brothers always tried to be the first to spot the huge eagle's nest that teetered precariously at the top of the tallest skinny pine. Out of habit, she still looked, knowing that eagle was long gone, but his white-hooded heirs could still be spotted soaring overhead or scouting for food from the tops of tall trees.

An old green truck was pulled into a cut-out in the palmettos. Abbey knew the truck and its owner; she slowed and picked her way through the meagre space between the truck and the palmettos. An old black man lifted a fuel can into an army green jon boat.

"Good afternoon, Roosevelt." The white-haired man looked up with a question on his face. "It's me, Abbey Bunn."

Roosevelt's smile revealed chalk-white teeth. "What'chu doin' sneakin' in here like a bobcat?"

"I was running and saw your truck. I figured you'd be fooling around with that boat and thought you might need a hand putting it in."

He gazed at her for a minute, looked serious. "I thought maybe you'd found another somebody in the river needed help."

"I guess you heard."

"I saw Sarge other mornin'. He told me what happened. You seem to have a knack for findin' folks in trouble, Miss Abbey." Roosevelt put his hands on the bow of his boat and began to push it toward the creek. Abbey grabbed hold of the stern and pulled.

"Roosevelt, were you pulling your crab traps Saturday morning?"

He tied the boat's painter to a tree; its stern swung around with the current. "I was. Did my usual run. When I got out to the river, I saw two fellas in a big powerful boat tearin' it up. Sun wuddint even up good and that feller drinkin' beer like it was Saturday night 'stead a' mornin'."

"Which way were they headed?"

"South, far as I could tell."

"Do you remember anything about the boat?"

"It had a Georgia registration on it. I saw that much."

"You have good eyes, Roosevelt."

"Yep. That's one of my parts still works like it's s'posed to." Roosevelt hopped into his boat and started the motor. "That feller y'all saved gonna make it?"

"I think so." Abbey tossed the painter into the bow and the boat caught the current. Roosevelt waved and went on down the creek.

Watching him go, she thought about the night a year ago when she and Roosevelt pushed off from that same spot and went out into the river and waited and watched as an airplane dropped two bales of marijuana almost in front of the Taylor's Point dock. What a night that had been. She held this old man in very high regard and trusted him completely. After what he'd just said she was pretty sure the suspect fishing boat was out of St. Marys.

At Taylor's Point, she walked out on the dock and spat in the river, then watched the small bubbles move on the incoming tide. There were many things she did automatically without even thinking about why she did them: tooting the horn three times to announce your arrival, looking for the eagle's nest, and drinking from the pipe at the sulfur spring.

Water. I need a drink of water. Her running shoes patted the soft sand. Though there was plenty of tree cover here, it was August and it was plenty hot. Perspiration seemed far too gentle a word to describe the rivulets of salty sweat pouring from her body; her tongue tasted like the tarmac at the Atlanta airport in the middle of the day. On the edge of the woods sat a mossy bathtub into which a pipe spouted cold, clear water from an aquifer. It had been there as long as she could remember, and she had taken a sip every time she had passed it. Another family thing.

Mid-sip, a white Camaro convertible blew past and left her in a cloud of white, powdery dust. "Damn." She clamped her eyes shut and held her breath. Dust enveloped her. "Damn, damn, damn." Tears streamed down her cheeks as grit eased between her eyeballs and her contact lenses. *Shit fire.*

She ran a finger beneath each eye, careful not to dislodge a lens, then applied slight pressure to her eyeballs. Only a lens wearer would understand. She threw cold water on her face, wiped her nose and beneath her eyes on the tail of her t-shirt. She began to walk, then trot. When her eyes finally watered and her vision cleared, she slow-jogged. *Who the hell was that?* She fumed and spat grit for the rest of her run, cursing the unthoughtful driver of that car.

As she approached the bluff, she saw the Camaro parked at the club dock in front of her cottage. *Son-of-a...* The car had a Florida tag. A man in a colorful Hawaiian shirt, with a young woman nearby, stood out on the dock snapping photographs all around as though doing a photo shoot for a magazine. He didn't see her coming down the wooden walkway; she took a deep breath. She had seen that man in person before—twice.

"Excuse me, but I don't believe I know you." Turning toward her, he lowered his camera; his mouth opened and he stared but said nothing.

"I couldn't help but notice your Florida plates." Crossing her arms, she leaned against a handrail on the river side of the dock. "My name is Abbey Taylor Bunn, and you are..."

"Yeah, uh, my name's Bart Croek. I'm developing a piece down the road in St. Marys, and I'm just checking things out, you know, getting to know my neighbors." He waved his camera around. "This is pretty nice, what I've seen, anyway."

"*A-hem,*" the young woman with him interrupted. She smiled and fluttered her fingers toward Abbey. "Hi. *A-hem.* I'm with him."

Arm Candy must have something stuck in her throat. Abbey recognized the rings as those on the hands that had been wrapped around the man in the sales trailer. *Bart Croek, Vickie's husband. Scumbag.*

"Glad you think so. We do too, that's why we have two signs at the gate: No Trespassing and Members and Guests Only. Guess you didn't see them, or maybe you're someone's guest."

"This is some kind of club?" Bart looked around with a derisive smirk on his face.

"Yes. That's what 'Members Only' implies."

"Oh. Well, maybe I want to join your club. How about that?" Abbey uncrossed her arms and shook her head, but Bart kept talking. "We drove around a little. There's not much to it. I'd take a match to most of these shacks and knock down these dilapidated docks and start over, new everything. This place could be dynamite with these views."

Bart looked at Arm Candy, who eased her pink short-shorts off the handrail, then spread her feet and planted her fists on her hips cheerleader-style. "Yeah," she said. "He could do it too. That's what he does for a living."

Abbey glanced at her. "Rah-rah."

"What did you say?" One splay-fingered hand went to her thigh. "What's that supposed to mean?" Arm Candy looked at Bart, but his eyes were on Abbey's.

"Private, as in members only, like the sign says."

"Well, what the hell," Arm Candy said. "This place is in the middle of nowhere and we're just—"

"Trespassing," Abbey said with a look that made the woman sidle up and behind Bart.

A wet, squishy squeak proceeded up the ramp from the floating dock. Abbey knew the sound without looking.

"Y'all best be moving on," Sarge said at the top of the ramp. He spat a long brown stream over the rail.

"Eww-yick." Arm Candy grabbed her throat.

"Who the hell do you think you are?" Bart said. Sarge stepped toward him. "What the—" When Sarge kept on coming, Bart grabbed his date's arm and pulled her squealing from the dock and all the way to the Camaro.

Sarge turned back toward the ramp.

"Thanks, Sarge. What a jerk."

"Yep. World's full of 'em."

Abbey watched the Camaro storm through the front gate and down the paved road. *What the hell did Vickie tell him to get him poking around here?*

TWENTY-SIX

The next morning, the river was as glassy as a lake, and it was a good thing. After Bart's visit Wednesday and a fitful night thinking about Vickie's screwed-up life, Abbey had some serious anger to work out. Today she would retrace Saturday's row to see if anything came to her about Doc's rescue. The tide was coming in and though it would not be exact, she wanted to see how long it took her to get to the sound where she had found Doc.

Twenty minutes later, she stopped parallel to the shell bank where she had stashed her boat while they pulled Doc from the water. Terkoff's partner was right. Why didn't she remember more about the fishing boat except that it was big? A lot of help that was. She had been focused on the man in the water and not so much how he got there. Far out in the sound, three shrimp boats were silhouetted against the sky, much farther away than the fishing boat had been.

She stared at their unmistakable shapes for several seconds and realized they stood out because there was nothing behind them but more open water and sky, no dark background, no land or distracting trees, only their ghostly presence in faint outline. Three cutouts backed by blue-gray sky. Sitting silently, she tried to let her memory fill in details. Stern Man had on some kind of dark shirt, and the boat's driver had on a white one. And there was something else she couldn't put her finger on, a flag or something up high, color.

At first it had been the man's angry voice that had gotten her attention, then the yelling. Was it the boat's driver or the man standing in the stern? Doc didn't strike her as a yeller. No, he looked like he probably was a guest on the boat dressed in his Brooks Brothers shorts and shirt, not a real fisherman. She imagined one of the other men yelling at Doc. But why? Why would you take a guest out fishing and then yell at him?

Certainly you wouldn't do that to an inexperienced fisherman. You would show him what to do. So maybe the yelling was about something else, something serious enough to make the lunatic run over Doc and leave him for the sharks. What could possibly make a man that angry? Money and women were things men often fought over.

She tried to reconstruct the other yell she had heard, the one after the argument broke out and right before that awful boat-hitting-body sound. Looking around, she saw there was no one near enough to hear so she yelled, "Ehhhhh," but that sounded more like she had just smelled a dead animal. "Ahhh," she tried from the back of her throat. That was closer, like someone taken by surprise or shocked that a boat was coming at him at full speed. But why would Doc have been in the water in the first place?

She squinted at the slick, silver water as though it would give her the answer. Had someone yelled "No," or was she making that up? There had been an emphatic one-syllable sound like *no* or *oh*, just before the yelp or cry. She was almost certain. Stern Man kept staring out of the back of that boat like he was looking for something, looking for the man they had just run over. Had he been as shocked as Doc at the turn of events? If he had, that man could be the weak link they needed to break, because the driver obviously had known what he was doing.

Rowing toward home, she imagined Doc and Stern Man enjoying the ride in the back of the boat. An argument broke out. Back to money and women. Doctors usually had money, so assume the fight was about money. Then something happened and Doc ended up in the water, either because he was knocked in or he jumped in. Knocked in was simple; he could have been punched in the face and fallen or simply lost his balance. But why would he jump in, unless he felt threatened enough to take his chances, same as people who jumped out of burning buildings. Someone pulled a knife or a gun, and Doc decided to swim for the shore. He wasn't that far from it when she found him. He cut and swam.

Back at Kings Bluff, she rinsed her shell and put it away, then got cleaned up and called the hospital. Doc had been agitated all morning, which was a good sign. He was trying to figure things out, fighting with disconnected information in his head and trying to put things in order. She left the number at the cottage. "Please let me know if anything changes."

Still aggravated with Bart, she couldn't sit still, so she called the B&B in St. Marys. The manager was in. With a brief explanation of why and what she needed from him, Abbey said, "And the hat I pulled from the river was from a Philadelphia clothier, and it had D-O-C written in it in indelible ink. I know the chances are slim to none that this man was staying in your inn and that his car is one of the rentals I saw in your lot, but it's all I have to go on, Mr. Smith. I have racked my brain since I found him on Saturday, so I hope you'll help me see if my hunch is correct."

Why would he give her this information? She was nobody. "And for your information, I'm working with Sheriff Terkoff of Camden County on this. He's the officer in charge of the investigation."

"Goodness, Ms. Bunn, okay. I see. Maybe I can bend the rules here a bit. If it was me or a friend of mine, I'd hope someone was doing what you're doing. I guess it won't do any harm to share what little information I have." Abbey heard a drawer open and papers shuffle. "Here we go."

Smith clicked his tongue. "Okay, well, it looks like I might have something here. One of the cars belongs to a Dr. Ed Pressman from Philadelphia. How about that."

Abbey held her breath. "That's interesting. When did he check in?"

"Well, last Friday afternoon. Oh, dear, I remember now. He asked me where to go for good seafood. He was a delightful fellow, anesthesiologist, I believe. I should have made the connection sooner, Ms. Bunn, because he wore a hat with an eagle on it. Philadelphia Eagles, of course. My word. I'm slipping. But this sounds rather hopeful, doesn't it? I don't feel right giving more information to a citizen, but of course I will be happy to share it with your sheriff."

"Wonderful! Thank you so much, Mr. Smith. I'll call Sheriff Terkoff right now and we will probably head your way." She called Terkoff and they agreed to meet at the B&B at eleven o'clock.

TWENTY-SEVEN

Abbey parked on the street to wait for Terkoff. Moments later he pulled in behind the B&B and met Abbey out front. They went inside and the Osprey Inn's manager handed the sheriff a copy of a registration sheet. Terkoff looked it over, then handed it to Abbey and said to Smith, "Have you seen Dr. Pressman in the last couple of days?"

"No, sir. Not since Friday when he checked in. I went off duty about the time he would have gone to dinner that night and I came in around ten o'clock Saturday morning and never saw him again."

"Is that unusual, not to see him at all?" Abbey said.

"Not really. Some of our guests prefer to go for breakfast on their own, and that's really the only time I would have seen him. There is so much to do here that our guests come and go as they please, and we rarely know who is here and who isn't."

Abbey said, "You're right. When I have stayed in B&Bs I loved the breakfasts, but if I stayed here I'd be checking out places down by the water."

Terkoff took the registration sheet from Abbey and said, "May I use your phone, sir? I'll try the numbers here." The manager passed the phone over and Terkoff dialed. "Answering machine picked up on the doctor's home phone. There's another one here, another doctor with same last name. Maybe his brother or father." Terkoff dialed then gave a thumbs-up. He explained who he was and why he was calling.

"Yes. He was rescued and he's in the hospital in Jacksonville, Florida. I am going to give the phone to the woman who found him. Her name is Abbey Bunn. She can give you more details than I can."

Abbey took the phone. "Hello, this is Abbey Bunn."

"Abbey, this is Ed Pressman's brother, Dr. Adam Pressman. Please call me Adam."

"Hello, Adam." Abbey told the man exactly what she knew and how she had come upon his brother in the river.

When she finished, Adam said, "Thank God you were there. I came home for lunch or I would have missed your call, but I'll make arrangements to get to Jacksonville the minute we hang up. I won't be able to leave until tomorrow because I have meetings all afternoon and I'm on call tonight. How shall I contact you?"

She gave him her number. "This is the number at the cottage where I'm staying and there's a message machine there. If I miss your call, leave me your flight information and I'll plan to pick you up at the airport. You can probably get a direct flight to Jacksonville from Philadelphia. Hold on just a second."

She held the telephone at her hip so Adam could still hear. "Mr. Smith, since Doc's room has been unoccupied, can his brother stay there until we work something out?"

"Certainly," Smith said. "As long as he needs it. I'll just shift some things around and he should be good to go. He will just have to pick up an extra key and sign in."

"You're all set with a place to stay, Adam, and I bet your brother might have left a car key in his room," she said, looking at the manager.

"Let me go look," the manager spun away, as though eager to contribute to the plan.

"The manager's going to have a look for your brother's car key."

"Thanks, Abbey. And tell him not to bother to change the sheets. They were only slept on one night."

Abbey chuckled. "I'll pass that along."

"So I won't need to rent a car."

"Your brother has one sitting in the parking lot here at the B&B. That's how we found you. When you get here, you can call the rental folks and work it out with them."

The manager returned dangling the car key for her and Terkoff to see and said he would have housekeeping put all fresh linens in Doc's room anyway.

"We have the keys so there's a car here for you." She listened to Adam for several seconds. "No, it's no trouble. Believe me, I am happy to do whatever I can to help your brother. At least we're getting somewhere now."

Terkoff gave the manager his contact information and they walked out. "Get going and let me know when Adam calls. When he gets here I'd like to meet you at the hospital."

"Will do." She stopped. "Oh, I almost forgot. I have something for you." She pulled Doc's hat from her front seat and handed it to Terkoff. "Here's the hat I found." She showed him the clothier's label and the handwritten DOC inside. "Take good care of this. I think I know who's missing it."

"You got it." Terkoff folded the cap in his hand, started to walk off then turned. "And, Abbey, good bit of detective work."

"Thanks. I'm working on it." *That and trusting my gut, among other things.*

TWENTY-EIGHT

lthough St. Marys was safe, Vickie didn't want to leave her new things in the car at the office. Besides, Bart didn't need to know she had been shopping again. It served him right, though, what with the embarrassment the last time she'd tried to use his card. His new one worked today just fine. This would be a quick stop so she pulled up in front of the house and gathered her purchases. She fiddled with her key in the front door. *Damn lock!* Dashing up the stairs, she dumped her things on the bed and out of breath, she removed the plastic and shook the hangers to remove wrinkles, then crammed everything into the end of her closet. She'd straighten them later. Shopping was thirsty work.

After a look in the mirror, she freshened her face before going downstairs to the kitchen. She grabbed a cold drink from the fridge and popped off the top on the metal Coca-Cola opener on the kitchen cabinet. As she turned and walked toward the window over the kitchen sink, the bottle moved to her lips. In the back yard, the pool's aqua water sparkled. Before the Coke made it to her mouth, the green bottle in her hand lowered and then clinked on the counter when she set it down.

Surrounded by luscious tropical plants in oversized ceramic pots, the pool looked like a tropical paradise and beside it lay a sea nymph warming in the sun. Bic's tan was rich and deep and complete from hairline to toe. She lay elegantly on a lounge chair, a full-grown woman with all the shapes and curves to prove it. Fit, too. *I used to look like that.* Bic prided herself on her flat belly and muscular thighs, yet every inch of her was smooth golden muscle. There were two opened beer bottles on the table under the umbrella. A pile of clothing and a pair of large running shoes lay on a chair. Vickie craned her neck and tried to see the blocked portion of the pool.

Bic threw her head back and laughed; her bare breasts jiggled. A little line creased her midriff at her belly button when she sat up. Vickie gasped. Her eyes widened and her hand went to her mouth. *Oh, my gosh, he's... he's...* Vickie's hands gripped the edge of the sink, her knuckles white. She watched.

TWENTY-NINE

Clouds eased across the pale sky. Rain was predicted for the weekend. Abbey hoped it would hold off long enough for Adam to fly in.

"Hey." Abbey turned to see who had spoken.

"Oh, hi, Cliff."

Beach Boy's smile broadened. "Yeah. You remembered. Still thinking about that fishing boat?" He sauntered over, his flip-flops tapping softly on his heels as they slipped down the sandy sidewalk, threads from his baggy cutoffs stuck on curly blonde hairs on his tanned legs. It looked like that would itch.

Abbey scratched her shin with the toe of her shoe. "Nope, still looking."

"I have connections if you want some help." The toothpick between his teeth traveled from the right to the left and back, then flipped inside his mouth with a quick maneuver of his tongue.

Abbey grimaced. "Aren't you afraid you're gonna swallow that thing?"

"Nah." His smile was bad-boy cocky. "Wanna go grab a beer and talk about boats? Or books? Or whatever you want to talk about?"

"Gosh, thanks, but I can't. I'm meeting a friend tonight. I'm just killing time until I have to go get ready."

"Huh. Too bad. I'm heading across the street for a cold brewski." Cliff nodded toward the café.

"Oh, Cliff,"—he looked at her hopefully, as though he thought she had changed her mind—"after we talked yesterday, I picked up a map of that new development in St. Marys and drove around out there. Are you familiar with the old house on the creek?"

"Yep. It belonged to a couple from Atlanta. They owned all of that land."

"So I heard. I drove out there and saw a light on in the house." *One time.* "And a white Range Rover was parked in the carport." *Another time.* "I thought the house was vacant."

"It was, but what I heard was the developer's partner is living there until he builds. I think they call him Cutty or something like that. Before him, though, the developer and his wife lived there while their house was being built."

So Cutty is Bart's partner. "Okay. That explains it. It's his electric bill, so I guess he can leave a light on if he wants. It doesn't look like a bad house. I bet it was great when it was kept up."

"Hell, a house on that creek? I'd take it in a minute if they needed someone to house-sit."

"Okay, thanks, Cliff. I need to get going."

"Gotta get dolled up, eh," he grinned. "But if your plans change you know where to find me." Cliff smiled, tucked his hands into his back pockets and flopped away. He turned once and gave her another smile and a little salute.

"Take it easy."

Cutty and Bart. Partners. I wonder what Bart was so angry about that he pounded the table with his fist.

THIRTY

White contrails crisscrossed the sky as Abbey pulled to the curb at Jacksonville International Airport Friday morning. Smelling highly of hot asphalt and jet fuel, the air stirred enough to flutter the strappy leaves of palm trees like giant cheerleader pom-pom shakers. Keeping her eyes on the door, Abbey looked for someone who matched the way Adam had described himself when he called her the night before: tall and dark-haired and pulling one small green roller bag. A stream of people came through exit doors and there were several possibilities, but only one flipped a Phillies baseball cap onto his head as he walked to the curb, a cap just like the one she had given to Terkoff for samples. Hopping out, she walked toward the man she hoped would be able to answer a whole lot of questions.

"Doctor Pressman?"

"Yes." He walked toward her and shook the hand she offered.

"You're right on time."

"It was a good flight. Thanks for picking me up. I could have taken a cab."

"Oh, no. I wouldn't dare. I'm delivering you right to your brother's bedside." As she drove, she explained what she knew, starting with how she had found his brother five days prior.

"If you don't mind, Doctor, I need to make a call. I promised a certain policeman I would let him know when we were headed to the hospital. He's a Georgia cop and he's the investigating officer." Abbey pulled over at a gas station and called Terkoff as they had agreed the day before.

"We're on our way to the hospital," she said when the sheriff picked up. "Right. It was on time. No, we'll grab something later. I'm sure he's starved, but he's pretty eager to see his brother. Okay. See you soon."

When she got back in the Jeep, Adam was staring at one of her business cards, which he had picked up from the stack she kept in a small open compartment below her radio. "You know, during the entire flight this morning I tried to figure out why Ed was here in the first place." He held up her card. "I think I just figured it out. Real estate. We were shoveling his driveway last winter, and he said he might start to look for a place in a warmer climate so he could escape the cold winters up north."

"Could be," Abbey said. "There's certainly plenty to choose from here, and Jacksonville is booming."

"Mind if I keep this?" Adam held up her card.

"It's yours."

Traffic moved along at a steady pace for a weekend. Terkoff met them at the hospital in his usual pressed uniform and starched stature. Another cop stood beside him.

Abbey made introductions, and Terkoff introduced the other cop. "Mic is my contact here in Florida in case I need any local assistance." Terkoff looked at Adam's hat. "Guess I won't have to run any tests on this." He pulled the identical cap from his back pocket and handed it to Adam, who took it, studied it, eying the DOC written in it, and looked around the attentive group.

"And you found this…"

"In the river. That's one of the things that made me real curious about the noise I heard. It's a lucky hat."

Adam held it like it was precious. "We went to the Phillies' first home game this season and bought these." They obtained visitor passes and got on the elevator.

Maurine looked up when they approached the nurse's station. "I bet you're the brother who is going to fill in some blanks for us." Abbey had phoned the hospital that morning and informed the nurse about Doc's identity and everything else she had learned. She introduced Maurine to Adam and they walked down the hall.

"I bet your parents were happy when you two graduated," Maurine said to Adam.

Adam smiled. "They were used to it. They're both doctors."

"Ah. So how's that working for you?" Maurine gave Adam a crooked smile.

Adam looked uncertain, but then he noticed Abbey's chuckle and realized the nurse had a dry sense of humor. "Some days better than others. Family dinner conversations are fairly predictable."

Maurine led them down the hall to Ed's room. "Now, don't push him. Why don't you two uniforms stay by the door and let Abbey tell Doc his brother is here. He responds to her voice."

When they walked into the room, Doc looked their way. Except for the tinges of bluish-purple on his face and what peeked through his hospital wrap, the patient looked pale. "What's going on," Doc said.

Abbey responded. "Doc, we have a surprise for you. Your brother Adam is here. He's going to get you out of this place and take you home." Doc adjusted in the bed and mumbled something incoherent.

Adam went to the bedside and placed a hand on his brother's shoulder. "Hi, Ed. It's me, Adam. I'm here now with Abbey, the one who pulled you out of the river."

"Guess I was right, calling you Doc," Abbey said. Ed's mouth twitched and he looked from Abbey to Adam.

Adam said, "I take that as a smile. What happened, old man, did you tell someone one of your lousy jokes and he tossed you in the drink?" Ed mumbled deep in his throat, then his hand inched up the sheet toward Adam's until they met halfway.

"Don't know. You're Adam? You look familiar."

Adam looked at Abbey and Terkoff. "Familiar. He has conveniently forgotten how I used to beat him up all the time when we were kids. Familiar. That's good." He took a deep breath. "He's going to be okay. I know it. We just won't know for a while if there's any long-term damage, but he's a brilliant man and he'll soon realize he has to work hard to get it all back."

"Mind if I talk?" Terkoff said, more to the nurse than to anyone else in the room.

Maurine nodded. Adam said, "Certainly."

"Okay." Terkoff stepped forward and assumed his tough-guy interrogator stance, crossed arms and all. Abbey shot him a look, pointed at his feet and shook her head slowly, pressing both of her palms down to tell him to relax.

Terkoff eased. "I'm going to start at the beginning. I know Abbey filled you in, Doctor Pressman, but I want to walk through what we have been able to put together so far. We think your brother here was out fishing."

Adam said, "He just put a little pressure on my hand."

Abbey looked from the brothers to Terkoff, who mouthed, "Tell him what happened."

She cleared her throat. "Hi, Doc. It's me again, Abbey. I heard the collision, when the boat hit you. I was out rowing and I found you floating on your back in the river. You held onto the rigger of my shell and—"

"Big squeeze," Adam said. "Ed rows in Philadelphia. At some level, he was aware of what you wanted him to do. It must have made sense to him."

"Okay. That's why he didn't flip me. He just held on and let me pull him. What I can't figure out is how he got out of the way of that boat," Abbey said. "He must have a hell of a set of lungs."

"He's a competitive masters swimmer too," Adam said. "My little brother the jock."

"Lucky for him. When I got to him, he was conscious and floating on his back like he knew his life depended on it, and I guess it did." She took a deep breath. "I think I saw the boat that hit him. There were two men in it, and they were leaving the area just about the time I saw Doc floating."

Doc's mouth twisted as though he was trying to work something out but couldn't quite come up with the answer.

"Whoa. Good squeeze," Adam said.

"I'll be damned. Look at that," Terkoff said. Tears spilled from Doc's eyes and streamed toward his ears. Adam grabbed a tissue and staunched the flow.

"I think those are good tears," Adam said. "He has probably been holding them for a while, waiting for things to make sense to him."

"Yeah," Doc said. He looked at Adam. "You're finally here."

"I'm finally here," Adam said.

"This is the most I have seen out of him in days," Abbey said, "and I was just thinking about something."

Terkoff studied Abbey's face. "What were you thinking?"

"Well, he's coming around and he will be leaving the hospital, so he'll be safe. What if you run something in the newspaper, something vague about a hit-and-run on such-and-such a day and how the injured party was unconscious but is coming around and has started to talk. That might flush these guys out, scare them a little, maybe make them so nervous they do something stupid."

"I like it," Adam said, "and so does Ed. He just squeezed. But there can be no mention of his name or where he is hospitalized or where he lives, any of that. I'll take him home the minute the hospital gives him the okay, but give us a day or two after we leave. I'd hate to have these people try to find him."

"Damn straight. Damn straight. Damn straight," Doc said.

They all looked at each other and smiled. "Well, I guess that's that. Let's do it," Adam said.

Terkoff said, "I know someone at the paper who will run the story, so you let me know as soon as you have an okay from the hospital, and I'll get it in the paper and on the nightly news the day after you two clear out of here. Only problem is I don't write worth a damn." He looked from Maurine to Abbey. "Pardon my French."

"Hold on." Abbey walked out and returned several minutes later with paper and pen and pulled the rollaway tray table to the window. She jotted several lines, read what she had written, then added and incorporated suggestions from the others and handed the paper to Terkoff. "There. See what you can do. Put your name and stuff on it so it looks official."

Abbey drove Adam back to St Mary's. Smith, the inn manager, had already run everything by the car rental agency so all Adam had to do was call them to confirm and give them his credit card number. She handed Adam a five-dollar bill.

"What's that for?"

"Hang on to it, Adam. I want you to do something for me for Doc. I'll let you know what when you call me from the airport on your way home."

She used the phone in the lobby and checked at her cottage for messages. There was one from Vickie, a reminder that they were having lunch, and one from Tom. His put a smile on her face.

THIRTY-ONE

Friday morning, Bart's black Cadillac and Cutty's Range Rover were parked in front of the office, and Bart's door was closed. Vickie threw her purse in the drawer and tiptoed over to assume the position she had perfected of late. She wanted to know what was so important all of a sudden that Bart had to keep his door closed all the time. It made her feel she was no longer part of the team, and she wanted to know why. She was getting good at this and rather liked getting the inside scoop; attuned to what was going on in there, she could even tell where Cutty sat because she heard air rush out of the cushion of the chair he preferred, and Bart's leather chair creaked when he moved a muscle.

Bart said, "What the hell happened to you? You been on a bender or something?"

Cutty said, "Late night."

"Son-of-a-bitch," Vickie muttered. *He's waterlogged.*

"Lightweight," Bart said. "Where'd you go? Somewhere around here?"

"Nah. A friend cooked dinner. She had some great wine… and lots of it." There was a belch. Vickie assumed it was Cutty. "But that was after the Depth Chargers."

"That little bitch," Vickie hissed between clenched teeth.

"Damn. I haven't done those in years. That tequila will kill you, or blind you. I don't mess with that stuff," Bart said.

156

"No, this was good stuff, really good stuff. Smooth going down, but…." Cutty groaned, "man, oh man. I'm hurting."

"So you want to die, sissy-boy, right," Bart said, but Cutty didn't respond. Talking seemed to take too much effort for him. Bart suggested several hair-of the-dog remedies and then recounted drinking adventures from his past, adventures that always had a woman at their core. "I got a lot back then." Vickie rolled her eyes and huffed.

"Listen, dammit. I'm drinking too much, Bart. Thinking about all of this shit is driving me crazy and that great big toy of yours out back makes me sick. Hell, when did you dream up that crazy scheme anyway? There had to have been a better way."

"Shut the hell up. Not here. We have nothing to worry about."

"Maybe," Cutty said, "but we're dying here. We need cash or we're going belly-up. You have any more great ideas?"

"Hell, I'm working on it. You got any, partner?"

Vickie heard Bart circle round and round, squeak, squeak, squeak. "Vickie is driving me bat-shit, asking questions all the time. Anyone can see we're in trouble and she brings it up every damn day, subtle ways sometimes. Hell, she tried to use my American Express card the other day and was turned down. That went over big. Shit. Then I come in here and you start crawling up my ass." Vickie frowned and wrapped her arms around her waist.

"You told me the other day Vickie was from money, right? Why don't you ask her to ask her folks for a loan? We'll pay them back when we get this thing rolling."

"Dammit, there're already in as much as they ever will be. They gave me some money to get started."

Vickie jerked up. *Started? My father paid for this damned place!*

"Maybe if you cut her old man in on the deal," Cutty said.

"Her parents are dead, and Vickie's in about as much as she ever will be. I pay her for her time here and she's happy with that." Vickie bit her bottom lip.

"Well, hell. When you brought me on you told me you bought this place with your own cold hard cash. Those were your exact words. Damn, Bart. It was all her money, wasn't it?"

Bart didn't deny it. Vickie's cheeks burned with anger and without thinking, she reached for the doorknob. "Now I really feel bad for her, Bart. She didn't deserve any of this." She dropped her hand.

There was silence, then Cutty said, "That's really something, partner. You have a wife who's rich and pretty, and she deserves a good life and none of this stuff you've done even comes close to bothering you, does it?"

Her emotions changed from angry to confused. She leaned in closer, wanting him to tell her exactly what more Bart could have done.

"Oh, so now it's what I have done, and you had nothing to do with it. I see. It's all my problem. Well, thanks, pal. What the hell can I do about it now, Cutty? What's done is done." Vickie squinted as though that would help her to understand what they were talking about.

"Yeah, and my poor helpless wife. She had it all: clothes, money, that damn horse, but she always drove shitty cars. Can you imagine? All that dough and she drove shitty cars. Go figure. Spoiled rotten, did whatever in hell she wanted to do but always driving some shitty car." Bart's leather chair squeaked. "When I married her, I told her she would never drive a shitty car again and she hasn't."

"For crying out loud, Bart. Cars are things. Some people don't care about things."

"Yeah, well, thank goodness my daughter took after me. Except in her looks. In that department, she took after her mother, which ain't all bad, as you know." Vickie's lip quivered and a tear rolled down her cheek.

"Look here," Bart said. "Of course, you met her the other day at lunch, but I keep this little reminder close to me." Vickie knew what he was doing. He kept a photograph in his wallet, Bic's annual picture from her senior year in high school. "She's special, that one. She'll be something someday."

Cutty didn't say a word. Vickie dug dents in her palms with her fingernails and took deep breaths. She imagined Cutty staring at the photograph and getting all hot and bothered. He said nothing; she remembered what she'd seen. Cutty knew Bic very well. A little too well.

"Damn, man. You getting a hard-on over a picture?" Bart laughed. "Your hand's shaking like a leaf. Maybe you should go home and have a beer and take a nap. You're worthless today."

Vickie had heard enough. She grabbed her purse and didn't bother to close the front door.

THIRTY-TWO

It was before the lunch hour so the deck was empty. Vickie was at their table and had already consumed half of her glass of pink lemonade. *She must have had a tough tennis lesson.* Abbey sat down and studied Vickie's unaccustomed frown. "Are you okay?"

"No. But this helps." She tipped her glass toward Abbey, then took a healthy gulp. "Fair warning. I freed the virgin today. This is the real deal."

"Oh. Those bartender experiments usually pack a punch, so be careful." *Well, this is new. Either she found out about Bart's girlfriend or something else has happened.*

Vickie polished off the drink and motioned to the waitress for another.

"What's going on, Vickie?"

The waitress appeared with an iced tea and a pink lemonade and said, "Watch these, hon. They're pretty potent and they'll sneak up on you." She glanced at Abbey and shrugged as she walked away.

Vickie muttered, "Thanks for the warning." Her lip trembled as she picked up the fresh glass and sipped. "I'm not going back to that office today. Can't."

"Vickie, what has you so upset?"

Vickie sniffed. "I just need some girl time."

Abbey thought for several seconds. Needing girl time usually

160

had something to do with a man, but then, Vickie was a mother, so that too was an option. Vickie huffed and puffed several times. "Vickie, talk to me. What's going on?" She imagined any number of things. Vickie wouldn't meet her eyes so she pushed. "Look, you asked for my help, so I need to talk to you about Crooked Creek. You know it's in trouble." That worked. Vickie looked at her.

In for a penny, in for a pound. "I checked around. The development is in arrears on the construction loan and who knows what else."

"Utility bills," Vickie offered. "Plus, no one has set foot out there in ages." She sniffled.

"How about the taxes? You get behind in those and you'll hear from the IRS in a hurry."

Vickie looked at her lap and thought for several seconds; her head moved slightly from side to side. "Daddy must have had an inkling about Bart from the beginning. He took care of the property in his will. I never even saw a tax bill. After Bic was finished with school in Orlando, Bart decided he wanted to try his hand at development. Of course, I owned the land in Georgia and Daddy had made sure that property was mine and only mine. Thank God I had enough sense not to give Bart any ownership in it. As it was, I had to co-sign every loan he was able to finagle. I guess I should get in touch with Daddy's banker and lawyer." She continued to stare at her hands and Abbey let her talk.

"No wonder Bart has been so impossible lately. He could use a day off, a round of golf or something. He needs to relax and get his mind off of that place." She shook her head. "He gets all huffy and short with me. The other night he told me he was trying to keep a roof over our heads." She wiped her nose with a lace handkerchief. "He said he didn't have time to go out to lunch with friends like I did."

Abbey wondered how much Vickie had told Bart about her. She didn't like the way he looked, the way he acted, or the fact that he was a developer in trouble who was two-timing his wife and snooping around Kings Bluff. She didn't trust him as far as she could throw him. "Do you tell Bart when we're getting together?"

"Are you kidding? My time is my time. As you so aptly pointed out, he controls enough of my life as it is. I sure as heck don't want him to know how I spend my free time."

"I'm rather private, Vickie, so I'd just as soon he not know a whole lot about me."

Vickie's face dropped and she swallowed hard. "He mentioned you. I don't know, he must have seen us together or something or maybe he saw your car and noticed the Atlanta tag." She sipped her drink. "You should try one of these. They're really good, not too sweet."

"No, thanks. It's a bit early for me. We have had lunch several times, Vickie, but that's about it." The pancake makeup wasn't as obvious as before, but maybe it had powder over it this time to blend it in better; even that, though, did not totally cover the bruise. "What *have* you told him about me?"

"Well, he asked who I was meeting for lunch and I told him my new friend from Atlanta."

You told me several days ago you told him I was a friend of a friend. "Did you tell him I had a place near here?"

Vickie bit her lip and squinted her eyes. "I don't think so. I don't even know where you stay. I figure it's close though, because you get here in such a hurry."

She's probably lying, but she has all of those old newspaper clippings. He could have found them and figured it out.

Vickie cleared her throat. "I have been naughty."

Oh, brother. Children are naughty. "How so?"

Several tables had filled. Vickie looked around the deck as though the other patrons were tuned in to their conversation. She lowered her voice. "I sort of listened in on them."

"On whom?"

"On Bart and his partner, silly. Cutty the cutie." Vickie licked her lips and fluffed her hair. Squinting her eyes as she leaned forward, she whispered. "I think they're scrambling, trying to figure out how not to lose their pants, and Cutty said they had bigger issues than money. I can't imagine what that might be—I mean, what can be a bigger issue than money for crying out loud. They're not stupid. They know things are at a standstill like you said." She took a healthy gulp. "I hope Bart isn't living on his credit card, but I wouldn't know. He pays his, I pay mine. Or he pays his most of the time, as I found out."

Time to put on the dumb act so Vickie wouldn't know she had done her own snooping. "So Bart has a partner in the development. Do Bart and this Cutty fellow have drinks here?"

"Every day."

"Tall, dark fellow who drives a white Range Rover?"

Vickie nodded. "Gorgeous, isn't he?" She thought for several seconds. "How'd you know?"

"I stopped at the package store the other day and he almost ran me over. I asked someone at the marina who he was." *She'll never know.*

Vickie pulled her arms to her middle and pooched out her lips. "So, what did you think?"

"About what."

"About Cutty."

"I don't know. I think it's a weird name." Abbey shrugged, not certain where this was headed. "He's a good-looking guy if you like the tall, dark, swarthy type."

"Huh." Vickie relaxed, then her eyes darted back to Abbey's. "Cutty is his nickname. William Cuthbert Faulkner. No relation to the author, he says, but with a name like Faulkner, his mother said she had to do it. He's single, you know. Interested?" Vickie's chest heaved. She looked like a hell-cat in heat.

"No, I'm not." But maybe Vickie was. "So they admit the development is in trouble."

"Yes." Vickie's head bobbed up and down. "I came here from work." She flipped her hair out of her eyes and leaned in even closer as if sharing top secret information. "Something's going on, Abbey, I'm sure of it. Our conversations have made me look at things a little differently and I'm thinking really hard, and I'm watching. And listening. I think Bart was in a fight or something."

"What makes you think so?"

Vickie dabbed at her forehead with a napkin and sat back. "Well, out of the blue, Bart told Cutty I was driving him crazy. He knows how I am. I'm interested, I want to be part of everything. I ask questions. I'm not trying to be a pest." She shook her head.

Abbey nodded.

"Bart has been very intolerant lately. It started a couple of days ago when Cutty parked in Bart's space. Bart went ballistic. He's a total bully about stuff like that, possessive like you wouldn't believe. Spoiled is more like it. Then Cutty laid into him about some brawl he was in. Can you imagine grown men duking it out? I admit, my husband can be a real shit when he wants to be, Abbey, and I don't doubt for a minute that he would take a swing at someone." Whether she meant to or not, Vickie put her hand to her bruised cheek.

"I have heard them talk about this fight before. That is, I assume it's the same one." She giggled. "I don't know, maybe Bart goes around picking fights with people all over town." She took a long sip. "Then out of the blue, Bart told Cutty I was always asking questions. Cutty couldn't get off of that stupid fight. He said something like there had to have been a better way to get the money. That part didn't make much sense to me, because how could this fight have anything to do with money? But they sure as heck need money. I agree with that." Vickie blew her nose into her destroyed napkin and signaled the waitress.

Abbey thought about one of the scenarios she had worked out

while she was rowing that had involved a fight. *Heck, some men fight.*

"I need food," Vickie said. Abbey ordered two shrimp salads and two iced teas.

"What do you call those things she's drinking?"

"Tornadoes," the waitress said.

"Like a New Orleans Hurricane. How appropriate," Abbey said. "Sorry, you were saying…"

"I think they're going to hire a temp. I can't believe it after all I've done to try to help them get that place off the ground." Vickie took a deep breath. "Now after what you told me, I think Crooked Creek is going under. And I'm out all of my money."

I wonder how much she's out of pocket. A lot based on her mortgage guy. "So you're out some money. What else is bothering you?"

"Well, this is sort of embarrassing, but I feel I can confide in you." She surveyed the crowd of diners again. "It's Cutty." Vickie stared at Abbey as though looking for some sort of reaction. "You know, Bart is gone a lot and Cutty, well, Cutty kind of takes advantage of that. Do you know what Bart had the nerve to say to me when Cutty accidentally on purpose touched me the first time?"

Abbey held up one hand and her mouth dropped open. "Whoa. He touched you? What happened?"

The fingers on Vickie's right hand pressed the knuckles on her left. "It wasn't too long ago. Bart told me he'd say something to Cutty. He said it was really 'no big deal.' Told me to get over it." Vickie looked at her hands clasped in her lap. "He said Cutty was his partner and he couldn't afford to rock the boat."

Abbey said nothing. *And here Bart is fooling around.*

"I think that… that… I don't know what I think. It makes me feel dirty." Vickie bit her finger hard enough to leave small tooth prints in the skin. "Maybe it was a test to see if I would say something to Bart, to see what Bart would do."

"Did you actually tell Bart what happened?"

"Part of it."

Abbey shook her head. "I'm so sorry," she said. "Do you want to talk about it?"

Vickie stared at the river.

As long as we're on the topic, maybe I can loosen her up. Abbey placed both elbows on the table and steepled her hands beneath her chin. "There was an agent who sold some lots at Crooked Creek. Did Bart mention a restraining order to you?"

Vickie looked away for several seconds. "No. I don't think so. Why would he? But I don't put a whole lot of stock in the young women these days. They're very forward, you know, and they throw themselves at anything in pants, especially if the wearer of the pants is attractive. There were several who were at the development all the time showing property, and I guess they stopped but I figured they were just showing other places. Real estate is a tough business, as you know. You agents have to show your clients everything. I put mine through the wringer in Orlando, so I know. What was it I heard about buyers not always being totally honest about what they will be willing to consider?"

"Buyers are liars. A client swears she doesn't want to do a lick of work on a house, then she gets angry at her agent for not showing her the house her best friend bought, which needs total renovation," Abbey said.

"Really?" Vickie stared wide-eyed.

"Really." Abbey's eyes held Vickie's. "Those two agents you were talking about. One quit showing at Crooked Creek because Bart acted inappropriately. He made unwanted advances so she took out a restraining order on him. You don't remember being called about this?" She watched Vickie's expression go from what could have passed for curious to definitely furious.

Vickie's hand went to her mouth and then both arms crossed over her abdomen. Her bottom lip all but disappeared under her top teeth. "Vickie." Abbey hunched down to make eye contact. Vickie looked up, so she tried another tactic.

"What started this business with Cutty?" Abbey reached across the white painted metal table and placed her hand on Vickie's forearm. *Compassionate Abbey.*

"Oh, I don't know. Bart was out one day. There was a knock on the front door. I thought it was the lawn service or something, so I went to see who it was." Vickie's voice was halting. "When I saw it was Cutty, I told him Bart wasn't home, and he said he knew." She dabbed at her eyes with a balled wad of paper napkin. "Bart apparently told him he had an extra set of golf clubs Cutty could borrow."

Abbey looked away to give her a minute.

"The door was barely open, but he just walked on in." She hesitated. "He sort of brushed my breast with his arm and nudged me aside. I thought it was a mistake. I mean, he's a big guy. I was sure he didn't mean to do it, so I offered him a glass of iced tea, because it was awfully hot that day. Then he walked on in and kind of checked everything out like he had never been in my house before. I don't know, I figured he had been inside with Bart. He walked to the family room and went right to the fireplace where we have a lot of framed photographs. I felt so awkward.

"I started pointing out pictures of Bart and me on trips we'd taken, tried to make small talk." She hesitated and took a breath. "He brushed by me again from the back this time, and his hand slid across my bottom." Vickie's hand went to her throat; she looked on the verge of losing it.

"What did you do?"

"I... I, well, I turned so quickly I spilled iced tea on... on my blouse. As fast as that he pulled out his handkerchief and... and then he blotted the spill off my breast before I could do anything. Really, it was that fast."

"You should have punched him. I would have given him a swift kick you know where."

"I told him he'd have to leave before Bart got home." Vickie sipped her drink. "He just—he just looked at me with this disgusting—this disgusting grin on his face. And... and he said it would be better if we kept his 'little visit' to ourselves. Like we'd planned it or something. You know?"

Vickie had never stumbled over her words like this before. Either she was terribly upset or was making things up as she went along. *I'll play along, but this sounds rehearsed.* "Bastard," Abbey said. *I don't believe her for a minute.*

Vickie shrugged. "It was so strange. Later, Bart actually told Cutty that I was giddy after he dropped by for the clubs. He actually said that, that I was giddy." She reached into her bag and poured something into her hand from a small brown plastic pill bottle.

Abbey watched the bottle drop into the cavernous purse. There was the same BB rattle she had heard before, and these were not Tic Tacs. Vickie popped the pill into her mouth and then took a long pull on her drink.

"Vickie, it's none of my business but you shouldn't mix medication with alcohol. The side effects can kill you."

"I know. It's just that some days are tougher than others. I was thinking before you got here that maybe Bart and I deserve each other."

"How's that?"

"An old girlfriend of his warned me about his temper when she found out we were getting married. She said he knocked her around when he started to drink, but I figured it was her fault, that maybe she didn't do what he wanted her to do. I guess that's why I let him control me like I do, or that's my excuse anyway. But I got to thinking, I'm no prize either. Remember I told you about my first love?"

Abbey nodded.

"The night of the accident we went to a party. Billy had a couple of beers and I sipped on a Coca-Cola. It was raining hard by the time we left. I'll never forget it. He asked me to drive, but I made up some excuse, like I hadn't gotten much sleep the night before because I was up studying. I told him I was too tired to drive." She finished off her drink and signaled the waitress for another. Tears gathered in her eyes and she looked away from Abbey. "I actually told him since he was the man it was his responsibility to drive us home." When her drink arrived, she picked it up and cradled it in her hands.

"There was a bad curve a block from where I lived. The car skidded off the road and hit a tree. He went through the windshield and I got dumped on the floor in the rear. I had been asleep on the back seat. He broke his neck and died instantly. I walked away from it. Not a scratch. Not even a bruise."

It had begun to sprinkle, so Abbey and Vickie waited for change inside. The white Camaro Abbey had seen at Kings Bluff the day before eased down the street. Bart had on the white straw hat. Abbey's eyes stayed on the car while she listened to Vickie's prattle about how guilty she'd felt after the wreck. The Camaro paused beside Vickie's car and Bart looked up at the deck. Abbey eased back until she could no longer see him, and he eased on down the road.

THIRTY-THREE

Watch Dog met Abbey at the door and dashed off after a squirrel the minute she opened it. Tom had called the night before to confirm that he was heading her way first thing Saturday morning and he was ready to eat some crabs. She took chicken backs from the freezer, went to the pump house and grabbed two small, square wire crab baskets like she had used as a child. They were more fun than the big traps you could leave in for days, and this would give her something to do while she read on the dock.

It took several minutes to acclimate to the moist heavy air after being in the air-conditioned Jeep. Kings Bluff had a smell of its own. Breezes blew across the river and mixed with cedar, sulfur and pine, air so heavy and full of earthy aromas you could taste it. Abbey inhaled deeply and ran a hand through her hair, which felt thicker in the salty moisture. She tilted her head toward the sun's subtle afternoon warmth. It felt divine. Fluffy white animal clouds drifted slowly overhead herded by transparent wind forces.

Elusive marsh hens hidden from view eh-eh-eh-ehed in tall grasses along the river bank. Now and then one popped out from cover momentarily, then ran back into hiding. Grandmother Taylor, Boonks's mother, loved to shoot them on full moon tides. Abbey never figured out why her grandmother hunted them and never thought to ask her. It didn't look like there was much there

170

to eat, and judging by what the hens probably ate, who'd want to eat them anyway? Must have been all about the hunt. Go figure; Grandmother Taylor was an outdoors woman.

She baited her baskets and dropped them off the end of the dock about twelve feet apart, allowing the cotton cords attached to the baskets to spin off of foot-long sticks she tied onto the handrail. Sitting on a wooden bench, face to the setting sun, she listened. There was so much to hear, but you missed it if you didn't stop and get quiet. The salty estuary was alive with new life. Creatures jumped, flittered, and popped. Spartina grass decayed silently to become part of the nutrient-rich mud and to flavor the air. These waters fed the entire East Coast and acted as a nursery of sorts, where baby shrimp, fish and oysters were protected from rough seas and feeders out in open water. Quiet here was of a different sort, bird song, rippling tide, and breeze-rustled pines. Lovely. Peaceful. She waited for the familiar *whoosh* of a spouting dolphin or the gentle flap of a stingray's wings as it fed in the mouth of a tributary.

A diesel engine hummed across the marsh. She recognized the sound. When the deadrise made its way around the bend, Sarge stopped at each buoyed milk jug to pull a trap, shaking it so crabs tumbled into a basket on the deck of the boat. As he moved along, the jugs bobbed in his wake like fat white seagulls. His thick body moved slowly as he worked. When he looped back toward the dock, Abbey went down the ramp to the floating dock to meet him.

"Afternoon, Sarge. Coming in?"

"Yup." His blue trousers were tucked into the tops of his white rubber boots. All crabbers wore those boots. The boat rocked in its wake. Bushel baskets of blue crabs filled the deck, their bubbling mouths audible to those who recognized the soft sound. As the boat bumped the dock, Sarge picked up a rope.

"Toss it," Abbey said. He did. She secured the bow line to a cleat, then walked to the stern of the boat and held up her hand for the second line and fastened it. Sarge carried a basket to the side of the boat.

"I'll take it," Abbey said. And so it went with the remainder of the baskets. By the time Sarge had turned off the motor, hosed off the deck, and gotten things in order, Abbey had carried all the baskets up the ramp to the covered portion of the dock where she waited.

Sarge's exit was slow and practiced. He grimaced when he stepped over the gunnel and onto the floating dock. Her father and uncles had served in World War II. Grandmother Taylor had told her Sarge was in the infantry in the war and he caught shrapnel in both legs. Obviously, they still bothered him. One swollen-knuckled arthritic hand grasped the handrail of the ramp while the other held the handles of a stack of white plastic buckets nested into each other. He took his painful time.

Sarge lowered himself to the bench with a groan, looked at the six bushel baskets on the floor between him and Abbey and then looked at her. Perspiration plastered his shirt to his back. Buttons gaped over his basketball-sized beer belly. His cheek bulged and a brown line marked where his lips met.

"Looks like you did pretty well, Sarge. You didn't have to spend your time rescuing anybody today."

Sarge thought for a minute. His belly moved in and out. "Yep." Maybe that was a laugh. He looked at her from under a doughy wild-haired brow and nodded, then worked his chaw and let one go into the river. He swiped the sleeve of his shirt across his mouth.

Abbey had watched him before. She knew his routine. "Want help culling the females?"

Sarge's mouth dropped open to expose a brownish pink tongue. He looked at her like she had just asked if he wanted her to weed his garden.

"I'd like to help." He continued to stare. "You helped me, I'll help you."

"Huh." Sarge separated four of the white buckets from the others and handed her two and kept two.

"Male keepers go five inches point to point. They go in there." He pointed to the bucket by her left foot. "Females in there. Except ones with eggs." He pointed to the bucket by her right foot. "Little ones there." He jabbed a thumb over his shoulder at the river. "And mommas full of eggs too. Gotta hatch babies."

They didn't talk, they sorted. Sarge rubbed his shins now and then. She wanted to ask him about the war, about his injuries, but she didn't want to pry or disturb the atmosphere of their unusual companionship. "Did you go shrimping this morning?"

"Yep." Sarge stopped sorting. He rested his elbows on his knees. "How'd that feller end up?"

Abbey looked from the bucket between her feet to Sarge's face. "You mean, the one we rescued?"

His brow creased into a question as though Abbey answered his question wrong.

"We saved him, Sarge. He's seriously injured but he's alive. He has a long way to go, but there's a good chance he will fully recover, I think. He's still sleeping it off. He's awfully bruised, but there were no cuts or anything. We located his brother in Philadelphia. He's here now, came to take his brother home." The look of melancholy on Sarge's face reminded her that the old soldier had probably seen and heard a whole lot more and a whole lot worse.

"He'd probably be dead if you hadn't come along and helped me get him back over here. We rescued him. We saved his life, Sarge. You know that, don't you?"

Sarge stared at the bottom-slick tennis shoes that had replaced his white rubber boots. After several seconds, he said, "Huh," and that was it. No talk of being in the right place at the right time or luck or any of that. It was just a done deal. They got back to work. When the crabs were sorted, Sarge shoved the bucket of large, eggless females her way.

"Can't sell females. Here's your supper."

Oh, yeah. Supper. I forgot all about supper. Her little baskets could wait 'til later. "Thank you, Sarge. I love crab better than anything."

She helped him load the white buckets and the empty bushel baskets onto a dolly and walked with him to his truck. "Well, thanks again for everything, Sarge."

He dipped his head and flicked a dismissive wave as he got into his truck.

As she turned to leave with her bucket of females she heard him mutter, "Rescued that feller, saved him," like he was trying the idea on for size. Somehow it felt good to know this big old war veteran country man was on her side

THIRTY-FOUR

t five-thirty that afternoon, Abbey prepared her side dish for the Friday night dinner at the clubhouse. She turned the ingredients of her salad over and over to mix them thoroughly and if an errant pea or kernel of corn or bit of onion hit the floor, Watch Dog was quick to scarf it up. "Oil and rice wine vinegar okay with you?" Watch licked his chops, his eyes smiled. "I know you love your vegetables, but let's get you some protein."

She filled his water bowl and a white ceramic chow bowl with his name on it and placed them on the floor, then scratched between his shoulders. "When I get back we can take a stroll, big guy." She dared not say walk or he wouldn't let her out the door without him. While he was occupied with dinner, she put a dish towel over her salad and sneaked out.

The dinner would be well attended, judging by the number of cars, trucks, and golf carts parked outside the clubhouse. Inside, men stood in groups or sat at tables and talked while the women pulled napkins, plates, and silverware out of drawers and arranged the bowls and platters that everyone had brought to share. Abbey made room for her salad in the cold dish section.

Snag Privit, the club president, blessed the food then asked that announcements wait until after dinner. Abbey had just joined the end of the loose line that had formed when the door opened and a white-bearded fellow with a faded baseball cap pulled low on his head walked in.

"Sorry I'm late," he said, "but I'm glad y'all didn't wait. I was catching my contribution." He held a large bowl with long, wispy whiskers and dead black pop-eyes protruding from the top.

"Oh, man, Cap'n. Look at that," someone said as the newcomer set his bowl on the serving table.

"I just pulled 'em out of the river. Thought that might make up for my tardiness." His teeth were as white as his beard. Boiled shrimp aroma filled the room. "Sorry I didn't head 'em but that's the way I cook 'em. Heads add flavor."

Abbey was the closest. "Wow. These look great." She grabbed a handful of whiskers and plopped the fat pink shrimp onto her plate.

"You enjoy those, little lady."

"Oh, don't worry. I shall."

Thirty minutes later, dinner was done and the desserts had been decimated. Snag thanked everyone for showing up and bringing their dishes, then he asked if there were any announcements. Abbey raised her hand.

Snag nodded to her and said, "For those of you who don't know Abbey here, her mother is Boonks Taylor Bunn, one of the longest-standing members of the Kings Bluff Club. Abbey's granddaddy Taylor was one of our co-founders, and her grandmother Taylor could out-fish and out shoot anybody sittin' in this room. Abbey and I grew up at Kings Bluff, though I might have a year or two on her."

Someone yelled, "More like a dozen," and people laughed. Snag motioned to Abbey to stand.

Someone tapped a glass with a knife and the chatter stopped. "It's good to see all of you. As Snag mentioned, I am Boonks Bunn's daughter, so you know I'm not an outsider. I go by Abbey Taylor Bunn same as my mother, but so as not to confuse, she uses

Boonks, a nickname her daddy gave to her but which I never picked up. That would have been a little too confusing." Smiles and gray-haired nods went around the room. "Most of you live in south Georgia, but my family calls Atlanta home so you can imagine why Kings Bluff is so important to us."

"You got that right, Miss Abbey," someone said. There was a titter of laughter.

"Don't I know it," she said. "Kings Bluff has always been our second home. I came here summers growing up and probably took it for granted, but now that I am older and I sell real estate in Atlanta, I realize what a precious jewel we have here." She recognized faces to which she couldn't attach names; some had grown old since the last time she had seen them but they were all familiar. It was important they know she was one of them.

"Saturday morning I left the dock in front of Mother's cottage early, just as the sun was coming up. I was in a rowing shell, the skinny boat some of you have seen me in."

"Damnedest thing I ever saw," one elderly man said to the younger man by his side, but loud enough for everyone in the room to hear. The young one patted the older one on the shoulder and held a finger to his lips. "Well, it is," the older man said. The younger man looked at Abbey, shrugged and mouthed "sorry."

For the benefit of this room full of fishermen who had more than likely never seen a racing shell, she gave a quick description of her boat and how it worked. "As I said, I left the dock when it was barely light. It probably took me twenty minutes to get to the cut that comes in at Taylor's Point. Remember, I sit backwards in my boat so I look over my shoulders every five or so strokes to see where I'm going." Many of the men screwed up their faces as if trying to imagine how to do what she described.

"I heard this loud noise and knew immediately a boat had hit something. I had heard a motorboat out in the sound earlier, so I worked my way from the creek to the open water and I saw a large boat high-tailing it away from me; I also saw something in the water that I couldn't make out at first. Turns out, it was a man. I have to assume the boat I saw had hit the man, because we were the only boats out there until Sarge showed up." She nodded at Sarge. "The man was alive. We got him into Sarge's boat and he contacted the DNR, and we met them here. That's what all that fuss was about the other day."

"Is he dead?" one old fellow asked.

"No, he's in the hospital in Jacksonville. Still in and out of it, but he's talking a little and we have located his brother." She didn't go into any details about how that had come about.

"Which day you talking about?" another man asked.

"Saturday morning, early." It seemed like it had been a month ago.

"Most of us decided to fish a good ways out that morning, else we might have seen them," one man said.

Snag said, "Well, has anyone seen anything that might help us out here?"

"You said Saturday?" Cap'n said.

"Yes, sir, early Saturday morning."

"Well, hell, yes, I saw somebody, three somebodies to be exact. I went flounder gigging Friday night right out there beyond Taylor's Point and didn't feel like coming in. Night was beautiful, sky full of stars. I had my bedroll and my buddy Jack to keep me company, so I didn't see any need to leave such a wonderful setup. Figured I'd reserve my spot so none of my good friends here would beat me to it in the morning. Right about sunrise, after I tied on some new leaders, I heard a boat coming, fast. When it got close enough to make out who it was, I didn't recognize any of 'em. Good thing. This dumb-ass—excuse me, ladies but that's the only name for someone like that—this dumb-ass come runnin' down the river hell-bent-for-leather headed toward the sound. Can't figure out what he was doing in our creek unless he was lookin' for a quiet place to fish, but like I said, I didn't recognize any of 'em.

"Driver was pullin' on a beer like it was middle of the day. Wuddin' but six, six-thirty in the mornin'. I'm tellin' you what, he was dangerous. Waked me out big time and never even looked my way or waved an apology or nothin'. Wasn't from here, that's for sure. No manners whatsoever."

Abbey said, "You said there were three of them. Suppose they were going fishing?"

"Reckon so. Rod holders was full."

"I saw the boat too, but I was too far away to really make out anything," Abbey said. "Don't suppose you noticed the make or anything."

"Shoot," Cap'n said, like that was the dumbest thing he had ever heard in his life. "It was a twenty-four-foot Grady White and it had five rods rigged and ready. Anything else you want to know, little lady?"

"No, sir. That about does it." Abbey nudged hair behind her ear. "Thank you."

Sarge and Abbey exchanged a look. *Wonder what he's thinking? Doc's laid up in the hospital and two men think they got away with murder.*

THIRTY-FIVE

After an early morning row and a swim and a quick trip to the grocery store, Abbey and Watch Dog stood at the kitchen counter and breakfasted on chunks of juicy cantaloupe. A puddle pooled under Watch's mouth as he awaited each bite. She rubbed his ear. "It's Saturday and our buddy is coming today."

While Watch busied himself with his real breakfast, Abbey sneaked out the back door and hopped into her Jeep. Tom wasn't wild about the fact that she carried a weapon, so it was better that she practiced at the club's firing range before he arrived. Warm cedar-tinged air blew through the open windows and smelled as soft as it felt. An osprey scanned the forest for prey from the top of a tall skinny pine. Sarge stood at the gas pump at the boat hoist at the far end of the bluff and acknowledged Abbey's wave with a nod. Interesting man.

Driving slowly to keep down the dust, her eyes searched the woods for wild turkeys, pigs, raccoons, armadillos, deer, and snakes. They were there. All you had to do was look. When she arrived at the firing range, it was empty so she grabbed her gun bag and a full body outline target from the back of the Jeep and placed them on the firing platform.

The wooden wall at the end of the range was too far away for her purposes. If she needed to protect herself, it would more than likely be at close range. Jerking a battered real estate sign from the ground halfway down the range, she walked off seven yards from the firing platform and stomped the sign into the soft sand. Full body targets were great. With enough practice, you could be pretty sure where you would hit a live target; if she ever had to fire at someone, she didn't plan to wing him. She'd take him down. Separating her feet at an angle, she moved them until she was happy with her stance, looked at the target's face, and raised her weapon to look down her sight. There would be none of this careful sighting in a real-life situation; it would be aim and fire, so that's how she practiced.

A year ago almost to the day, Abbey had been in a shoot-out with an arsonist who was intent on burning Kings Bluff to the ground. In the process, Tom, who had come on the gas can wielding man first, was critically wounded, and a bullet intended to take Abbey out had parted her hair and bloodied her scalp. Though she hit her assailant and knocked him down, his bullet had hit her at almost the exact same time and possibly made her jerk her weapon. If there ever was a next time, she wanted to take out her target before he had a chance to get off a round.

She attached the target to the sign with wooden clothespins from her gun bag, the very same pins she had used to hang clothes on the line at her Grandmother Taylor's home. Though an avid sportswoman, Grandmother Taylor never came to the firing range, having preferred to do her practicing in season on wild game. Abbey had no doubt her grandmother would approve of her working on her marksmanship, though she would have been horrified to think her granddaughter had been in a shootout. But Abbey knew her grandmother had kept a loaded pistol by her bed at night, so she had been prepared too.

Abbey put on ear and eye protection, then loaded five .38 caliber shells into her new Smith & Wesson revolver, a birthday present to herself that year. She took her time to aim on the first five rounds. Five holes peppered the image's waist. Not bad. That would take down an assailant, but she wanted to be between the gut and the chest so she inserted five more shells, then raised the weapon, looked down the barrel and fired, pop-pop-pop-pop-pop. Holes circled the chest. "Good," she muttered and loaded five more.

Twenty minutes and a box of shells later, she crushed the mutilated target and threw it in a garbage can, packed up her equipment and headed to the cottage. After a quick dip in the pool, she showered and changed, wishing the old shower house still stood. A square affair with metal sides and roof and a concrete floor, it was well used by dirty, stinky fishermen and crabbers, and it was the best way in the world to get the children to actually use soap and water. Maybe she'd suggest to her brothers that it was time to build a new one

THIRTY-SIX

Old Bay seasoning, salt, pepper, and one dried jalapeno pepper from last year's Atlanta garden were on the stove in a large pot of water. Abbey had cleaned up the house the night before so she stripped the bed and put on fresh linens. Boonks threatened to build a new cottage with a laundry room and air conditioning, but for now, linens had to be taken to a laundromat in Brunswick or St. Marys or home to Atlanta and brought back. It was a pain in the neck, but a small price to pay to have this place. No one in the family complained. A quick once-over in the bathroom and she was almost ready for company. Ceiling fans whirred and a good breeze blew off the water and through the shotgun hallway.

The phone rang. "Hello, Abbey, this is Adam."

"Hi, Adam. What are you up to this afternoon?"

"We're at the airport in Jacksonville. It took all morning, but Ed was released around noon. I arranged flights last night so we're out of here around five o'clock."

"That's terrific, Adam. I hate that I won't be able to say goodbye to you two. Would you do me a favor?"

"Sure. Name it. We owe you more than a favor."

"You know that five dollars I gave you? Please buy Ed a beer when you get on that plane. He asked for one when I was getting him out of the river, and the opportunity just never arose."

183

Adam laughed. "You got it. And would you do one for me?"

"Glad to."

"Please send me a copy of the article when it comes out."

"Absolutely. I'll send you a stack of papers."

"And by the way, I called Terkoff before we left the hospital. He's having the paper release the story Monday or Tuesday to give us plenty of time to get out of town and get settled at home."

"That's great. I'll let you know what shakes out after that."

"Please do. I don't think this will be our last conversation."

"Nor do I. Have a safe flight. I have your numbers, Adam."

It was going on toward three o'clock by the time she hung up the phone. Tom had left a message, at ten o'clock that morning. He'd been delayed at his office but was leaving right then. If he did, in fact, leave at ten o'clock, he'd arrive any minute. There'd be plenty of daylight left for them to enjoy the afternoon. The toot-toot-toot of a horn sounded. Tom had adopted Boonks's method of announcing his arrival.

Yip! Watch Dog scrambled to his feet and the two of them dashed outside and intercepted Tom as he opened his door.

"You lost, Mister? This is a private club, members only."

"So I heard." Tom grinned as Watch Dog accosted him with wet kisses. "Sometimes you are too sassy for your own good, woman." He grinned as he unfolded from the car and reached out to pull her into a bear hug. "Doggone it, I missed you." He kissed her hard.

Several seconds later, she pushed back. "Oooooweeeeee. You must have. What will the neighbors say, Mr. Clark?"

"Who cares?" He pulled her back and pecked her on the forehead. "You, my dear, look fantastic." He held her at arm's length. "You have just enough color. Rowing every day suits you."

"Not every day, but weather and time permitting, I have been out there. Let me help you with your things."

"What's this 'time permitting' stuff? I thought you were on vacation."

"I am. But I picked up a new client down here, remember?"

"Yeah. We'll talk about that later." When they walked into the cottage, Tom sneezed, then sneezed again. "Wow. What's on the stove?"

"Vinegar, Old Bay, black pepper and a jalapeno. Sorry, it's potent. Put your things in the bedroom and come on back."

The water in the large pot bubbled to a gurgling boil. Abbey had iced the crabs overnight in a large cooler, then returned them to Sarge's white buckets for ease of carry. With a long-handled tong she grabbed and lifted a crab. Another one grabbed a dangling leg of the first crab with a claw and held on for dear life.

"Okay, you two, hang on, hang on, don't drop on the..." She swung the dangling duo toward the steaming pot and released the tong's grip, but the first had grabbed the tong. She banged the handle on the pot until the claw finally let go. "All right." Mesmerized, Watch Dog sat at her feet licking his chops. His head followed the tongs each time she dipped into the bucket and lifted to the pot.

Tom returned. "What's that about? Why is that one hanging on to the other one?"

"Misery loves company. I guess they don't want to boil alone."

Tom grimaced. "Guess not."

Abbey smiled. "No matter how much people love to eat crab and lobster, no one likes the part about dropping them into boiling water."

"Do they scream?" Tom draped an arm over her shoulders.

"Nope. They just hang on to each other like they know what's coming." She reached up and grabbed his head in both her hands and pulled him down for a kiss. "I'm glad you're here. I missed you. A lot."

"Good."

"Good that I missed you? You like me to be unhappy?"

"Sure." Tom headed to the refrigerator. "Means I'm making headway. Want a beer?"

"You're impossible."

"No, just determined." He picked up two bottles and inspected the labels. "Traffic getting out of Atlanta was a bear."

"I don't miss it for one second. I'll have a Killian's please, O Determined One."

Tom grinned and opened the beers. "You have been busy. Did you stay home all day to catch my supper?"

Abbey picked up her tongs and snapped them at his nose. "Nope. Today I went for a row, a swim, and to the grocery store." *Never mind the firing range.* "I had a business appointment yesterday, but I helped Sarge when he came in from hauling his traps. These are a gift from him. You didn't meet him last summer." She pulled a crab from the pot with the tongs.

"What are you doing?"

"Just checking the color of his shell. He's still green. I want him nice and orange. They need more time." The crab dropped back into the pot. "Sarge was away last year when you and I were playing cops and robbers."

"Oh. He's the one who helped you pull the man out of the river the other day, right?"

"Yes."

"I'd like to meet him. Can we have an early dinner? I'm starved."

She grabbed a fistful of scuppernongs from a bowl on the counter and handed them to him. "Eat these. Crabs have to cool after I take them off the stove anyway. Let's say dinner around six. We'll get you a snack, but start on those. They're great, very sweet."

He sucked the juice and sweet meat from the grape. "Ooh, these are good. I picked up several nice wines at Pearsons. Shall I refrigerate a white?"

"Hmm. Sounds good. It can chill while we go for a swim. The crabs will be cooked by the time we put on our suits and I can get them off the stove to cool while we're at the pool."

"Sounds like a plan, ma'am."

~

Two and one-half hours later, after they swam and retrieved Abbey's crab baskets from the dock, Tom poured two glasses of wine and handed one to her. "Here. You're on vacation. Now that's a refreshing pool. It's always cold."

"It comes from the aquifer so it never heats up in the summer."

"I really missed you, Abbey." Watch Dog's tail thumped on the wood floor. Tom stooped down and gave the dog a hug around the neck. "Yeah, you too, buddy."

"Tom, do you want to shower before we put on dry clothes?" Abbey's hair dripped on her shoulders and a wet towel sagged around her hips.

"Do we need to? The pool water doesn't smell chemically," Tom said.

"There's no chlorine."

"So, I'm clean," Tom said. He walked over to Abbey, looped a finger under her bathing suit strap and gently lifted it off her shoulder. "I have never been skinny-dipping in that pool before."

"There's a first time for everything, Mr. Clark, but I suggest we wait until dark. Maybe an after dinner dunk."

"Arggh." Tom squinted one eye shut.

Abbey burst out laughing. "Oh, no, the pirate returns to port. Remember when we were caught on the dock in the rain?"

"Remember?" Tom looked incredulous. "How could I forget—rainy day, beautiful woman running through the house dropping clothes on her way to the shower… Whew. Remember? Yes, I remember." He took a large gulp of wine. "Which reminds me. Follow." He beckoned with a crooked finger. "I have something to show you."

Abbey said, "You didn't tell me to pick up dessert."

"Oh, but come with me. I think it's in here."

In their bedroom, he dropped his towel and wet trunks and stood there wearing nothing but a smile. "Well?"

"Well what?" Abbey said with as much incredulity as she could muster.

"Well, how are you liking me so far?"

"You big goof." She stepped closer and backed him to the bed, then pushed so he flopped onto the mattress. He raised up on his elbows, grinned and watched as she dropped her towel and slowly peeled off her swimsuit.

"Arghh. Is this the part where you have your way with me, lady?"

"Shhhhhhhhhh." She moved closer and whispered, "You must be the invading pirate from the north I've heard so much about, the one who came down here to terrorize the women. I'm here to collect bounty what's owed me and my people." Abbey tapped his leg and he made room. She lay down beside him and lengthened out on her side and propped her head on her hand.

"Aye, but there's only one woman I'll be terrorizing."

"Well, go on then," Abbey said. "What are you waiting for? Terrorize me."

"Oy, shiver me timbers."

"Your timber isn't shiverin', mate."

～

With a platter of boiled crabs between them and the orange setting sun framed by the window, Tom poured the remainder of the bottle of wine into their glasses. He picked up a crab body and turned it over and over as if looking for the magic button to open it.

Abbey broke a body in half, then pressed the half shell with her fingers to crack it in half again. She gently worked out the lump of meat at the back flipper leg. Tom watched and looked about ready to drool. "You and Watch Dog."

"Would you please show me how to do that again?" He stared at the clump of white meat on its way to her mouth.

She slowly moved the succulent morsel to Tom instead. He took it with his teeth.

"Oh, man. Tom Jones doesn't have anything on us."

Abbey smiled. "Now watch. Each leg goes to a chamber in the body that is filled with meat." She broke the shell and worked through the mystery of extracting meat from the body of the blue crab.

"Damn, that's good," Tom said. "Tell me more about Vickie."

"Where to start. At first she came off as a flake, clueless and helpless. Not so much now. Maybe *that* Vickie wouldn't see how being married to the developer might be information I'd want, but I think there's more to it. She's using me for something, to get me on her side or maybe even to make me curious enough to check out her husband on my own. She's no dummy. She made sure I knew enough about him to piss me off.

"My guess is she's sort of a social climber. She had it all when she was young, then she lost her love and her parents; she grabbed Bart because she thought he was going to make it big and put her back on her pedestal. Along the way she figured out he was a los-er—maybe she even thinks he's up to something. In her own weird way, she has implied as much. My guess is she wants to look for something in Atlanta before everything comes crashing down in St. Marys."

"Do you think she's honest?"

"When she wants to be."

"Sounds crazy. So you think she's using you."

"Sort of."

"Doesn't that bother you?"

"No, it makes me curious. I think I know why she called me."

"Why?"

"Our first lunch, she brought up all of these newspaper arti-cles she had read about the drug bust you and I were involved in. Then she told me I was much more than a real estate agent." Ab-bey shrugged. "Like I said, she might be suspicious of Bart and she doesn't want to be left holding the bag, she wants to go after him but doesn't know how. Enter real estate agent who now has a history of going after bad guys and winning. She thinks she needs me on her team, and she might be right."

Tom picked an orange flake off his place mat and flicked it onto the pile of shells in the middle of the table. "Plausible. I had an intern at the firm do some research on Bart." Their eyes met and Tom wasn't smiling. He told her what he had learned.

"So he really is a womanizer," Abbey said. She told Tom about Bart and the woman she had seen him with in the sales trailer and at Kings Bluff. "He's not just having a fling; this is what he does. Poor Vickie. But I still can't figure out why she wanted me to find out that he was a developer on my own. She said he dabbled in real estate."

"I'm sure she has her reason, Abbey. I think you're on to something here and I want you to be careful. People like Bart and Vickie don't just all of a sudden do things, they usually have histories of doing things or, if not histories, they come together and realize they have the same goals. I'm not saying they're in cahoots. Each might have an agenda. But in the back of your mind, hold on to the idea that the two of them might be scammers."

"Yeah. I know. Vickie is heavily involved in that development financially, and it's obvious it's in trouble. She also has a house in Orlando. So that's two houses plus the development, but she told me the Orlando home is on the market. I bet they have to sell it. That's a lot of real estate to hold."

"I'd watch it with her. You never know what people are really after." They cleared the table.

"Would you mind terribly if I played golf tomorrow? A friend from law school invited me over to St. Simons to play a round."

"That's great, Tom. Do it. This is your vacation too."

"Okay, good. And if it's okay with you, I might try to track down that agent who my intern said had supposedly disappeared."

"Be my guest," Abbey said. "That's a little beyond my job description."

"The other night you mentioned you visited the guy you rescued. How's he doing?"

"Great. His brother took him back to Philadelphia this afternoon. You know, I acted on a crazy idea I had about rental cars and I got lucky." She told Tom about the B&B and finding Doc's brother.

"You have good instincts, Abbey, and you're good at cobbling together information. Run with it. I don't know what I would have done without you and your ideas last year. You see things differently, and it's good." He patted her hand. "What is it with you and developers?"

"I have wondered the same thing."

Tom folded newspapers filled with empty crab shells into a roll. "What shall I do with these?"

"Put them back in the bucket and dump them off the end of the dock. They'd stink up the trash, and something in the water might want to nibble on them." They dumped the shells off the end of the dock. "It's getting dark," Abbey said. She made a face and scrunched up her shoulders. "I'm kind of hot and sticky after picking crabs. A refreshing dip before we call it a day would be nice."

"Of the skinny variety?"

"First time for everything," Abbey said.

"Certainly," Tom grinned.

THIRTY-SEVEN

Early Sunday morning after a good long jog to and from Taylor's Point, Tom, Abbey and Watch Dog settled on the porch for a light breakfast. "You are off to St. Simons for golf this morning, right?" Abbey set down two mugs of coffee and pecked Tom on the cheek.

"Yep. What are you up to? I hate to leave you so soon. I feel like I just got here."

"You did. Don't worry about it. I want you to see your friends, and hopefully we'll have time to do some things together later in the week. Somehow I'll manage without you today," she teased. The phone rang. She dashed to get it and returned several minutes later.

"Don't worry about little old me. That was Snag. He wanted to take *us* fishing, but I told him you had other plans so I'm going." Tom looked disappointed. "Ah, so sorry. Maybe he'll ask us again." She ruffled his hair.

"That makes me feel better anyway," he said.

"Are you playing tomorrow too?"

Tom scowled. "Yes, but we'll do something fun the day after, I promise. I didn't come down here just to play golf. Do you want me to pick up anything for dinner on my way home this afternoon?"

"I don't think so. I hope I'll have some fish and there's salad stuff we need to eat, and I'll make a pot of grits. Sometime this week we can go for a boat ride in the Okefenokee Swamp or have lunch in

St. Augustine or Fernandina and poke around. I'll come up with something fun."

"I'd like anything you want to do. This is your part of the world, so show me what you think I need to see. Let's make this a real vacation but no Weeki Wachee mermaids or anything like that."

"What do you know about Weeki Wachee's mermaids?"

"My family went to Florida once when I was a kid. Once was enough."

"I'll take that off the list then," she said sarcastically, then glanced at her watch. "Don't you have an early tee time?"

"Yep. I'll take a steam and shower over there before we play. Better run. See you this afternoon." He hugged her and left her on the porch.

Mid-afternoon, Tom thanked his friend for the golf game and walked to his car, thinking how nice it was to be able to spend time with a friend and know he wouldn't get the third degree when he got back to the cottage. Abbey was easy like that. She wanted him to enjoy time with his friends, and she wanted to enjoy time with hers. His wife had been totally different, demanded to know who he was with, where they were going, and what they were doing, an insistent need-to-know about almost everything he did.

She had played him like a poker hand; he'd been blind to her true intent. Now, of course, it all made sense. How else could she entertain two lovers unless she knew where Tom was every minute of the day? Even now, one year after her death, he hated to think about the fact that her murder was her own doing and there was nothing he could have done to stop it. She had been checkmated by a lover he knew nothing about until it was too late. Sadly, he doubted he would ever forgive her.

Before his appointment, there was enough time to make a few wrong turns, which he did, but things started to look vaguely familiar when he passed the small airport on his right. Several minutes later he arrived at the St. Simons Island pier, found a parking place, and went up to the deck at Brogan's and surveyed the crowd. A pretty young woman wearing a green Masters visor sat at a high table sipping an iced tea. "Sam," Tom said with a question as he walked up to her.

She made eye contact and smiled. "Tom?"

"Yes." Tom sat on the stool opposite her. "Sam. Short for Samantha, I suppose. Were you supposed to be a boy after a string of sisters?"

Sam nodded. "How'd you guess? My poor daddy wanted a boy so bad he whispered into my mother's belly every night, 'Good boy, Sam, good boy.'"

Tom chuckled. "Did that make you a tomboy?"

"I don't know if that's what did it, but it worked. I throw a mean spiral, I still have the shotgun Daddy gave me when I turned twelve, and I can filet a redfish with the best of them." Sam took a long look at him. "But you didn't get my friend to set this up so you could ask me about my name."

Tom ordered iced tea. "No, I didn't. As your friend probably told you, I practice law in Atlanta and date a real estate agent there. Her name is Abbey Bunn and she was contacted by a woman from St. Marys who wants to look at property up there."

Sam nodded. "Okay, I get it. My friend here didn't tell me much, but she said I needed to talk to you because you were looking into Bart Croek. Am I to assume Bart has something to do with the woman who contacted Abbey?"

"Good assumption," Tom said. "I'm not officially investigating him. Let's just say I am interested in Bart because if Abbey is working with his wife, she could very easily come in contact with him at some point. I want to make sure he's not a Ted Bundy kind of a guy."

Sam clasped her fists together, leaned her elbows on the table and rested her chin on her knuckles. "I'm going to level with you because I don't want to waste your time. I want you to do whatever it takes to take that guy down. At first, I thought Bart was cute. He was charming, good-looking, and rich, or so it seemed. My friend Joy, another agent, asked me to go with her to show property at Crooked Creek, because she was afraid of Bart. He apparently put the moves on her. I thought she was being a wimp so I agreed to go with her. I have to admit he was very friendly, too friendly, but he didn't bother me. I thought he was just a flirt.

"The development was beautiful, had loads of potential, so I started showing out there. Bart insisted on being present when lots were shown, so I figured he just wanted to make sure agents told prospects all the great things his development had to offer. At the time, I thought he was single. He never wore a ring and he certainly didn't act married. When I took my first offer to his office, he hugged me. I thought that was a little odd but, like I said, he was a friendly guy.

"After we closed on that first lot, he sent a present to my office. I returned it to the jeweler whose name was on the box, and they gave me the third degree, said the bracelet had been stolen from their display. When I told them it had been a gift, they wanted to know from whom. God, if I'd only known then what I know now, I would have told them immediately. But I was sure there was some mistake and I didn't want to cause trouble." Sam took a deep breath and ran her finger down the moisture on her glass.

Tom could tell she was deciding how much to tell him, so he let her think.

"I'll spare you the gory details, but suffice it to say that I let things get out of hand. Bart is very persuasive, and he's also very, umm, he's very..." A tear rolled down her cheek.

"Are you okay, Sam?" She nodded and wiped her cheek with her fist.

"Abbey's lucky she has you to look out for her."

Tom didn't know what to think, but it reminded him of the first time he and Abbey had their first serious talk about her ex. "Did he get rough with you?"

Sam blew out a little *huh* and shook her head. "He played mind games, that sort of thing. At first, I have to admit, he turned me on. He teased me and I caved. I had never met anyone like that before. I let him seduce me. Once we'd been together a few times, he laid a guilt trip on me like you wouldn't believe, said I knew exactly what I was getting into and he knew how much I wanted him. This went on for a while. We'd go to that old house his partner uses. It has a couple of bedrooms." Sam shook her head. "God, what a slut. I hated myself like you wouldn't believe but he worked this guilt thing on me."

Tom let her talk. "He got rougher and rougher as time went on, and eventually he started to scare me so I made up excuses. There was always an appointment or I had to get back to the office for floor duty or to meet a client. I'd say something. Anything not to have to be with him. This went on for a while, and I thought he got the hint. Then out of the blue he said he wanted to show me where the new marina was going in. We were in his car and there was no one else around."

Sam's eyes told Tom how much she hurt. "I wore a skirt that day. He forced himself on me." She looked away. "I was sobbing and screaming and pounding him with my fists. When he was finished, he started to cry. He blubbered like a fool and told me he needed me desperately because his wife had cut him off." She looked back at Tom. "That poor excuse for a human being raped me, Tom, and then tried to blame it on the fact that his wife had cut him off. I was petrified. I was literally scared he would do something else to me in the state he was in. He acted crazy, like he was on drugs or something." She took a long swig of her tea.

"You're the first person I ever told all of that. Dammit, I didn't even know he was married. I knew I had to get away from him."

"Did you keep showing at Crooked Creek?"

"No. Are you kidding me? Not after that. But I had several closings scheduled. I went to them only because his sister always represented him at closings. We were in attorneys' offices, so I knew he couldn't come in and pull anything. He still sent presents, expensive presents but I sent them all back to his office. I should have returned them to the jewelry stores and told them I thought they had been stolen, but I didn't. I just wanted to be done with him."

"Did you report this to the police?"

"No. He would have sworn the sex was consensual, and I knew how convincing he could be. No, I couldn't have stood the publicity though I wanted to hurt him so badly. Some days I wish I had."

"You didn't see him anymore?"

Sam bit her lip. "I wish. Several weeks after my last closing, I was at my apartment when the doorbell rang. I looked through the peephole, but no one was there so I opened the door a crack. There was a huge bouquet of red roses there in a vase. I leaned over to pick them up and he swooped out of nowhere and backed me into my apartment. I was terrified. The first chance I got, I jammed my knee into his crotch, slammed the vase of roses into his face, and was out the door before he knew what hit him. I had just been for a jog so I took off and ran as fast as I could to a guy friend's house, an attorney. He suggested I take out a restraining order so I did."

"Bart sounds dangerous, Sam. You did the right thing. Did you move after that?"

"You bet. I don't want that nutcase knowing anything about me. I took enough psych courses in college to know a sicko when I see one. He steals, he lies, and he doesn't care about anybody's feelings. The guy has no conscience. That jerk's a walking, talking sociopath. I think he could flip any minute and really hurt someone. You have every reason to be protective of your friend."

THIRTY-EIGHT

Fishing that morning had gone well. When they returned mid-day, Snag fileted trout, drum and flounder, and gave half to Abbey, which was way more than she and Tom could eat in a week, so she wrapped several choice filets in paper and drove to her cousin's house an hour away in Wayside. Having not caught up since their grandmother's death the previous year, they had a good long chat while they strolled around the cousin's farm and fed carrots to her horses. The afternoon slipped away. Eager to hear about Tom's game, Abbey drove back to Kings Bluff. Her fingertips drummed the steering wheel until she turned onto Kings Bluff Road, two lanes that ran between pine plantations and marsh flats.

As always, she pictured the marsh tacky horses that grazed on the coarse grasses of the sand flats when she was a child, flats now inhabited only by fiddler crabs and pocked with their dug-out homes. A small figure in a red plaid shirt ambled toward her on the edge of the road. Hongry had been a fixture at the Bluff as long as she could remember, and well before, according to Boonks. She pulled over on the side of the road and rolled down her window.

"Hi, Hongry. You want a ride home?"

"Yessum. I'd 'preciate it."

Abbey whipped a U-turn on the deserted road and pulled beside him. Aromas of cherry pipe tobacco and cedar oil entered the

198

Jeep with the little man, whose rich mahogany-colored skin was as wrinkled as a raisin. Change jingled in his pocket. Hongry only accepted silver coins because he knew paper was worthless. Smart for an uneducated woodsman. It sounded as though his day had been profitable.

"I hope your new septic system is working okay, Hongry. Have you gotten used to it yet?"

"Oh, yessum. I likes it just fine. Specially in the winter time." He chuckled. "You tell yo momma how much I likes it fo' me."

"I will, Hongry. She was very happy to put that in for you." The previous year, after Grandmother Taylor passed away and left Boonks and her two brothers an ample sum of money, Abbey's mother had a septic system installed behind Hongry's home to replace his ancient outhouse.

Abbey pulled in to the next dirt road and stopped in front of a ramshackle little house, which looked to be pieced together with assorted trash dump materials much like a patchwork quilt. Hongry's garden overflowed with bright yellow sunflowers and lush green vegetation. "My goodness, Hongry, you really have a green thumb, don't you?"

"Iz jus chicken shit."

"What?" Abbey glanced at him.

"It's not me does it. I told Mr. Tom. Iz chicken shit whut makes stuff grow."

"You talked to Tom?"

"Yessum. Long time."

Abbey grinned. *Well, good, Tom and Hongry. Gotta be a story there.* "Chicken shit fertilizer, eh. I'll remember that. Thanks for the tip." Hongry nodded vigorously and smiled. "You take care of yourself, okay?" *Wonder when he saw Tom?*

The little man nodded and hopped out. "Thank you." He walked to his garden and picked up the hoe leaning against the fence.

Chicken shit. What a character.

Tom was on the screened porch at the cottage enjoying a beer and a paperback. "Hi." She pecked him on the cheek and grabbed a rocker. "What are you reading?"

"A friend suggested my education would not be complete until I read *To Kill a Mockingbird*." He gave her a crooked smile. "She could be you, you know. Scout. There's a picture of you in that fat photograph album of yours you showed me one time in Atlanta. When I'm reading this, I picture that little barefoot girl in the photograph."

"Funny, a guy friend in high school told me the same thing. I want to hear about your game."

"Come with me," Tom said as he laid down his book and stood. "Why don't I put something together for dinner while I tell you a little about my day? I didn't spend it all on the golf course." They went into the kitchen.

Abbey sat on a stool. "Tom, guess who I gave a ride home just now."

"Who?"

"Hongry, and he said he talked to you. Did you two get together to reminisce about old times or something?" Old times began the previous summer, when Hongry was key in saving Abbey and Tom from the gun-wielding arsonist.

Tom took a bottle of wine from the fridge and opened it. "On my way back from St. Simons, I stopped by Hongry's house and pulled him out of his garden. I told him I wanted to make sure he had returned that wounded eagle to the wild. Poor guy thought I was fussing at him until I told him I was only kidding, that I really did want to know how the eagle was doing. He laughed and then told me the whole story about how he had been hiding behind a tree and saw one of the drug dealers shoot the eagle and then go back to fishing with his buddy.

"Hongry said he watched the eagle fall to the ground, so he

tossed a marshmallow on the bank near the two men, and this big old alligator he calls No Mo—and that's another story altogether—came up out of the pond to get his treat and nearly scared those two dealers to death." Tom laughed.

"I think you have a loyal little friend there, Tom."

Tom pulled a plate from the fridge covered with waxed paper and placed it on the counter. Abbey watched as he turned on the gas burner and then poured peanut oil into a cast iron skillet. "What's this, Tom?"

"Crab cakes."

She lifted a corner of the wax paper. "Did you pick out the rest of the crabs in the fridge?"

"Sort of."

"How do you sort of pick out enough crabs to make these huge, gorgeous crab cakes?"

"I could lie."

"Or..."

"Or I could tell you that Hongry and I spent an hour or two this afternoon together and he gave me a lesson. Mostly I watched, but I kind of got the hang of it after a while. Those little hands of his are fast!"

"Did you actually make the crab cakes?"

"Hongry supervised."

Abbey put her arms around Tom from behind and gave him a squeeze. "I wish I had been a fly on the wall so I could have watched. That explains all the change in his pocket. I am very proud of you, Thomas Clark. Those are the most beautiful crab cakes I have ever seen. How can I help?"

"Hongry brought us yellow squash and zucchini from his garden. See what you can do with them."

Vegetables compliments of chicken shit. Abbey washed and sliced and tossed the squash and Vidalia onion in a bit of olive oil then put them in the oven to roast.

"Hongry told me about how he fertilizes his vegetables, but he didn't breathe a word about the crabs. How did you pay him?"

"Quarters, of course," Tom said. "I took a cue from your grandmother."

"Thanks. I bet you made his day."

~

It was a typical August night, hot and still and filled with chirps, buzzing, and creature croaks. Heat lightning flickered silently in the deep purple sky. Abbey and Tom clung to a black rubber inner tube retired from some tractor and kicked slowly around the pool. "When I retraced my rescue row the other day, I half expected to hear that fishing boat bearing down on me. It kind of freaked me out."

Tom flicked water into her face. She stuck her tongue out at him. "I'm trying to be serious, Tom. One time Mother told me it wouldn't hurt to appear a little helpless now and then. She says I'm too independent. What I really think is she's afraid I'll run you off if I act strong all the time." Tom disappeared below the surface. Abbey squealed as she was pulled off the inner tube and under water. Large bubbles burped to the surface followed by their two heads.

"Interesting, Tom. Exactly what was that?"

Grinning, he thought for several seconds. "It was a high school science experiment."

"And you were trying to prove what exactly?" Her face said "I don't believe you" and his said "it was pretty funny." "Unh-hunh. And where and with whom did you work on this so-called experiment?" Abbey treaded water and waited.

He looked ultra-serious. "Well, it was all guys and it was the end of the school year. We dissected our guinea pigs and had a few minutes before the bell rang, so we started talking about what we were doing that summer and we sort of came up with this idea to embarrass girls. I forgot about it until now and figured I'd give it a try. We called it the... unh, the blowfish."

"You're one sick puppy." She chuckled and swam to the side. "I'm getting cold. Why don't we get decent and go in for a nightcap to send us off to la-la-land."

They went back to the house and changed and Tom uncorked a half-full bottle of Chardonnay. "I'm glad you figured out who Doc was. They'll find out who did this to him and things will come together pretty quickly. I told you you're good at this."

"Let's sit on the porch to finish our wine," she said. "It's too pretty to be inside."

Watch settled between their chairs. Tom said, "Remember I told you I wanted to see if I could find the agent who took out the restraining order on Bart?"

"Yes. Did you, Sherlock?"

"I met her right after my golf game." He reminded her of how Fast Eddy had researched Bart Croek for him earlier that week. "Anyway, Eddy's girlfriend is from St. Simons. I called her yesterday and she put me in touch with Samantha, the woman who took out the order." Tom filled her in on what he had learned from Samantha about Bart.

"That jerk. Vickie has a bruise on her face. I'm sure he knocks her around. No wonder she wants a place in Atlanta. I'd bet good money if you tried to trace the money the buyers of those lots put down, you'd have a hard time finding it. I guarantee you it's not in any trust account."

"If you want me to, I'll make some calls."

"Be my guest." Abbey's cheeks burned. "Damn him. Now tell me about your game today."

Tom regaled her with his good shots, bemoaned his bad, and shared several off-color jokes he'd heard. The man he played with was someone he'd met in law school and who was now married to his high school sweetheart, with three sons and a baby on the way. "He's hoping for a girl. I'll never catch up with him." Tom picked up the fingers of Abbey's left hand.

"I want kids, Abbey. And I want them with you. Promise me you'll think about it. We're not getting any younger."

She squeezed his hand. "I know. We'll talk about it soon. I promise." One Chuck-will's-widow on the edge of the woods seemed to plead for his lost love. Abbey knew it wasn't fair to keep putting Tom off, but it had only been a year since the horrible turn of events when she thought she had lost him for good, and to a damn bullet, of all things. It wasn't until last Thanksgiving that she knew he was out of the woods. She told herself that by this Thanksgiving, three months from now, she would tell him yes or no. "I think those birds know when it's going to rain."

"You're great at changing the subject," Tom said. They were quiet for several minutes.

"Tell me more about this new prospect of yours—Vickie."

"She's kind of a head case, but if I was married to Bart I would be too. It seems to me she needs a friend, and she needs someone to help her sort out what that lunatic of hers is up to."

The phone rang. Abbey looked at her watch. "It's ten o'clock. No one would call this late unless it's Mother checking in on us."

"Tell her to come down. I haven't had her chocolate sheet cake in ages."

Yes, and you two could strong-arm me to the altar. "I hope it's not Vickie. Come save me if I don't come right back." Abbey hurried to beat the machine.

THIRTY-NINE

Abbey picked up the phone and said hello.

"Abbey, I'm so glad you're still up," Vickie said.

Abbey rolled her eyes. *Good grief. She's drunk.* "Yes, Vickie, I'm still up. What's going on?" Why did people drink when they're on the phone? Did they think you couldn't hear them? It sounded like she was slurping ice cream from a spoon.

"Bart's out. Went to dinner, I guess."

Abbey pictured Vickie's loose red curls all in her face, her make-up a little smudged, lipstick around the rim of her wineglass and none on her lips. She grabbed the legal pad and pencil she'd left by the phone and stretched the receiver over to the dining room table and sat. She hoped Tom would remember to come save her.

Tom walked into the kitchen. She held up her glass and mouthed "Vickie." Tom nodded, filled their glasses with the last bit of wine and sat beside her. Abbey tilted the phone toward him so he could hear.

"Does he do that often, go to dinner without telling you or including you?"

"Sometimes," Vickie said. "No, yeah, pretty often. Cutty doesn't like to cook so the two of them go out a lot."

"Cutty drives a Range Rover, right? He's sort of a dark Crocodile Dundee type, isn't he?"

Vickie responded with a not-so-dainty slurp. "Ohhh. Yeah. I told you he was cute, didn't I." Without waiting, she said, "I would have given him a run for his money—if I hadn' met Bart first of course." Abbey waited. "I shouldn't tell you this, Abbey, but he made another play for me."

Tom raised his eyebrows. Abbey thought, here we go again, so she played along. This could get interesting. "Really. Did you tell Bart?"

Vickie ignored her and jabbered on. "Today I asked Bart if we could have lunch tomorrow so we could talk." She sniffed. "He blew me off, Abbey, said he had an appointment. So I came right out and asked him what was going on with the development." Another sniff. "Do you know what he had the nerve to say to me? He told me to stay out of it. I helped him get started with this place. Heck, I have time and money in that damned development and he treats me like a nobody."

Abbey jumped in. "Vickie, this is exactly why you need a lawyer. Have you called any of the names I gave you?"

"Does he think I can't see what's going on out there? The bloody nerve of him, Abbey. It makes me so angry."

Abbey scribbled two stick figures on her pad. Vickie blew her nose, and wine gurgled from a bottle. *Oh, boy.* As she drew, one figure developed loopy electrified hair on its round head, then a turned-down mouth and great big eyes. The chest sported enormous melon boobs and a little cartoon heart. A cloud floated near the booby one's mouth. Abbey wrote *Bart's a boob gosh darn it.* The second figure had a peanut-sized penis and a donkey's head with huge, furry ears. The cloud by his mouth said *Hee Haw, Screw Ya.* Tom pointed at the figure and gave her a thumb-to-finger okay sign. "So, what did you say to him?"

"His damned partner came over right in the middle of our discussion. I don't know what that jerk Bart's up to, but I don't like it." *Jerk? Is that the best you can do? How about rapist?* Abbey waited.

Vickie was cranked. "We need to talk. Something's definitely going on here."

Abbey finished off her figures with appropriate footwear. "I was thinking. How long has this Cutty fellow been in the picture?"

"Gosh. I don't know, but I know how I can find out." The phone clunked on a hard surface. Abbey shrugged at Tom. Moments later, another phone picked up. "I'm at Bart's desk. I have his calendar here. Let me see. Here it is. Febrerry sixteenth last year. Calendar says 'meet Cutty, partner' followed by two little bitty question marks. Oh, wait—"

Abbey listened but there was no sound. "Vickie?"

"Oh, hi, honey," Vickie no longer spoke into the receiver. This time Tom shrugged. "I'll be there innaminute. I'm on the phone, Baht." Vickie then said into the mouthpiece, as though having a conversation, "No, I don't think I have anything planned for tomorrow. Same place? Noonish work? Sounds *gooood*."

Abbey pictured Bart swaggering into the room. "Hang up, Vickie." She didn't, so Abbey listened.

"What are you doing in my desk?" Bart said in a loud voice. Tom mouthed uh-oh. "And you're drunk. Dammit, Vickie, is that my calendar? Why the hell are you messing around in my desk?"

Not so clearly, Abbey heard Vickie but it was muffled as though she had the phone against her body. Then, "Okay, hold your horses, Baht. For cryin' out loud. The one in the kitchen is off the hook. I'll hang this up and go in there."

Several seconds later, Vickie picked up. "Okay, you still there?"

"Yes. You had better go."

"Guess so," Vickie whispered. "Can you do lunch tomorrow, usual place?"

"Sure. Noon."

In a slurred whisper, Vickie said, "Great. I'm so glad you're my new bes' friend. I really need your help. See you tomorrow." She hiccupped, then hung up.

Abbey and Tom finished their wine and called it a day. At two o'clock in the morning, she sat straight up in bed and shouted, "No!" as the big, powerful boat bore down on her in her shell.

Tom stirred. "Abbey, what's wrong?"

"Nothing. Just a dream. Go back to sleep." She patted his hand, and it turned over and held onto her fingers loosely. She closed her eyes, and the monkey scrambled her thoughts into senseless dreams.

FORTY

Monday morning after Tom left for golf, Abbey straightened up the house, then watered the azaleas surrounding the cottage. New bright green growth had sprouted on branches that had been pruned in March after their early spring flowering. When the neighbor's children came to take Watch to their doggie daycare, she headed to the firing range and took her time running through a box of shells. Pleased with her accuracy, she cleaned her pistol right there at the range and headed to St. Marys.

A little early to meet Vickie, she decided to stretch her legs. St. Marys' street presence had not been grossly altered over the years by overly zealous renovators or clever architects. Structures were old and charming and well maintained, for the most part. After Atlanta, where houses were torn down left-right-and-center to make room for the new and grand, this was a refreshing change. Abbey walked and aired her thoughts.

Some people vacationed far from home and had guides lead them around from one attraction to the next, while others chose unstructured adventures that presented challenges far different from those in their daily lives. Abbey felt she was an offshoot of the latter persuasion, though her adventures of late presented themselves in such a way that she either had to get involved or had to turn her back on them completely. Rod Serling and "The Twilight

Zone" crossed her mind; she hummed the theme song and played a scenario in her head where she stepped through an invisible portal in the old shower house at Kings Bluff and entered an atmosphere littered with other peoples' problems, problems she felt an irresistible urge to fix. *Spooky.*

She circled back to her car and hopped in. The map of Crooked Creek was on her passenger seat. The land on the far side of the development belonged to Weyerhaeuser, the big paper company that raised pine trees for pulp wood. Curious, she drove, following the map into the interior of the property, where the marina was supposed to be built. Trees and brush had been cleared and piled on the edge of a large swath of land where a huge footprint was marked by orange plastic surveyor's tape attached to short wooden stakes.

Abbey parked and walked to the edge of the creek. Cumberland Island's lush bump in the ocean looked close enough to row to with no problem. There were no permits or other signage posted on trees to indicate work in progress. She wondered about the status of the marina permit. Cutty's temporary housing was close by and she wanted another look. The last time she had tried, the security guard appeared and forced her to make a hasty retreat.

Everything was eerily quiet. There was no one and nothing about, not a deer, an armadillo, or a wild turkey. Following the road along the creek, she arrived at Cutty's house, where a golf cart was parked in the carport. She lowered her passenger side window and slowed. A black labrador retriever lay on the concrete between the golf cart and a metal support column where the dog's leash was tied. The dog looked up and seemed to consider standing.

"Shushhhh," Abbey whispered. "Good boy. Don't bark." A large silver bag just like Vickie's occupied most of the passenger seat. She kept driving. *What's Vickie's purse doing there? Interesting.* She departed and drove by the sales trailer on her way to town. The white Range Rover, Ashley's red Mercedes, and a golf cart were in the lot behind the trailer. It was time for lunch.

FORTY-ONE

he table on the rail with the unobstructed view of the waterfront might as well have a sign on it: Reserved for Vickie and Abbey. Vickie's erect posture had wilted to a slump, and her red coif looked like it had been through a wind tunnel. The normal purse prop was absent—but it, or one just like it, was on the seat of a golf cart at Cutty's house. Occupying its place in a chair of its own was a red, rectangular patent leather wallet.

Abbey decided to goose her lunch mate's apparent malaise. "Hey. What's going on?" Vickie's head drifted upward to reveal glassy, bloodshot eyes that looked like they had foregone sleep for an extended crying jag. "Uh-oh. What happened, Vickie." *Try the truth.*

Large glasses of iced tea and pink lemonade appeared. "I'll come back for your orders in a minute," the waitress said. Vickie grabbed her arm.

"I need a big-girl drink today—martini, dry, extra olives. Please." It sounded like she had ordered one or two of those in her life. She closed her eyes and massaged her temples with both hands.

"Sure, hon." The waitress cut concerned eyes to Abbey's and raised both palms in an "I don't know what's going on" gesture as she walked to another table of diners.

After the head massage, Vickie's hair looked like a 1960s tease job that never received the requisite bouffant smooth-over. Abbey expected the usual finger fluff but it never came. Moisture, either tears or perspiration, collected under the reddened eyes. "I'm so angry I could scream." Her lip quivered; crossed arms jammed into her midriff and bolstered her cantaloupe breasts over the top of her white tank top to the point of spillover. "Or rip someone's head off. Or another vital part, if you catch my drift."

"Ouch. Did you hear something you didn't want to hear at your office?"

Vickie screwed up her mouth. "Well, that too. There are a lot of things. Mainly personal." She grabbed her lemonade and sipped. Her brow wrinkled. Maybe she'd been thinking about that martini and the sugary sweet lemon surprised her, or maybe she was trying to decide what or how much to share. Abbey waited. She didn't want to disturb whatever was going on in Vickie's head.

"Oh, I don't know. For starters, my daughter has overstayed her welcome. Jeez, she's been here since Thursday. What's that saying about fish and company? Believe me, it's true." Vickie shook her head. "And Bart and I had a little dust-up this morning." Exasperated, air blew between her lips from puffed cheeks.

Abbey did a quick information check: It had been obvious at their first lunch meeting that there was tension between mother and daughter, when Vickie reacted oddly to Bic's photograph. Vickie and Bart argued that morning. Daddy's little girl is getting on Momma's nerves, so that could have fueled an argument, especially if Bart was playing favorites. Abbey glanced at Vickie's bulging wallet. Maybe Bic had her mother's purse and that's why it was sitting on the seat of the golf cart at Cutty's.

"I bet it's kind of tough when Bic shows up—two grown women in the same house. When I went home from college, I used to borrow my mother's things all the time. My parents had a lot of social engagements so Momma had great clothes, and though I was much bigger than she, somehow I squeezed into those beautiful dresses of hers."

Vickie rolled her eyes. "She never asks, she just takes." She pushed her lemonade aside and looked for the waitress. "I have gotten used to that. But Bart. Damn. He must have seen some scribbles I had left by the kitchen phone. I doodle when I talk. Anyway, he said he knew all about you and where you came from, that private hunting club and all." Her cheeks flushed and she looked at her lap.

Abbey took a measured breath. "Yeah, I know. He showed up over there the other day."

Vickie's head snapped up. "I'm so sorry, Abbey. I know what you said, and I was careless."

"If he comes snooping around there again with his developer hat on, I'll dig up every piece of dirt on him I can find and I'll make his life miserable."

The waitress put a large martini in front of Vickie. "Atta girl. Touché," Vickie said with a nod, a wide, knowing smile, and a tip of her drink toward Abbey followed by a closed-eyes sip. "I'm so sorry."

"That's okay. I'm a big girl. I can take care of myself."

Vickie gave her a questioning look as though she wanted to know what Abbey meant by that, but was distracted when the waitress came back and took their lunch orders. Vickie looked on the verge of something akin to a breakdown, so Abbey assumed a calm, even tone she would have used talking to a skittish animal. "I told you I drove around Crooked Creek the other day. I guess it's handy for your staff to use those golf carts I saw at the sales trailer. Saves burning gas just to tour the property, doesn't it?"

Vickie's head jerked up; her lips almost a snarl. "There are two of them. Bic thinks they're toys at her disposal." She all but spat the words.

And there's one at Cutty's right now with your purse in it. She leaned over and plucked a long, coarse black hair off Vickie's shoulder with her thumb and forefinger, then flicked it away. Vickie scowled as she watched the hair float away on the breeze.

"She always brings her dog, then expects me to take care of him. That's one use I found for those damned carts. Sometimes I leash him and let him run along beside me. I'll be damned if I'm going to walk him. He's strong and he pulls like crazy. And he sheds like a darned oak tree. I have to vacuum twice a day when she's home." Vickie put a hand to her forehead and pinched above her nose.

"Have you and Bart talked about Cutty's advances again?" *As long as she's talking, why not ask.*

"No, but we need to this time."

"You mentioned something last night when you called."

Vickie signaled the waitress for another drink, then she stared at the waterfront. Her mouth opened, then closed. She said nothing but she squirmed. "This is embarrassing. I ran by the house for some reason. Oh, I remember. I had just gone shopping and wanted to drop my things off at the house. I grabbed a Coke from the kitchen and went out by the pool and just started piddling around, you know how you do. Sometimes you just get distracted. I gathered spent blooms and leaves and things to add to the mulch pile. It was a beautiful day and I was so happy. I was humming, not a care in the world." The waitress put the second martini and two salads on the table. Vickie took a long sip, then ate an olive.

"Bart wasn't home. I never get the house to myself anymore. Bic has been coming up from Jacksonville lately—a lot." Vickie licked her lips and tapped a nail on the table, thinking. "I love to poke around in the garden. Earlier that morning I had positioned a sprinkler so it would douse the vincas and the pentas in the flowerbeds. It's amazing how they perk up after a good long drink. I turned off the sprinkler and looked at the pool. It was like a tropical blue hole on a deserted island."

Abbey sipped her tea and jiggled her right leg. *Vickie loves details. Wonder where this one is going.* Vickie's eyes were fixed on something far out in the water.

"There's a six-foot privacy fence we had installed when we built the house. Hyacinth bean vines crawl all over it. I love their purple flowers and seed pods. They're so pretty. We assumed we'd have neighbors with children." She sipped her drink again. "Bart and I swim au naturel and that fence…" Vickie paused. "I like to be comfortable when I sunbathe."

"So anyway, I dipped a foot in the water. It was perfect. I stripped in the shower house, grabbed a towel and dove in. I was… you know, I was swimming to the shallow end when I heard tires crunch out front. Then a terrific force hit the water really loud. Water splashed everywhere. I spun around and saw something or someone swimming toward me under water. I knew it wasn't Bart because the person was very dark, but it was definitely a he, I could tell that much. I was terrified. I had no idea who…" She seemed to be collecting her thoughts. "I backed toward the wall and covered myself with… with my hands, as well as I could, standing there in my… well, you know, just standing there."

Softly she said, "I only realized it was Cutty when he burst to the surface, and I asked him what the hell he thought he was doing there and he laughed like it was the funniest thing he had ever done and he swam toward me. I didn't know what to do. I inched toward the steps in the corner, but my… my towel was at the deep end near the ladder. I'm a good swimmer so I thought about how to escape and moved closer to the steps. He grinned and continued toward me. I finally pushed off and went for it." Vickie suddenly looked into Abbey's eyes as though she wanted to make sure Abbey was paying attention.

"I swam as fast as I could and was halfway to the deep end before he realized I wasn't in front of him anymore, and then in one movement, he was out of the water trotting to the deep end. He was stark naked. Oh, my God, he's so…" Vickie seemed to forget where she was in her story. A moment passed. "He did one of those silly lifesaving rescue jumps and landed with his face out of the water. He looked funny, like a little kid messing around with his girlfriend." Vickie gasped, then emptied her drink.

"I mean his friends. Like I was one of his friends. Then he grabbed me into his arms and I... and I kicked him. I kicked him hard, you know where. I remembered you said that's what you would have done." She was breathing as though she had just run around the block. "That's when I... when I escaped and ran inside the house."

FORTY-TWO

Abbey sat there astonished and realized her mouth was open. She closed it. *Wow. Are you kidding me? Did he really do this or did you only want him to?* She had begun to think either Vickie had difficulty recalling and relating facts or she had a vivid imagination. But why would she make up this nonsense about Cutty? "You definitely need to tell Bart." *Would he even care?*

Vickie shook her head. "No. Bart would kill him, and I'd die if Bart got in trouble on account of me or went to jail."

And what would you do if you knew about Bart and his girlfriend? She thought what Tom would say. *Don't get involved. Change the subject. Business only.* "Huh. That's awful, Vickie, but I'm not the one you need to talk to about this. Let's keep things on track here. I have some ideas about places in Atlanta for you."

Vickie did her little wiggle and her eyebrows went up. "Okay, but before we get to that, this was kind of weird and I want to know what you think. Bart and Cutty were talking so loud the other day that I could almost hear them from my desk."

"About what?"

"Oh, the usual, I guess, but for some reason Cutty said he's sick and tired of looking out back at Bart's toy."

"What, Bart parked one of his cars at Cutty's or something?"

"No, silly. There's a creek behind his house. I think Bart parked his big old boat over there." Vickie looked perplexed. "I can't imagine why he would do that when he pays for one of those places over here at the marina. That's one of the main things he's excited about at the development. He'll have a place to keep that doggone boat."

"I didn't know Bart had a boat."

"Oh, sure, big fancy thing. Boys and their toys, right? It's usually at the marina, and I guess sometimes it's at Cutty's." Vickie waved a hand toward the marina. "They park them over there on trailers, I think. Did you know they don't leave boats in the water all the time?"

Abbey nodded and thought about Bart and his boat. Another big expensive boy-toy. Most men in this neck of the woods had a boat.

"I figured if it's a boat, it belongs in the water, right?" Vickie pressed her fingers into her eyebrows.

"Got a headache? Do you need an aspirin or something?"

"What I need is my purse." Vickie dropped her hand in her lap and managed a weak smile. "I honestly know nothing about boats."

"If they sit in salt water, they get barnacles and crud on the bottom. You have to take them out every now and then to clean them."

"Still doesn't seem right not to keep a boat in the water." Her nervous giggles were getting on Abbey's nerves. "But it's like his cars and houses. It's a statement. He told me he bought the darn thing because Crooked Creek is going to be a boating community and he wants to set an example and get the ball rolling. They plan to put in a marina with storage for tons of boats. That's supposed to be a huge selling point, you know, but you have to jump through hoops to get this permit thing, and once we get it, he will put his boat at the new marina. Set another example, be the first and all that." Vickie thought for several seconds. "Hey. Why don't you buy a lot and keep your boat there?"

"That wouldn't work for me."

Vickie glanced around at the sparsely populated deck, then licked her lips and leaned toward Abbey.

Here we go. More top secrets.

"I think they have done something bad, maybe really bad."

Abbey looked at her to see if she was teasing, but she looked serious. "Why do you say that?"

"Remember the lawyer who called and wanted to talk to me? I finally called him back this morning from home. It's about this deposition thing—like I have any idea what that's all about." Vickie tapped her nails on the table. "I asked him if whatever it was had anything to do with the development, and he said yes, and I asked him if it wouldn't be better if he talked to Bart, and he said no, he wanted to talk to me." She screwed up her mouth like she was going to cry. "Why on earth does he want to talk to me? I don't know anything about that darned development."

"Vickie, he wants to ask you some questions, that's all. My guess is it has nothing to do with you specifically and everything to do with Crooked Creek. When does he want to see you?"

"He said as soon as possible, but I don't know how I feel about all of this. Why doesn't he just talk to Bart? Bart knows everything. He's the developer."

"It's your land, right? So you and your money are involved. You need to do this no matter what Bart says, and you need to do it right away. It's very important. Do you understand?"

"Yes, I think so." Vickie stuck a finger in her mouth. The fake nail was gone and she had chewed and whittled down what was left of the natural nail until it looked like a broken bit of bone. "Remember I told you about some fight?"

"Yes."

"Well, Cutty said maybe nobody cared, so I figured he meant about the other guy. That part didn't make a whole lot of sense to me. But I've been thinking. They talk about this stupid fight all the time, and it almost sounds like Cutty expected it to be in the newspaper or something." She blew her nose on her napkin.

The foot of Abbey's crossed leg jiggled back and forth, something she did when she was bored. *Newspaper.* The article about Doc should be in the paper by tomorrow. She hoped it would scare the living daylights out of the scumbag who drove that boat.

"It's funny, though, Cutty sure doesn't look like the nervous type. That's what seemed so odd to me," Vickie said.

"When would he or they have gotten into a fight and who would they fight?"

"I don't know, Abbey. I suppose it could have been last Saturday."

"Why then?"

"Because Bart was an absolute bear Saturday night and I mean B-E-A-R, and Cutty showed up at the house early the next morning and started talking about this fight and they have both been on edge ever since. Bart left way before my eyes opened last Saturday, and I know he planned to be out with Cutty all day. You know I don't get up until—"

Abbey couldn't take it any longer. "What were they doing out so early on Saturday and why would that have anything to do with this fight, Vickie?"

"Well, I don't know, but they have been talking behind closed doors all week about this, and it's obviously bothering them. And it all started after they went fishing Saturday morning just like every other man down here."

"Do they go fishing often?"

Vickie rolled her eyes. "I can count on one hand how many times Bart has been out in that elephant of his. I think it's all for show, just like his cars." She held up two fingers. "First time was about six months ago, a shake-down cruise or whatever they called it." She waved a hand in the general direction of the marina and grabbed her middle finger. "Second time was last Saturday. Same day as the fight, I guess." Her features gave way to wrinkles as she appeared to think about that day. "I don't know, maybe they knocked each other around, but they're not bruised or anything."

Wheels turned. *Okay, so they went fishing Saturday morning like thousands of other men—but they went from here. Oh, good Lord. Right in front of my face. There are no coincidences.* "Fishermen love to brag. Did they catch anything?" Abbey crossed fingers under the table and barely breathed.

"I guess not, except a bad temper, because he sure had one when he got home. I would have preferred fish. But that's mean. If they caught anything they must have given it away, maybe to the other fellow who went with them."

Abbey sat straighter. Cap'n saw three men. "Yeah, probably. Who was the other fellow, a friend?"

Vickie touched her bottom lip with a fingernail and thought. "No, some investor. Seems Bart said he was from Pittsburgh or, no, Philadelphia. I always get those two mixed up, but I remember thinking when he said it that I had been to a horse show near...." Vickie continued to jabber but Abbey no longer listened. *Bart's big toy behind Cutty's house.*

Abbey looked for their server and waved to get her attention. Her hand shook. "Check please?" she mouthed to the waitress.

FORTY-THREE

She flattened the Crooked Creek map on her steering wheel and located Cutty's house. Sure enough, there was a dark dash mark in the creek behind the house. *Damn. Of course that house had a dock.* Without a thought as to what she would do if Cutty was at home, she headed to his house. She wanted to see that boat. Too bad she'd left her back-up at the cottage playing with kids.

Images swirled through her head. Bart and Cutty. The whole thing made sense now. Dark-skinned Cutty was in the stern, probably shirtless, showing off his bod. Bart drove. It was his boat. That figured. Control. He left Doc to die. *Immoral son-of-a-bitch. Damn.* She glanced in her rear view mirror as she sped along, hoping no cop was out to make his monthly quota.

She felt stupid. What better place to hide a boat than a dock obscured by a bunch of overgrown bushes. The creek looked small on the map so it was probably shallow and not navigable at low tide, so other boaters wouldn't go in there unless they had to or knew which tide would allow it. And Cutty's house wasn't exactly on the beaten path. The old road to get to it was neglected and overgrown.

From what Vickie had said, Bart had probably argued with Doc, and somehow Doc went overboard and then Bart ran over him. Intentionally. Otherwise, they would have gone back to pick him up. An investor would want nothing to do with Crooked Creek once he saw how little progress had been made on it after so many months.

Maybe Doc never even set foot on the property. Bart could have pitched the fishing trip to soften Doc up, see what he was willing to spend without ever intending to show the property. But something went wrong on the boat. Bart had proven himself to be volatile. Doc probably read Bart right off the bat, and the dirt bag took care of business his way. Didn't matter. The partners were getting ready to get nailed.

Questions pelted her brain as she drove onto the Crooked Creek property. Was Cutty in on the scam, or was he sucked into it by Bart and his lies? Had all of that stuff Vickie spouted been an intentional distraction to steer Abbey away from Bart and Cutty, and possibly from Vickie herself? And why had Vickie gone on and on about Abbey's involvement in the drug deal? Snow job, probably.

Abbey doubted Vickie saw her as a threat, more like an ally—but then why did Vickie give Bart an alibi after the restraining order if she was trying to take him down? None of it made sense. Then the way she related the bit about the pool incident sounded totally fishy, almost like Vickie made the whole thing up as she went. Why would she create a story like that unless she was trying to get back at Cutty for something? Or maybe she was angry with him.

Better yet, maybe she had a crush on him and he paid her no attention. He was much younger. But the silver purse. Bic borrowed things and it was her dog beside the golf cart at Cutty's house. Remembering the first time she had seen Cutty, she tried to imagine him doing the things Vickie had accused him of, but she couldn't. At the café he had looked like a cool, post-college young man having a drink with his boss. No, the image Vickie painted didn't fit. And why would Cutty risk fooling around with the boss's wife in the boss's own house? It made no sense at all. Vickie had said she wanted to jump his bones when Abbey said he was good-looking, and maybe she tried and was rebuffed. That made sense.

Approaching Cutty's house slowly from the front, she saw no vehicles there. Grass was flattened coming out of the carport as though it had been run over that morning. There were no lights on. Hopping out, she sprayed with Cutters before wading through the tall grass. A twig snapped to her left. She stopped. Rattlesnakes and copperheads were all in these woods. A yellow painted turtle turned his head her way, blinked, then continued to amble toward the woods. The carport where the golf cart had been parked was empty except for a large metal trash can with its lid ajar. Stink escaped. Abbey put her hand over her nose and mouth and held her breath until she got out of range.

What remained of a screened porch ran across the back of the house, its bottom flapping in the breeze. Animals had easy access to what used to be a great place to have a leisurely drink. Paint peeled from shutters. The real estate agent in her decided the repairs needed were minor, mere lipstick and rouge, not structural. It looked like a neat little river cottage.

An overgrown oyster shell path led through the bushes to a meandering creek, crooked indeed. Tied up alongside the dock was a large boat. *Hot damn. That's it.* Her ears tuned in to the slightest sound. She hurried. Fishing rods protruded from racks in the stern of the boat. Cap'n said he saw three men. *This is gonna flip Terkoff's sunglasses.*

Rot had claimed most of the wooden walkway, but there were enough solid boards to allow her to pick her way to the dock. Rods and reels worth hundreds of dollars had been left out in the elements. Her brothers would have had a fit that the fishermen hadn't rinsed them off. These guys had been in a hurry. Following her nose, she nudged the top off of a bait bucket with her toe. Dead bait shrimp floated in the murky water. She replaced the bait well's top, then walked around the boat searching, not certain what she expected to find. Sand gnats attacked exposed skin and flew up her nose and into her eyes. So much for Cutters.

Above the water line, there were no marks from the hit-and-run. Inside the boat, there were several empty beer cans, an empty cooler, and several padded seats. Imagining Doc, the guest, sitting on the cushiest spot, she lifted the lid of what doubled as a seat and storage box and saw a towel rolled around something. She picked up the bundle and opened it. Inside was a pair of size ten Topsiders, the typical shoe worn by boaters because of their white soles. Doc was barefooted when she found him in the river.

Shoes in hand, she jumped off the boat and jogged to her Jeep. If this didn't put the noose around Bart's neck, she didn't know what would.

FORTY-FOUR

Glancing at her rear view mirror, Abbey saw no one in hot pursuit. The Jeep slid to a stop beside the sheriff's car and she ran inside the police station. "I need to see Sheriff Terkoff." Her voice was way too loud and excited.

From behind the large desk the cop seated there said, "Please have a seat."

"I can't sit. This is urgent. Please tell him I'll be out front." She paced around the parking area, alternately looking at the front door of the station and her watch. "Come on, come on, come on." Terkoff finally sauntered out the door as he placed his hat on his head, then adjusted it. *Costume complete.* She walked toward him.

"Hi." His smile faded the minute she got close enough for him to see her face. "What's wrong?"

"I know who the hit-and-run driver is." She spoke so fast and with such body language that both of Terkoff's hands went palms up as if he hadn't a clue.

"I'm talking about Doc, the hit-and-run victim, you big dope. I know who was driving the boat."

Terkoff grinned. "Really? And what has your totally legal and no doubt very thorough investigation turned up now?"

Attitude again. She was steamed now. "These," she thrust the Topsiders toward him.

"And those are supposed to implicate someone... how?" Ter-

226

koff folded his arms across his chest and stepped into his tough-guy stance.

"They were on Bart Croek's boat. And if you want to play fairytale I bet you can slip them on Doc's feet and they'll fit like a glove." She shook the shoes in front of Terkoff's face again with one hand. "They're his. Just like the hat is his. I don't know what happened out there but somehow a shoeless Doc ended up in the river, lost his hat, and was hit by a boat driven by Bart Croek."

"Whoa. Whose boat?" He adjusted his glasses. Now he at least looked curious.

"The developer of Crooked Creek's boat. I found these on Bart Croek's Grady White, which is tied up to the dock behind the original owner's house, which is where Bart's partner lives currently, and I can explain it all but you need to go check out that boat now. I know Doc was on it the morning he was hit. Bart Croek's wife, Vickie, more or less confirmed that when we had lunch today. Why those idiots haven't gotten rid of the boat before now is anybody's guess but you had better hurry.

"I think Bart is jumpy and he's suspicious. He showed up at Kings Bluff on Wednesday with one of his bimbos. Since he's a developer, he might have been scouting out real estate to buy but I know he has asked his wife about me—and there's no telling what she has told him, but I bet he pumps her for information and assuming he has, he could be suspicious of me." She took a deep breath.

"Or of her. She told me a lawyer wants to talk to her, and I bet that has Bart losing sleep. Who knows, but we can't afford for him to put two and two together just yet. You have to get on this now, Terkoff. We have to stay ahead of them. Don't give them time to make a move."

"Yeah, but hold on. You're friends with his wife, right? Maybe she mentioned Kings Bluff and he was curious about it. I mean, he is a developer, Abbey, and aren't developers always looking for something else to develop?"

Abbey dropped clenched fists to her sides. "Come on, Terkoff, you're not listening. We don't have time for this. I just had lunch with his wife. She told me her husband and his partner took an investor fishing last Saturday. A doctor from Philadelphia. That has to be Dr. Ed Pressman. The hat was his and I bet these shoes are his. What more do you need? I found the damn boat that was involved in the hit-and-run, but I certainly can't impound it. Go get it before they move the damn thing!"

"Abbey, a lot of people around here go fishing and a lot of them wear Topsiders and probably more than one has left his shoes on a boat. That's no proof." Terkoff pushed his sunglasses up on his nose.

"Dammit, Terkoff, are you not listening? They wanted money from Doc. Get it?"

"It's difficult to prove intent, Abbey." Terkoff's arms crossed, his feet spread in a familiar stance, he grinned and worked his gum hard.

Abbey stared at him with laser eyes. Both of her hands, all ten fingers crooked, flew in front of her hips and jabbed the air with frustration. His eyes bulged. "Ugggggghhhhh." He folded over; his hat plunked to the pavement. "What the hell—"

He actually thought...Oh, please. "Okay. I think I get the intent thing now. You actually thought I intended to grab you. Right?" Terkoff let out a huge held breath. "Let's run with that totally absurd thought. I might have intended to really hurt you or I might have intended that as foreplay, right? I see what you mean now about how difficult it is to prove intent. You had no idea what I had in mind just then. Confusing, wasn't it?" When she saw her sarcastic remark hit home, she turned and headed back into the station. "Maybe there's someone in here who will take me seriously and act on this."

Terkoff sucked air through his clenched teeth. "Hold on, dammit. I was jerking your chain this time. Payback. I'll check out the damn boat."

Abbey turned back. "And just a little further proof, I went to a dinner at Kings Bluff the other night. One of the men had been fishing the morning I found Doc. He saw a boat flying down the creek with three men on board. He said it was a Grady White. I got that stuff off of Bart's Grady White. Come on, Terkoff. Doc was barefoot when I pulled him out of the river. Those are his shoes."

"Okay. I'll get on it—as soon as I can breathe." He straightened up slowly, his shoulders not as square as usual. Slowly his fists went to his hips and he exhaled. "Damn, woman."

"Ah. Are we going to play nice now, Terkoff?" She gave him narrowed eyes. "Hurry, will you?"

As he turned toward his car he said, "Watch the eleven o'clock news tonight and pick up a paper in the morning."

Tom found Abbey reading on the porch when he returned from his golf game. He kissed the top of her head. She looked up and inhaled the familiar odors of beer and sweat. "You smell like my father did after he mowed the lawn and cooled off on the porch. Nice memory."

"What's up? I'm surprised you're not in the pool."

"I'm waiting for a call from Terkoff. Why don't you pour us some wine and join me and I'll tell you what I learned today." When he returned, she filled him in.

"I had lunch with Vickie again today. Maybe I mentioned this to you before, but she has been eavesdropping on good old Bart at the office. She thinks he and Cutty are into something, because Cutty has been all over Bart about some fight. At lunch today, she said the two of them had been out fishing last Saturday—the day before she first heard them mention this fight.

"Today was the first I had heard about Bart having a boat. Vickie said he keeps it at a dock behind the cottage where Cutty lives. I went straight over there after lunch and there it was—a Grady White, with rods still in the holder, no less."

Tom frowned. "And I'm sure you didn't go on board, did you?"

"You know I did. I had to. And there was a pair of Topsiders in a bin rolled up in a towel. Doc was barefooted when I found him. It all fits together perfectly. I was so sure they were Doc's that I took them to Terkoff, and finally he agreed to go take a look at the boat."

The phone rang and she dashed off to get it. Several minutes later she returned, shaking her head and muttering under her breath.

"That was Terkoff. They moved the damn boat. I can't believe it. It has been there over a week and now all of a sudden they get the bright idea to move it."

"Well, it figures, doesn't it? Somebody at the paper or the station could have mentioned the story to a friend or something, you never know. Terkoff will put out the word on that boat. They'll find it. It's hard to hide a boat, Abbey."

"Could have been someone at the paper or it could have been the security cop at Crooked Creek. He drove up several days ago as I was leaving there, and I saw him walk to the side of the house. I bet he said something to Bart and it took the idiot until today to move it."

Tom stood. "Could be, but let's not worry about it now. I've been walking on the course all day. Why don't we enjoy our wine for a minute and then put dinner together. I'm starved."

After dinner, they took Watch for a long walk, then settled on the sofa to watch the eleven o'clock news. Tom pulled her close. Doc's was the first story. When the newscaster moved on to the next story, Tom said, "Very clever the way that was scripted. She was pretty careful not to give away anything about Doc. Usually they try to give out all the gory details."

"I wrote something up and gave it to Terkoff, and he ran it by his contacts at the station and the newspaper. It was pretty much the way I wrote it but he added some cop jargon. If Bart and Cutty watched that or read the paper tomorrow, they'll think Doc has come around and spilled his guts. I imagine there will be some hand-wringing."

"Sweating bullets is more like it, Abbey. What idiots. I can't believe they left the boat at that dock."

FORTY-FIVE

Tom went to the hardware store Tuesday morning and bought a staple gun and new screening and got back to the cottage as Abbey was rinsing her shell in the back yard. He pecked her on the cheek. "I bet it was beautiful out there."

"Gorgeous. Can't wait to get you out in one of these."

"Sounds like a threat."

"More like a challenge. Are you hungry? I'm thinking pancakes."

Tom patted his stomach. "I could handle a short stack."

"Let's do it," she said. They left his purchases on the front stoop beside the fractured screened door and went inside to the kitchen. A red light blinked on the answering machine. Abbey frowned as she listened to the message, then jabbed the replay button and held the phone so Tom could hear.

"She sounds hysterical. Is that your Vickie?" Abbey nodded and played the message again.

"She is hysterical. Bart was in a foul mood the minute he hit the house last night, but she's so busy talking about what she thinks he's in a snit about that it's hard to tell what he actually said or did. I heard something about his boat." She looked at Tom. "Someone must have warned him or tipped him off or something. Did she say he hit her? I know he has done it before."

Tom shrugged. "I think that's what she said, but she's so worked up it's difficult to figure out what she said."

"Damn. I wish I knew what made him move his boat or if that was just a coincidence." She looked at Tom. His eyebrows gave her his answer. "I know. There are no coincidences." She thought for a second or two. "Maybe someone at the paper or the news station let it slip. Or maybe he overheard someone talking. What puzzles me is no one had any reason to connect him with a boating accident unless he or Cutty said something about it to them." Tom handed her a cup of hot tea.

"That stinking security cop might have been in on this. I told you he saw me outside Cutty's house. Bart probably thought he was in the clear after he moved the boat, and then the story hit the news last night. That set him off. There are televisions at the place where he and his partner drink. They grab dinner there a lot. He could have seen what we saw."

She sipped her tea. "I bet he's nervous as hell." She watched a truck drive down the road. "I wish we had a newspaper. Did you catch the thing about Bart and Bic?"

"Sort of, but I don't know who all these people are, so it was difficult to follow." Tom poured two glasses of orange juice and handed her one before popping two slices of whole wheat bread into the toaster. "You have to eat and I doubt you feel like making pancakes. I think it's going to be a long day."

"Bic is Bart and Vickie's daughter. She and her dad are tight; not so much, Bic and her mom. At lunch one day I saw a picture of Bic in Vickie's wallet and asked about her. It was obvious from Vickie's response they have a rocky relationship, the old mother-daughter competition thing. On steroids in this case. What I got from the message was that Bic got home late last night and lit into her dad about money. Bart was probably soused and he'd heard the news. I can only imagine how that one escalated. Did you hear the name Ashley?"

"Yes. That part was confusing because she was talking about Bic and Ashley, and I wasn't familiar with either of those names."

"Ashley is Bart's sister. She has a real estate license and sits in the sales trailer on the property. An agent in town told me she might be getting paid more than commissions. All I can tell you is she drives a very expensive Mercedes convertible. Maybe Auntie Ashley and Bic are both being subsidized by Bart. Who knows what's going on out there? I'd be very curious to know how many of those lots have actually closed and how many are pending.

"There could be a lot of money sitting in personal accounts that shouldn't be there. Vickie says Bart collects antique cars and you know they're expensive. I bet these folks are dipping into earnest money that should be sitting in a trust account. He wouldn't think twice about using other people's money to support his high-and-mighty lifestyle. We already know the man is unscrupulous."

"In his mind he's above the law, thinks he won't get caught," Tom said. "That's an amazing thing about the criminal mind. They convince themselves they're smarter than everyone else."

Abbey looked at Tom. "I guess our little ploy squeezed the worm out of the hole."

"I'll say. Good work, Sherlock."

"Did you catch the bit about her not understanding why Bart was so upset about the hit-and-run story?" Tom nodded. "If she only knew. I should call Terkoff, let him know Bart's getting ready to blow. Over and over Vickie said she had never seen him like this before, called him dangerous. I saw what his fist can do. She said he was going to Orlando."

"That's what I heard," Tom said as he handed her a piece of buttered toast. "Why Orlando?"

"They have a house there. Something bothers me. After he left, she said she checked the drawer in his bedside table and his revolver was gone. Why would she mention that unless she wanted me to know he had a gun—and even more, why did she look for it in the first place unless she wanted to see if he had taken it or she felt she needed to protect herself? Was she just letting me know or was she warning me?"

"Got me. Do you think she was drunk again? At this hour of the day?"

"No. Didn't sound like it. There were sniffles but no slurring. Pretty sure she was sober. She said Bart scared her when he was like that as though he gets that way often."

Abbey replayed the last of the message. Vickie's hysterical voice said: "Bart said he was so pissed off he was heading to Orlando, so while they yelled at each other like two alley cats, I disappeared and packed an overnight bag. A lady in my tennis group owns an inn in town and lives there, so I called and woke her up and got a room. I'm there now. Can you believe all of this damn drama? My mind's in a swirl and I sure could use a friend, Abbey. I need to talk to you. You're so level-headed, you can help me figure out what to do.

"Since he's probably nursing a major hangover in Florida, you and I could meet at the house this time. You need to look at it anyway. The way things are going we might have to sell it and you and I can discuss that while his royal highness is away. Can you please meet me at my house around noon? I'll assume you can, so I'll stop by the store and pick up goodies for lunch and we can eat by the pool." Vickie giggled. "Oh, and if that doesn't beat all, I had a flat tire yesterday so I had to borrow one of the company golf carts! Can't you see me racing around town in the middle of the night in a golf cart? See you soon, I hope."

Abbey looked at Tom. "Her Valium must have kicked in for her to be giggling about a damn golf cart."

Tom handed her another hot tea. "Is she a pill-popper?"

"Thanks." She took the mug. "All I can tell you is she carries a little brown bottle of something around in her purse all the time." She looked at her watch. "I think I had better go. If Bart comes back, I can at least back her up or offer moral support or something."

"Abbey, I don't want you getting into this. Call Terkoff and tell him what's going on. If Bart comes back, there's no telling what he'll do. You already know what he's capable of when he's not outraged, and now he's on the warpath."

"Well, I'm going. She has no one else."

"I don't know if that's a good idea. Remember the agent I talked to and what he did to her. Please give your cop friend a call." Watch Dog looked from one to the other.

"I will, but I won't leave Vickie in the lurch. I've gotta go." She grabbed her keys. Watch appeared with his leash in his mouth. Abbey looked at Watch and then at Tom.

"Why don't Watch and I both go with you, Abbey?"

"No, that's silly. You don't do domestic disputes. Why don't you go to Fernandina or something and go for a swim in the ocean? This was supposed to be our day to have fun."

Tom thought about it. "If you insist on going, it would make me feel a whole lot better if you at least took him with you." Watch Dog sat and looked at Abbey expectantly.

"Yeah, that's a good idea. Okay, boy, let's go." Watch trotted triumphantly to the door. She kissed Tom on the cheek.

"Are you sure you don't want me to come along?"

"Yes. I'm sure. This isn't your problem, but I might end up bringing Vickie back here if she's afraid to go home."

Tom held up his hands. "Your deals are way beyond my pay grade. You go play Florence Nightingale and do what you need to do. I need a swim in the ocean and a walk around Fernandina. I haven't been there in ages."

"If I see she's okay, we'll meet you on the beach in about two hours. Take a left when you get on the beach road and park anywhere near the first couple of houses. And don't wander too far. We'll find you."

"Right. Speaking of that moral support you wanted to offer. As much as I hate to say this, I hope your support holds about five rounds. I'm pretty sure you'll be carrying."

Abbey flipped him a salute and a smile. "Check. Just call me Annie Oakley. See ya."

FORTY-SIX

Abbey approached Vickie's house slowly. The lame gold Cadillac rested at an odd tilt in front of the house, and a Crooked Creek golf cart occupied the space in front of the pool gate. *Looks like she's back.* There were no other cars parked outside the house. If Bart had come home and parked in the garage, she didn't want to give him a heads-up that she had come to Vickie's rescue, so she pulled down the street a short distance in the direction of the to-be-built clubhouse.

She was surprised to see Bart's black Cadillac tucked behind a thick clump of palmetto bushes. *That's odd. He's obviously back. For someone so wild about his precious cars, that's a strange place to park.*

Rolling down all the windows enough so Watch could get out if he had to, she reached over the back of her seat and showed him a flattened hand, her signal for him to stay put. "Stay, Watch. You be a good boy and *stay*," she said forcefully with another hand signal.

Exiting the Jeep, she stuck her Smith & Wesson in the back pocket of her jeans and loosened her shirt to cover the pocket. Better safe than sorry. There was no one inside the Caddy. She put her hand on the hood and removed it at once. "Ouch!" He hadn't just been to the office, he had driven enough to heat up the engine. Maybe he'd been to Florida after all. Why was he hiding like this unless he was sneaking around and up to something?

Oyster shells in the driveway crunched under her feet and prompted her to move to the cushion of grass to be quieter. There was no telling what was going on in that house. *Dammit. I meant to call Terkoff.* Creeping to the garage, she gently pulled its side door open. Bart's Camaro convertible was the only occupant of the four available spaces.

Abbey looked around before she left the doorway, then walked past the golf cart and looked over the gate. No one was in the pool. Two glasses half-filled with a red liquid sat on the patio table. Melting ice cubes and lime chunks suggested two people had enjoyed Bloody Marys earlier. She continued to the door from the garage to the kitchen. It wasn't locked. Maybe Vickie and Bart had kissed and made up, had a lovely brunch, and were upstairs romping around their bedroom. Except if that was the case, why was Bart's car still hidden down the street instead of in the garage, and why hadn't Vickie's tire been repaired? No, something was off.

Wind picked up and blew hair in her face. She looked up. Gray clouds labored across a backdrop of black sky. Temperature dropped. Shuddering, she pushed the door open, entered, and pulled the door closed enough so the wind wouldn't blow it open or slam it shut.

Pop-pop. She jumped. "What was that?" she whispered. Her brain knew. Her body dropped to a crouch. *Not a double tap, two singles. A second in between to aim. Two hit or one twice?*

She glanced around. Red geranium plants on the tile floor. A pile of potting soil. Broken shards of a glossy green pot. Her mouth went dry. Last night's argument or today? A low bass beat throbbed against the wall to her right. Family room, Abbey guessed.

Perspiration clung to tiny pale hairs on her upper lip; her heart pounded blood and oxygen as though it knew something she didn't. Skirting the pile of soil and broken pot, she tiptoed past a counter. The wall phone receiver dangled to the floor on its uncoiled cord, the irritating buzz long since hushed. Vickie said she called a tennis buddy. *Don't touch anything.* Terkoff's dark glasses flashed in her head. She wanted to call him. She couldn't. A bag of groceries lay on its side. Cherry tomatoes lay helter-skelter on the heart pine floor, a still life for an artist. A clue for her.

Her right hand slipped into her back pocket. Assurance. The front door was closed. A piece of paper lay on the rug. She toed it. Grocery list.

Below the bass beat, a man mumbled. Cussed. Ice rattled. Someone poured a drink? Slowly she made her way to the closed pocket door to the other room. A door inside the other room squeaked open, then squeaked again. *Closed? Could be the door to the back yard.* She took a chance she was right. She'd seen enough new construction to have a pretty good idea where exterior doors were located. It made sense that one door in the family room, if that's what it was, opened to the pool area.

She pushed the left panel of the pocket door to the side a smidgen. Sound from the stereo was intense: sexy, rhythmic, Pointer Sisters singing "Slow Hand" as only they could. Small stereo lights blinked in the semi-dark room. A smell, gaggingly familiar, teased her nostrils. *Cinnamon. Vickie's the potpourri type.*

But another, more bold and base, overwhelmed. The partially opened back door confirmed her guess about the home's layout. Down the street, a large engine cranked and turned over, a well-oiled machine. *Bart's Cadillac.* The driver floored it. *Gone?*

She pushed the door open another few inches and entered the room. After she hit the power button on the stereo, she found a lamp and turned it on. Shutters were closed. An oversized green corduroy sofa blocked her view of the space in front of the fireplace. Thunder rumbled. The light flickered. Green-and-red plaid throw pillows lay strewn about the floor in front of the hearth where a bottle of champagne chilled in a silver wine cooler. It looked as though she had interrupted a party. *Two shots.* Sniffing the air again, other smells competed with the odor of gunpowder. *Sex?* She looked around. Not moving from where she stood, she tried to take in the whole scene. Everything was quiet, but wrong, somehow.

Needing light, she walked to the back door and opened it the rest of the way. Aqua water glistened in the pool. The new opening lit the room. A wing chair lay on its back on the far side of the fireplace. Apparently when it toppled it took out a floor lamp. The scene looked all too familiar, disarray created by the hand of a raging drunk, a scene from a life she had tried hard to forget.

Walking over to right the chair, she stumbled and leaned over to see what she'd stepped on. A lady's shoe this time, one of Vickie's Ferragamo flats, but at this level something else caught her eye.

She gasped. "Oh, my God. What the..." A four-legged confusion of bloodied naked bodies lay on the oval rug in front of the fireplace. "Vickie," she said softly as she moved.

Now the unpleasant odor made sense. A man's bare buttocks stared back at her; another body was pinned beneath him. A profusion of long orangey-red hair fanned out beneath the man's head. "Vickie, no. Oh, God. No," Abbey said in disbelief as she warily circled the bodies. What was left of the man's dark head was face down on the woman, but something didn't jive. Vickie was fastidious about her hair.

One perfectly aimed bullet hole in the woman's forehead accounted for the alarmed expression in her eyes, the only part of her face that showed. Shock. Or was it the look of someone begging for just a few minutes to explain? Hard to tell now. Abbey leaned closer and stared at the woman, puzzled. Death changed things, she knew. She tucked her toe beneath the man's hip, but before she could flip him over the back door slammed and the dead bolt threw. Abbey turned quickly.

FORTY-SEVEN

L et them wallow in their guilt," a raspy voice slurred from the door.

Abbey stared at Bart's face, tried to see his next move in his eyes, then glanced at his hand. He held something. He moved quickly for a drunk and was on her with the rope before she could decide which way to go. He breathed heavily into her hair. Body odor and the rank, overripe, sweet smell of bourbon surrounded her. "You keep quiet, dammit," he hissed into her ear.

"What are you doing, Bart?" She held her arms away from her body to make herself larger, but he yanked hard and looped the rope around her several times, pinning her arms to her sides. He stank of anger and hate.

"I'll ask the questions," he slurred. "What were you doing in my house?" Bart's voice grated like a rusty hinge. "Who's the trespasser now, Miss Real Estate Agent? Trespassers ought to be shot. Isn't that what you said?"

"No. That's not what I said. I came to check on Vickie. She called me because she was upset. I'm her friend. I was afraid for her. Why are you doing this? What have you done here, Bart?" *Keep him talking. He has flipped… and he has just gotten started.*

"Why? You can see what that whore did to me. I knew it. Oh, I knew it all along. The way she looked at him all the time." Bart grabbed Abbey around her waist and turned her to face him, then he fumbled with his zipper. She flipped her head forward and smashed his nose with her forehead.

"Damn you, bitch!" He shoved her to the floor and worked his zipper down with both hands. He was exposed, and excited.

Oh, God. Sicko. Think. Get out of here.

"You made her tell me about her and Cutty. She told me all about it. You told her to stand up for herself. Well, a lot of good that did the slut. She was after him from day one. I knew it the whole time. I could tell she wanted his sweet little tight ass."

"What are you doing, Bart? You'll never get away with this." She thought about Tom. What would he tell her to do? *Buy time.* "The police know about the hit-and-run, Bart. They're just waiting to pick you up. Don't make it any worse for yourself than it already is."

"Talk, talk, talk. All you bitches do is talk. She was getting ready to blab to a lawyer. I stopped her. She tell you about that? The big deposition? She thought she had me by the balls but I was on to her." He glanced at the bodies.

"Looks like a murder suicide to me. Happens all the time. And here, her nosey new friend was part of the threesome, blown away by the same gun. Imagine that. You must have walked in on them or something and got jealous they hadn't included you. Their party's over. Ours is just getting started Miss Know-It-All-Atlanta-damn-fancy real estate agent. Now you get to know me."

Breathing hard, Bart pulled a knife from his back pocket and knelt beside her on one knee. He fumbled one-handed with his newly tied rope but couldn't undo his knot. "Shit." He slit a loop with his knife. "There we go," he breathed.

Abbey shrank back. Each time he sliced through another loop, she tried to melt into the carpet, tried not to smell him, tried not to look into his wild eyes, focused on his labored breaths. He was drunk and clumsy. She could outthink and outwit him.

He held the knife to her heart and grabbed the front of her jeans.

Abbey yelled at the top of her lungs, "*Watch* what you're doing. You'll cut me. *Watch... Come!*"

"Shut up." He slapped her hard.

She turned her head toward the open back door. "*Come... on...* Bart. Let me go. You're *hurting* me!" she yelled.

"You know too much, lady."

She thought she heard a familiar whine. "And you think you can get away with this? You're dead meat, Bart." She raised her voice, "Someone's going to *come Watch* and look for me!" This outburst won her a backhanded slap.

He continued to fumble with her jeans. "You're lying, bitch. Damn, I can't get this damn thing undone. Stand up." Bart wobbled to his feet. "I said stand up."

Abbey got her feet under her and pretended to lose her balance so she could step away from him.

"Now, strip or I'll cut your clothes off." He wiggled the knife in front of her. "I'm kind of drunk. I might slip a little. It could get bloody."

She feigned modesty while she fumbled left-handed with the stubborn metal button on her jeans. *Thank you, Levis.* Her right hand moved under the back of her shirt. She heard a yip from the street. *Come on, Watch. Hurry.* "Hey, Bart," she said with a flip of her hair. "Doc Pressman sends his regards." *If I'm going down, he's going to know we've got him.*

Bart's jaw dropped and his eyes opened wide as they left the painfully slow strip-tease to focus on the mouth that said words he did not want to hear. "Whaddaya mean? Who are you talking about?"

"He's probably giving the cops an ear-full right now about how you and Cutty took him fishing and then tried to kill him." She half-turned her right hip away from him, then tugged the small Smith & Wesson to the top of her back pocket. A dog barked and

244 | TIDEWATER HIT

scratched at the front door. Bart's head jerked toward the sound; Abbey glanced at the open back door.

"Hurry up," Bart yelled. He changed his grip on the knife hanging by his thigh and moved closer to her.

"Hold it right there, Bart. *Watch, come!*" she screamed at the top of her lungs, then crouched and raised her revolver.

Bart growled and lunged. Without hesitation, she fired knee-high twice. In the past ten minutes, she had thought about taking him out and decided that would serve no purpose. It would be better to let the bastard live so he could stand trial, but live as a disabled gimp so he'd have a constant reminder he was a worthless human being. Bart howled and dropped in a moaning heap. His hands cupped his ruined right knee.

Watch Dog burst through the open back door snarling and went right for Bart. "Whoa, Watch," Abbey demanded in a stern voice. "Whoa. Sit, boy." He obeyed, and dropped to his haunches trembling. His attention dared Bart to flinch.

The front door banged against the foyer's chair railing. "Oopsey-daisey. Abbey, girlfriend, are you here? I didn't know if you could come or not but I saw your car parked down the street and... it's so dark in here." Vickie went to the panel beside the pocket door and flipped switches. The room flooded with light.

"What on earth are you doing in here of all places?" Vickie said. She clutched a large brown bag from the grocery store filled to overflowing.

Abbey looked from the bodies to Vickie. *That explains the hair.* She continued to hold the gun on Bart.

"Now that's better, we can see. Abbey, what's going on? Why are you holding a gun?" Vickie looked where the gun was pointed. "Bart! Oh, my God, Bart, what happened?" Vickie didn't move but stared at her husband lying on the floor. "Abbey, what on earth is going on here?"

Bart stopped moaning, his eyes glued to Vickie, who still stood in the doorway. "What are you... doing?" He stopped. "You're supposed to be..." His eyes jerked to the two dead bodies no more than five feet from his head. "But who's—"

"They look alike, Bart, but I think you got the wrong one," Abbey said.

His mouth opened to a great gaping hole. "*Noooooooooooo...* my baby girl... Nooooo, oh, my God. It wasn't supposed to be her. Cutty, you son-of-a-sorry-ass-bitch. What have you done to my baby girl?" Bart glared at Vickie. Drool seeped from a gaping mouth below contorted cheeks. His chest heaved. He gasped for air.

"What on earth is wrong with you, Bart? Finish a sentence for crying out loud," Vickie said as she finally walked into the room with her overnight bag and groceries and dropped them both on the sofa. Then she stopped.

"Oh-my-God-oh-my-God-oh-my-God." She walked slowly to the bodies and stood over them. "What happened?" Vickie looked from Abbey to Bart, then dropped to her knees. "Cutty? What on earth? Bart, what did you do? Abbey? Is that Bic?" Vickie's hands flew to her mouth and she screamed loud and long.

Abbey watched Bart get to his one good knee and crawl to the pile of bodies. Vickie leaned over them, her hands still over her mouth. Abbey moved in closer. Bart flipped Cutty over and revealed the destroyed face of his daughter. "*Noooooooooooooooooo,*" he howled.

Vickie's eyes grew wide. She screamed again.

Watch Dog stood his position beside Abbey. Still he trembled.

There was a siren. Tires skidded to a stop. Anxious voices at the front door. "Abbey? Abbey, where are you?"

"Back here, Tom. The family room."

Tom rushed in with Terkoff hot on his heels. "Are you okay?" He grabbed her by both shoulders and looked into her eyes.

"I'm fine. Bart needs medical attention." She looked over at Terkoff, who already stood by the bodies. "That's Bic, Vickie's daughter, and Cutty Faulkner, Bart's partner. Bart shot them thinking the woman was his wife. She's his daughter. They're all yours."

She leaned into Tom's chest.

~

Several hours later, after Terkoff had finished questioning Abbey and had moved on to assist his crew inside, Abbey, Tom, and Watch Dog sat by the pool under the large umbrella. For the longest time they didn't talk much, just stared at reflections of storm clouds in the water. Watch Dog sat on Abbey's feet, licked them now and then. His head moved back and forth, his ears alert to the plop-plop of the large raindrops which plinked the water's surface in the pool.

"I take it you never made it to Fernandina, Tom."

"No, I didn't. When you left Kings Bluff, I looked up the sheriff's office in the phone book and called Terkoff. I went to him and we came together." He grabbed Abbey's hand. "I guess you thought the woman on the floor was your friend Vickie."

"At first, but not really. I didn't have time to get a good look at her before Bart grabbed me, but I was puzzled. Her hair was wrong. Do you suppose Bart planned this all along, I mean, to kill Vickie? The deposition probably set him off to begin with. He had no idea what she knew. She could have crucified him. I think he wanted to silence her. I'm sure she knew more than she ever let on to me."

Tom squeezed her hand. "As much as I hate for you to carry that gun, it has saved my life once and yours twice. When did you realize the dead one wasn't Vickie?"

"When the real Vickie walked in the door. When I first saw the woman on the floor, I thought maybe Vickie's stories about Cutty making moves on her were true and that Bart had walked in on them in the act. But something wasn't right. When Vickie showed up, I realized what had happened. Bart almost had a heart attack when she walked in. He literally crawled over to the bodies to try to make sense of what he had done, but I don't think he really got it until he pulled Cutty away and Bic's horrified eyes stared back at him. He lost it."

Terkoff walked out. "Y'all can go now. I'll call you if I need you."

"Maybe Vickie should come with us," Abbey said.

"You can ask her. A change of scenery might do her good. Tom, I assume you'll catch a ride back to Kings Bluff with your partner there."

Vickie thanked Abbey for her invitation, but she had already called her friend who owned the inn. "I'll stay there a night or two. I don't want to be a bother for you, and it's probably best to be on familiar turf while I try to absorb the fact that I could be dead—and my daughter is."

She shuddered and Abbey patted her on the arm. "Bart thought he'd caught me red-handed with Cutty. He had every intention of killing me and instead he shot them."

"Did you know about Cutty and Bic? I assume they had been seeing each other," Abbey said.

Vickie wrapped her arms around her body and shook her head; she looked Abbey in the eyes. "I haven't been totally honest with you, and considering all that's happened, I need to be. Remember all that stuff I said about Cutty putting the moves on me?" Abbey met her look but said nothing. "I lied. He was a sweet man. I saw him with Bic in the pool not too long ago, and I guess that was the first time I realized they were serious. She had started coming to visit us more. I guessed there was probably a man involved to get her to drive up here from Jacksonville all the time, but I had no idea it was Cutty until I saw them in the pool. To be honest with you, I was jealous. I wanted what they had but I knew I would never have it with Bart, so I guess I fantasized about it. That's awful, isn't it?"

"All any of us wants is to be happy, Vickie."

"I can't believe he shot her. He killed our daughter." Vickie had acted amazingly controlled for someone whose husband had just been hauled off to jail for the murder of their daughter and her boyfriend, but it finally hit her. Abbey put an arm around her and let her cry.

"Call me when you're ready for a change of scenery. I'd like for you to come see me at Kings Bluff before I head back to Atlanta."

FORTY-EIGHT

Two mornings after Bart's drunken double hit, Tom made a grocery store run for lunch supplies. Vickie had called that morning to say she was ready to take Abbey up on her offer to come see Kings Bluff if it was convenient. Abbey invited her for lunch at the cottage followed by a tour of the club. When he returned from shopping, Tom joined Abbey on the screened porch. "Where's Vickie? I saw her car in back."

"Watch Dog is taking her for a walk. They hit it off the minute she arrived, and Watch seemed to know she needed some calming no-questions-asked company. He took her hand in his mouth and led her to the door, and they headed down the bluff. He even walked at a leisurely pace."

"How is she doing?"

"Seems okay, all things considered."

"How are you doing?" Tom patted her on the knee.

"I'm okay. I told her about Doc, in a nutshell, and she was horrified."

"I guess so. What did she say about how you found him?"

"I think she's going to commission a bronze statue of me, something along the lines of those Joan of Arc figures you see in parks, but instead of me sitting on a horse I'll be in a rowing shell."

Tom looked at her with knitted brows. "You're kidding, right?"

"Well, yes, but she did go bonkers over the fact that, and I quote,

249

'Bart almost killed a third person, you, who would have surely died if you hadn't had your gun and this precious dog.' She thinks she owes me something for saving Doc, said she'd give me one of Bart's cars or something but I talked her down to just buying something from me in Atlanta."

"I don't know, a statue of you in Piedmont Park would be nice." Tom nodded his head. "We could go to the park on holidays and put flowers in the boat. I can see it."

Abbey swatted him. "Stop. You do that at cemeteries. Vickie wanted to meet Doc to apologize and was upset that he had already headed back to Philadelphia. She wants to talk to him if I can arrange it."

"That should be interesting."

"I'd like to check on Doc anyway, so maybe I'll call Adam this afternoon while she's here."

Twenty minutes later, Vickie and Watch sauntered across the front lawn and joined them on the porch. "So this is where you go to get your head screwed back on straight," Vickie said.

"Best place I know to do it," Abbey said. Tom pulled up an extra rocker.

"You were awfully nice to let me come here today. Now I can imagine how you spend your days when you're here, but most of all I can imagine the little girl Abbey running up and down those wooden walkways to the docks and wandering from here to there on these old roads. Do you have any pictures?"

"Oh, yeah," Tom said as he hopped up and headed inside. He returned moments later with a dusty old framed collage, which he'd retrieved from the living room wall. "Here she is with her brothers and some cousins."

Abbey shook her head and Vickie squealed. "Is that you?" She looked from the black-and-white photograph to the blushing Abbey. "That is you, isn't it?"

Abbey nodded. "Afraid so." She stuck out her tongue at Tom but he just grinned.

Vickie said, "This looks so, so Southern, like it's right out of the page of a book with you barefoot kids, the fishing poles, the boys looking all sweaty like they just played a game of ball…"

"*To Kill a Mockingbird* or *Huckleberry Finn*, take your pick," Tom said.

"Yes! You're absolutely right, Tom."

"Okay, enough of the Rogues gallery. Why don't we take Vickie for a drive around the club and then we'll come back here for lunch. After that I'll try to get in touch with Adam and Ed Pressman."

"Oh, yes, please. I'm sorry I won't be able to meet the Pressmans to apologize face to face. I had no idea Bart was capable of doing what he did to that poor doctor. No wonder he had been so foul lately. My God. Who could live with that? And after he left that poor man to drown, he actually shot Bic and Cutty. In their heads, no less." Vickie's voice had become a whisper. Abbey's and Tom's eyes met. "I guess he's capable of just about anything." She grabbed Abbey's hand. "I could be dead instead of sitting on this porch with you." A tear rolled down her cheek. "I just had no idea what he was capable of, but you did, didn't you?"

"I have to be honest with you, Vickie. I had a bad feeling about him from the start."

"After I left the house the other day and got off by myself, I thought about Bic and the relationship we had. We knocked heads, sure, but we loved each other. I'll really miss that sassy little girl." Tears rolled down Vickie's cheeks.

"But Bart? That's another story. When I was packing the other day to go to the inn, I went in his closet to borrow the little overnight bag he always took on his business trips and guess what I found inside?" Both Abbey and Tom shrugged. "A little velvet box with a turquoise-and-silver cuff bracelet inside. It was engraved 'Happy Birthday' and the date of someone's birthday." Abbey had a pretty good idea who Bart's lover was, but sharing that bit of information served no purpose. "Not only was he going to kill me, but he already had my replacement. Who does he think he is, Henry the Eighth?"

Tom and Abbey laughed, and when Vickie looked up with anguish written all over her face, she laughed too.

FORTY-NINE

Two months later in Atlanta, the days were shorter and the nights were cooler. Abbey was at her desk at Dorsey Alston Realtors planning her showings for the following day. Fall was the time to get properties under contract for closings in the first quarter of the year, when her bank account always suffered. When she answered the receptionist's page, she sat back in her chair and grinned.

"Hello, Vickie. Of course I'll have lunch with you today. I have missed seeing you."

An hour later as she stood in the parking lot of her office, Abbey looked for the gold Cadillac. A silver two-door Saab convertible with tan leather seats pulled up beside her. The top was down, so Vickie's cute, short, dark brown curly hair was windblown. "Wow. The hair really suits you."

"Thanks. Hop in, girlfriend." Abbey studied Vickie's new look head to toe: un-dyed hair, slim jeans, green cashmere crewneck sweater, and white Converse tennis shoes. She looked like a kid home from college. "Henri's okay with you?"

"Aha, Vickie. You're getting to know Buckhead. Sure. I love Henri's. We can pick up sandwiches and eat at the duck pond."

"The duck pond. Now you have me. I only know things a short hop from my condo. Where is the duck pond?"

"I'll show you."

They bought lunch and went to the duck pond in Garden Heights off of Peachtree Street, where they sat in the grass and fed bread to the ducks and caught up. "Bart begged me to forgive him and to wait for him. He was so pitiful it was awful, but I told him not to even waste his time thinking about it because I wanted a divorce."

"Is he going to fight it?"

"Damn well better not, and he knows it. By the time he gets out he'll be a broke flabby old man and no woman will want anything to do with him. I don't feel one bit sorry for him because he brought all of this on himself. Of course, I still think about Bic. What a sad story. I'll never get over her death but there's nothing I can do."

"It sounds like you have moved on. That's good. Some women would get all hung up on what they could have done differently, but as far as I can see, you're not one to cry over spilled milk."

"Nope." Vickie smiled. "And I guess my apology to Doctor Pressman worked. Those two Philadelphia brothers were already involved in several properties in the South, and now that Doc is fully recovered, they want to have one of their tried-and-true developers take a look at Crooked Creek. And if he likes what he sees, the Pressman brothers are interested in investor roles in my new development. Can you believe it?"

"Vickie, I have learned not to be surprised by anything you say or do."

FIFTY

Tom, in a show of true decorum and Southern gentlemanly manners, told Abbey's nephews and nieces he wanted to sleep on a cot on the screened porch with them instead of in a bedroom inside like all the other "chicken" adults. Abbey was tickled. Boonks acted like it was the most natural thing in the world for a grown man to sleep on a cot on the screened porch with the kids, but Abbey knew her mother appreciated the fact that Tom didn't question her rule that beds were shared only by married couples. Boonks was a true Southern lady.

Mid-afternoon on Thanksgiving Day, they'd had turkey and dressing and all the trimmings they all loved. But today was Friday and dinner would be oysters roasted over an open fire and cold beer. Everyone was excited. Abbey watched Tom tend the fire, nudging logs so they got the proper flow of air and adding more wood when needed. Her two brothers hosed mud off the oysters that Roosevelt had harvested in the creek that morning and dropped off that afternoon. Tom's fire glowed red-hot and sparks drifted upward into the dark purple sky.

Through the kitchen window, Abbey watched Boonks pantomime for her sons' wives a reminder of how to use a rag with an oyster knife so as not to puncture their palms. When their lesson was over, Boonks handed each a metal tray on which she placed bottles of ketchup, horseradish, and Tabasco. She added sleeves of saltine crackers, small mixing bowls, and rolls of paper towel and sent them outside to the tall wooden table where they would shuck and eat hot roasted oysters. Oblivious to all of the preparations being done by the adults, the children rolled around on the living room floor with a very happy Watch Dog.

Unnoticed by the others, Abbey slipped away to the dock, aided by the light of a glorious full moon. Shiny white pinpoints of stars speckled the deep purple night sky. At the end of the dock she stood and listened for the little flutter sound she had come to expect in the river, a stingray who fed in the mouth of a small tributary that emptied into the river from the marsh. The night was cool, beautiful, and peaceful. Inhaling the salt air deeply, she wrapped her arms around herself and took it all in.

A board squeaked. "Mind if I join you?"

She turned. "I didn't even hear you, Tom. You're quiet as a cat. I was listening to the stingray across the river. He makes a little flapping noise when he flutters his wings."

"It looked like you were deep in thought."

"I was. I've been thinking a lot lately."

"About what?"

"That house you mentioned one time."

"Oh."

"And other things." There was no teasing in her voice.

He laid his arm across her shoulder. "Good things?"

"Serious things."

"Hunh. Do these things have anything to do with me?"

"Yep."

"Am I in trouble?" He dropped his arm from her shoulder and turned her so he looked into her moonlit eyes.

"Deep, deep trouble." She grinned.

"Son-of-a-gun, Abbey. Do you mean what I think you mean?"

"Yes."

"She said yes. Yes!"

ACKNOWLEDGMENTS

Thank you to all of you who have read my books and encouraged others to do so. Your comments, critiques, reviews, and book club invitations are great and always welcome and helpful to me as a writer.

Special thanks to:

Emily Carmain – my editor, my best go-to person, my friend with a knack for helping me to do it right.

Emily Clement Davenport – a friend and honest reader and part of the pod since fifth grade.

Linda F raser and Diane Gallagher – friends with critical eyes!

My ground game – thanks for your final edit suggestions and for getting the word out.

Al Segars, coordinator for SCDNR's ACE Basin National Estuarine Research Reserve – thanks, Al, for always being willing to talk about our beautiful and exceptional waters and who has jurisdiction where.

Deputy R. Jeremy Turner (Patrol Division), Camden County Sheriff Office – thanks for your comments about the police force. If I got it wrong, forgive me!

Steve Weeks – your art is exceptional and your blunt honesty about my writing is always appreciated.

Lowcountry Writers – who have listened, critiqued, and supported. Thank you all from the bottom of my heart.

AUTHOR'S NOTE

This is not a true story though an actual event stirred my creative juices and made me think I could fashion a story with at least as wild an outcome. Mark Twain said, "Truth is stranger than fiction…," and that's a fact. Just look at the newspaper or watch the nightly news and see what heinous crimes are committed every day.

If you read *Tidewater Rip* and have returned to see what Abbey Taylor Bunn's next challenge is, I thank you for your support. If you are new to my work, thank you for giving me the opportunity to entertain you. Mistakes are all mine.

M. Z. Thwaite
Beaufort, South Carolina

ABOUT THE AUTHOR

M. Z. Thwaite has held real estate licenses in Georgia, New Jersey, and South Carolina, though now she merely uses that part of her history as a story-telling tool. She grew up in Atlanta, Georgia, and earned a bachelor of arts degree from the University of Georgia. She is the author of *Tidewater Rip*, the first in her Tidewater series, and Flight, a short story chosen for *The Petigru Review 2015 – Volume 9*. She lives with her husband in Beaufort, South Carolina, where they both enjoy the beauty of the Lowcountry. For a glimpse of her work, go to www.mzthwaite.com.

Made in the USA
Lexington, KY
31 October 2017